PRAISE FOR OLIVIA MILES

"Olivia Miles is an expert at creating a sweet, romantic plot and setting endearing characters within it, which ultimately results in a delightful read."

—*RT Book Reviews*

Praise for *The Winter Wedding Plan*

"A charming holiday tale of fresh starts, friendship, and love with a heroine even Scrooge couldn't resist."

—Sheila Roberts, *New York Times* bestselling author

"This second book in the Misty Point series continues to develop the relationship between sisters Kate and Charlotte Daniels—and their cousin Bree—with grace and sincerity. Charlotte proves a compelling heroine, a single mom determined to rise above her past mistakes and finally make her family proud."

—*RT Book Reviews*, four stars

Praise for *Mistletoe on Main Street*

"The passion and tension between Luke and Grace are equal parts tender and intense, and their journey back toward each other is a sweet and nostalgic one. With a down-home feel throughout, this story is sure to warm any reader's heart. A delightful read."

—*RT Book Reviews*, four stars

"Sweet, tender, and burgeoning with Christmas spirit and New England appeal, this engaging reunion tale sees one couple blissfully together, artfully setting the stage for the next book in the series."

—*Library Journal*

Praise for *A Match Made on Main Street*

"In the latest in her Briar Creek series, Miles brings us a book filled with crisp storytelling, amusing banter, and charming, endearing characters. The love between Mark and Anna is genuinely deep, and the tension between them is fiery. Miles's modern romance will lure readers in and keep them turning the pages."

—*RT Book Reviews*, four stars

Praise for *Hope Springs on Main Street*

"*Hope Springs on Main Street* is a warm, tender story overflowing with emotion. With strong, memorable characters and a delightful small town, this book will surely work its way into your heart. Olivia Miles weaves a beautiful story of healing and second chances."

—RaeAnne Thayne, *New York Times* bestselling author

"Romantic, touching, and deep-sigh satisfying."

—Emma Cane, author

"Appreciation for the setting will gradually grow on you as it does on Henry, which is a subtle and effective draw. With a charming cast of characters, the touching connection of family, and the lovely bloom of romance . . . *Hope Springs on Main Street* is a sweet and worthy addition to your romance collection."

—*USA Today*

"This story is delightfully engaging."

—*RT Book Reviews*, four stars

"No couple deserved a second chance at love more than this pair."

—*Harlequin Junkie*, four stars

Praise for *Love Blooms on Main Street*

"Lighthearted storytelling laced with humor is the highlight of Miles's latest story."

—*RT Book Reviews*

"For those who want a deeper small-town read, I'd recommend *Love Blooms on Main Street*."

—*Harlequin Junkie*

Praise for *Christmas Comes to Main Street*

"Readers seeking a peppermint-filled, cozy Christmas contemporary will be satisfied."

—*Publishers Weekly*

Praise for *Recipe for Romance*

"Miles's heartbreaking second-chance-at-romance story features a guilt-ridden hero and bewildered heroine. The author's intuitive dialogue adds authenticity to her small-town setting as she keeps readers guessing until the end."

—*RT Book Reviews*

Praise for *'Twas the Week before Christmas*

"Miles debuts a holiday romance with more tangles than old Christmas lights: her grinchy hero with heart and elfish, Christmas-loving heroine entertain with their obstacle-course courtship as her narrative paints a Currier and Ives holiday scene."

—*RT Book Reviews*

The Heirloom Inn

Christmas at the Cottage
Still the One
One Fine Day
Had to Be You

Misty Point Series (Grand Central / Forever)

One Week to the Wedding
The Winter Wedding Plan

Sweeter in the City Series

Sweeter in the Summer
Sweeter Than Sunshine
No Sweeter Love
One Sweet Christmas

Briar Creek Series (Grand Central / Forever)

Mistletoe on Main Street
A Match Made on Main Street
Hope Springs on Main Street
Love Blooms on Main Street
Christmas Comes to Main Street

Harlequin Special Edition

'Twas the Week Before Christmas
Recipe for Romance

The Heirloom Inn

OLIVIA MILES

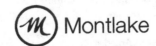

Published by Montlake, Seattle

www.apub.com

Amazon, the Amazon logo, and Montlake are trademarks of Amazon.com, Inc., or its affiliates.

ISBN-13: 9781662510816 (paperback)
ISBN-13: 9781662510809 (digital)

Cover design by Leah Jacobs-Gordon
Cover image: © Yevhenii Chulovskyi / Shutterstock; © Kirk Fisher / Shutterstock; © alb2018 / Shutterstock; © polinaloves / Shutterstock; © Dan Thornberg / Shutterstock

Printed in the United States of America

For Avery

CHAPTER ONE

LEAH

Leah Burke was doing a very poor job of forgetting the fact that she was on the wrong side of thirty-five and that, for the third time in her life, she was starting over again. The first time it had happened, she was a child with little say in the matter. The second round, she ran far and fast. Now, so many years later, when she'd thought she finally had her life settled, she didn't know what to do.

For lack of a better idea at the moment, she sat on the edge of her younger daughter's bed, watching as Annie tried to cram a third stuffed animal into the already overpacked suitcase. Ten minutes earlier, when twelve-year-old Chloe had made it clear that she didn't require any help preparing for their trip tomorrow, Annie had promptly followed suit, leaving Leah with the weary knowledge that she'd be up late tonight, replacing the impractical plastic princess shoes with the more functional leather sandals and canvas sneakers, ensuring that her daughter had enough bathing suits and shorts for the warm days and sweaters and hoodies for the cool nights.

But she knew she'd still worry. It was in her nature. Perhaps it was inevitable, destined by birth order and her place as the oldest sibling.

Or perhaps it was unavoidable, given that she'd lost her own mother when she was only Chloe's age.

Leah had very much still needed a mother back then. On days like this, she still did. A mother to tell her that everything would be all right, even when most of the time it didn't feel that way. Someone who would remind her that the girls weren't going to be alone; they were going to be with their father, who, while certainly the more relaxed parent, was technically an adult. But more than anything, especially lately, what she really needed was a hug.

With a frown, she realized she couldn't even pinpoint the last time that Ted had hugged her. They'd been separated for only four months, but the distance had started long before that, creeping up so slowly that she hadn't even thought to worry. Not until it was too late.

Annie contemplated her suitcase and finally met Leah's eyes. Leah gave her a knowing smile.

"I can't go away for a whole month without Bunny the bear!" Annie protested before the argument had even started.

A whole month. As if Leah needed a reminder. Pretend that they're going to sleepaway camp—that's what her best friend, Gina, told her every time Leah brought up her ex-husband's summer plans, which was often.

She hadn't noticed the cracks in their marriage at first, but these last few months, they were all she could think about anymore when the house was quiet but her mind wouldn't turn off. How she and Ted had drifted apart. How maybe they'd never been all that compatible from the start. How she'd rushed into a marriage that had only been another adventure for Ted. How, in the end, he'd left her behind.

"It's a big trip," Leah said to Annie. "I can take good care of Bunny while you're gone."

Annie wrestled with the decision, and it dawned on Leah that Annie felt the same anxiety over being parted from her favorite stuffed bear that Leah felt at not seeing her children for twenty-eight days.

"I don't think I can leave her," Annie said firmly.

"I understand." More than she was letting on. That's what this new arrangement called for: a stiff upper lip. "Just be careful not to lose her—"

"I would never lose the thing I love most in the world!" Annie said with the kind of innocence that came with having never really experienced a deep loss before.

Leah supposed she should pat herself on the back for that, protecting her children as much as she could, but she couldn't shield them from everything. She started rattling off the instructions she'd already given earlier that day but stopped when she heard a groan from the hallway. A moment later, Chloe appeared and leaned against the doorjamb, her dirty-blonde hair—the same shade as Leah's—loose at her shoulders, her brown eyes the same as her father's, right down to the impossibly long lashes. "We know, we know. Check our luggage tags before we walk off because the bags might belong to someone else, which seems impossible given that ours are hot pink!"

"I love pink!" Annie said happily, while her older sister muttered something about it being so embarrassing.

"It's practical," Leah said. "If I bought gray or navy or black, then your luggage would look like everyone else's." Good God, she sounded like such a mom, and she was only thirty-six years old. She should feel like she had her whole life stretching ahead of her, but instead, she felt more than a little lost. For fourteen years, her entire adult life had been centered around her husband, her children, and their home. Without lunches to pack or activities to drive to, her days didn't have much purpose.

"What time is our flight?" Annie asked.

"Early," Leah stressed. "So it's time for bed."

"But it's only seven!" Chloe insisted. She'd been pushing to stay up until ten since school ended last week, something that her friends apparently did, which led to countless arguments that replaced the previous ones about getting her the latest-model cell phone.

"Babies go to bed at seven," Chloe continued.

Leah bit back a laugh. Her babies certainly hadn't gone to bed at seven, and if they did, they were up again by eleven. Those days had been long, but now, looking at her two growing girls, she yearned for them, sleepless nights and all.

She checked herself right there. There was no sense in wishing for the past. She'd made that promise to herself a long time ago, and more than once.

"You have to get up at four if we're going to make it to the airport in time for your six o'clock flight," she reminded them.

"Why do we have to leave so early?" Annie pouted.

Why? That was the question Leah wanted to ask too. Why had Ted booked such an early flight, knowing the girls would be grouchy and tired? Why had he decided to end the marriage and disrupt their family life? Why had he stopped loving her?

There were many questions, and only one person had the answer. And at the end of the day, it didn't change a damn thing.

"Your father booked the tickets, and he'll be waiting for you at the airport bright and early!" She tried to feign enthusiasm even though the mere thought of seeing Ted, however briefly, only filled her with dread lately.

Annie clapped her hands with excitement. "And then we'll be on our way!"

Yep. Then they'd be on their way. While she . . . she'd be right here. Where she'd faithfully been day after day, year after year. Her home. Her safe place. So much for that.

While the girls brushed their teeth, arguing over the sink they shared in the bathroom that separated their two rooms, Leah quickly swapped the dress-up clothes for sneakers, T-shirts, and shorts. She hauled each piece of luggage to the hallway landing, deciding to leave them there until the morning in case there were any last-minute changes.

The water had stopped running, and she walked back into Annie's room to pull down the purple floral duvet and plump the pillow. Like Chloe's, Annie's hair was shoulder length and blonde, only she'd gotten

Leah's loose curls. Leah had always felt singled out by her hair as a child, and she'd felt a kinship with her younger daughter over this shared trait—a reminder that Annie wasn't just her child but her family. A new family to replace the one she'd lost.

Annie climbed under her blankets and pulled them up to her chin. "Mom?"

Leah smiled softly at her. She'd never tire of that sweet voice. "Yes, honey?"

"What are you going to do when we're away?"

Good question, Leah thought. She supposed she could clean out the linen closet. Maybe finally start putting a résumé together—even though she had no real work experience outside the home. Maybe she'd tackle the weeds in the perennial beds. She knew what Gina would say. *An entire month without all the responsibilities that came with parenthood, and now, single parenthood?* But Gina, with three kids of her own, was only fantasizing. Her summer would be defined by dropping the kids off at day camp, blowing up floaties for afternoon trips to the town pool, and hauling coolers, towels, chairs, and an umbrella to the shore of Lake Michigan every Saturday.

All the things that Leah yearned to do right now, even though at times they had felt downright exhausting.

"Oh, I'll probably just spend the days snooping through Chloe's drawers and reading her diary." She winked, and Annie giggled. Leah didn't even think that Chloe kept a diary, and she could only imagine the reaction her daughter would give her if she so much as entered her room without knocking first.

She was laughing as she flicked off the bedside lamp, but her heart felt heavy when she stepped into the hallway, wishing for just tonight that Chloe would let her tuck her in like she used to do.

"Night, Chlo!" she called out.

She heard a grumbled response from somewhere behind the door. The separation had been hard on Chloe, Leah knew, even if she didn't like to talk about it. And this trip, exciting as it would probably be for the girls, was hard on all of them. Even if they didn't talk about that either.

Downstairs, Leah started the kettle for tea and flicked on the television. She picked up the phone to see if Ted had sent any more updates on the itinerary, but there were only two text messages from Gina trying to cheer her up (Happy hour every night at five! No laundry piling up! The television all to yourself!) and another from her youngest sister, sent an hour ago.

Please call. That couldn't be good. Emma seldom reached out, and when she did, it was around the holidays or someone's birthday, usually full of cheer and gossip, with carefully edited stories of all that had been happening in Door County.

They didn't speak often, not in the way some of Leah's friends did with their sisters. It wasn't that they didn't like each other, more that they weren't close—or at least hadn't been in a long time. Once, it had been their six-plus-year age difference that separated them, leaving Leah feeling maternal toward Emma, especially with their difficult circumstances. But Emma was twenty-nine now, meaning that she was technically one of Leah's peers, even though it was difficult to shake old habits and think of her as a proper adult.

Maybe it was the fact that Emma still lived in their childhood home and hadn't yet settled into the normal set of responsibilities that had defined Leah's daily life by that age. Or maybe it was the fact that Emma lived in Fog's Landing, and that alone made Leah keep her distance.

Leah thought of her own two girls upstairs and hoped that this trip might bond them together. Hardship had a way of doing that, as her aunt liked to say.

Except, Leah thought with a pinch of her mouth, when hardship did the opposite.

With a strange feeling in her stomach, Leah dialed her sister's number and listened to it ring.

"Oh, Leah!" Emma answered in a breathless rush, and Leah felt all her parental impulses go on high alert.

"Did something happen? Are you okay?" It was her natural response these days—and maybe long before that, not that anyone could fault her. Her mind went to worst-case scenarios without much encouragement.

"It's Aunt Vivian," her sister said softly, and Leah closed her eyes, letting a deep sigh release from her lungs as she dropped onto a chair. She wasn't surprised, not entirely, and the words didn't come with the same shock as their parents' accident had all those years ago. She didn't need to ask for details or elaboration, even as Emma gave them. Another stroke, most likely, in her sleep. Emma had found her this morning. She'd been too consumed with the events of the day to call until now, which was only probably true. The bigger reason was that Leah was just an outsider now—not by choice, but that depended on whose opinion you asked—and Fog's Landing, Wisconsin, was full of locals with thoughts on the Burke sisters.

Leah listened to her sister's voice, so familiar despite the months that sometimes passed without a call or years without a visit, and she could almost picture her, standing in the kitchen of the big house on the bluff or sitting on the front porch, watching the lake water crash against the rocks, and she knew with certainty how she would spend the days that until this moment had felt so long and open and stark.

With the phone wedged under her chin, she walked back up the stairs to her bedroom, pulled one more suitcase out of the half-empty closet, and began filling it. Her children weren't the only ones going away tomorrow. She'd be leaving too. Or rather, returning. To the one place she'd sworn she'd never go back to ever again.

CHAPTER TWO

EMMA

Today called for lots of chocolate. Emma didn't even bother to measure it out like she usually did but instead coarsely chopped a good portion of the thick bar and mixed it into the batter.

Baking was something that Aunt Vivian had taught her, back when Emma and her sisters had first come to live here, in the big, strange house with the kitchen that was nearly as bright as the basement was scary. She hadn't been able to escape her grief in a sketchbook, like Leah, or a novel, like Sadie. She was lost. She wandered around the old house, pulling open drawers, finding hiding spaces where she would sit for hours on end with her favorite doll for company, until Aunt Vivian finally ushered her into the kitchen one day and handed her an apron, hand sewn from the floral fabric that Viv preferred and made just for her.

"Sugar. Butter. Flour." She'd winked at Emma, giving her that smile that said everything was going to be okay, at least for a little while, and then she taught her—about whisking, about sifting; that it was always better to underbake a chocolate cake so it wouldn't be too dry when it cooled; and that you couldn't frost a hot cupcake, no matter how impatient you were to eat it. "Good things come in time," she'd said.

She'd also shown Emma that if she measured carefully and followed a recipe with precision, she had a guaranteed outcome every time.

Baking was something reliable in a world that, back then, felt just as uncertain as it did now.

Emma slid the pan into the oven and set the timer; then she refilled her glass of wine, telling herself that she wasn't exactly drinking alone when her faithful dog was stuck at her side. Still, as she walked into the den at the back of the large Victorian home where she'd spent most of her life, Sully nipping at her heels with his little marching feet, she couldn't help but feel exactly that: alone.

She'd known this day would come, of course. Aunt Vivian had been her mother's elder sister by nine years, and while she wasn't exactly old, her blood pressure had been a problem for most of the time that Emma had known her. "Part of our genes," Viv used to say. Then, with a smile, she'd add, "Like this wonderful house."

Viv liked to get caught up in her various volunteer work in town—her quilting, her baking, her gardening—and she always had to be reminded to take her blood pressure medicine. And Emma had always reminded her, of course. If she didn't, who else would?

Staying in Fog's Landing was supposed to be temporary, at most a stepping stone, but then Aunt Vivian had had that stroke a few years ago, and Emma couldn't leave when there was always the threat of another. As the months and then years went on, she had dared to think that it wouldn't happen, that Aunt Vivian would go on forever, that she would . . .

Well, there was no sense in dwelling on what Emma had hoped for herself. Aunt Vivian was gone. In many ways, she was the only mother Emma had ever known. The memories she had of her own parents were hazy at best, and Vivian hadn't been one to share stories. There had been a falling-out, something she didn't like to talk about, even when they were baking and she tended to get chatty about the past.

Recipes did that, she'd liked to say. They stirred up more than flour and eggs. They brought back memories too.

A single tear slipped down Emma's cheek, and she brushed it away, feeling the tightening in her chest that had been there all day and probably wouldn't be going away anytime soon.

She solaced herself with the knowledge that there hadn't been any drawn-out illness, no real suffering, just a peaceful ending in Viv's sleep. She should feel comforted by that—or so Vivian's best friend, Linda, had told her when she'd run next door to her house this morning, out of breath, crying, and so panicked that she was shaking from head to toe, barely able to form a coherent sentence.

Aunt Vivian was gone. There was a silence in the house—an emptiness that she couldn't escape. The pillow on Aunt Vivian's favorite armchair was still fluffed from lack of use; the teakettle on the stove top was still heavy and ready for Viv's multiple cups of Earl Grey.

As the hours passed, the shock wore off, but comfort never came. Instead, she was left with a single emotion, so strong that it churned her stomach and made even her double-fudge brownies unappetizing; one that left her longing for the past nearly as much as she dreaded facing it again.

Guilt.

"What'll it be tonight?" Yes, she talked to her dog, a sure sign that she should get out more. Sully couldn't answer her, but she knew he held an opinion all the same. Anything but another viewing of *Jurassic Park* (the roar of the dinosaurs had left him hiding under the ottoman when Wyatt insisted on watching it two weeks ago). Emma settled on a lighthearted rom-com she'd seen at least a dozen times and eyed her phone, wondering if she should call Wyatt, if it might be good for her to have a little company tonight. But all Emma felt she deserved was to be alone. With her guilt.

Plus, she had already called Wyatt this morning. She needed to stop calling Wyatt.

She picked up her phone and checked to see if her sister Sadie had bothered to reply to her text. She had not, but then, Emma wasn't fully expecting her to either. She'd done her part, delivered the news. She could at least sleep with that part of her conscience clear.

Maybe she should call her friend Sarah, and she started to before she remembered that Sarah was working at the inn tonight—covering her shift. Emma's boss, Pamela, had insisted she take the next two weeks off, if not more, but Emma couldn't help but wonder if being at the front desk, answering phones and taking reservations, and politely managing the demands and complaints of the guests would be better than sitting here right now.

She sipped her wine as the first scene started, wondering why they didn't make feel-good movies like this anymore. Sully was already asleep beside her, exhausted from the chaos of the day, his gentle snores the only sound to be heard in the large, empty house other than the cheesy '90s song that she mouthed as tears started to prickle the back of her eyes.

She called Wyatt.

The phone rang, and instantly Emma wished she could have exhibited more restraint, but today was not the day for it. And today would be the last time. She owed Viv that, probably herself too.

Yes, definitely herself.

Besides, she probably wouldn't even be living in Door County much longer. Without her aunt, she had no reason to stay in Fog's Landing and many, many reasons to leave.

The number one reason for why she needed to leave this town answered on the third ring, and her traitorous heart turned over, like it always did, at the mere sound of his deep, gravelly voice.

She closed her eyes, feeling deeply disappointed in herself, but not enough to stop her from smiling when he said, "I was just thinking about you."

He had been thinking about her. But of course, he had been thinking about her. Vivian Stewart had passed away in her sleep. Everyone in Door County would probably be thinking about her right now.

Emma held her breath, hoping that she wouldn't have to come flat out and ask him if he wanted to come over and keep her company.

"Have you eaten?" Before she could reply, he said, "I was just about to order a pizza. Your favorite, of course. Sound good?"

It sounded more than good. It sounded like everything she hadn't even dared to hope to hear. He was coming over. With her favorite kind of pizza. Because he remembered things like that. Because he paid attention. Because he cared.

But was it because he loved her?

She knew that all evidence pointed to the contrary, that he was a friend, nothing more, and that she shouldn't even let herself hold out hope. And when she forgot that, when she slipped, Viv had always been there to remind her.

Emma disconnected the call and leaned back, emitting a long sigh and hoping that Aunt Vivian wasn't looking down on her and shaking her head silently, as she had been known to do when Wyatt's name was mentioned.

She could have sworn Sully gave her a judgmental stare from his spot on the couch before he stretched and hopped down onto the threadbare rug.

"Last time," she said, and this time she meant it. She left her wineglass on the coffee table and grabbed another from the kitchen, along with a bottle of red, which would go nicely with the pizza. The kitchen was clean, with only a couple of items in the sink from her breakfast this morning, before her world changed for good.

There would have to be arrangements; that's what Linda had said. She'd offered to help, but that wouldn't be necessary. Leah would be here tomorrow afternoon. Just knowing that made Emma feel calm enough to wash the single plate and mug, set them on the drying rack.

The doorbell rang when she was straightening up the den. She shoved the wadded-up, tear-soaked tissues into the back pocket of her jeans and hurried to the front hall, where Wyatt's tall form was blurry behind the frosted-glass windowpane of the home's original door.

Her heart did its usual traitorous leap when she pulled the knob. His grin, wide and slightly dimpled, did it to her every time. His murky blue eyes crinkled at the corners as he held out the pizza box.

"That smells wonderful," she admitted, realizing that she hadn't eaten since breakfast, even though every single person she'd talked to throughout the day had tried to ply her with tea, snacks, and a warm meal. Leave it to Wyatt to be the one to pique her interest. Even her stomach couldn't say no to the man.

She led him to the back of the house, to the den that housed walls of books and framed photos, an oversize and sun-bleached leather otto-man that doubled as a coffee table, and a well-loved chenille couch that was deep and soft and probably should have been replaced a decade ago but, like so many other things in the old, rambling house, was part of what gave it character.

He waited until they'd cracked open the box and each helped them-selves to a slice before asking the loaded question: "How are you doing?"

There were so many ways to answer that, she couldn't settle on just one. She went to the facts instead. "Leah's coming tomorrow. That will be good."

He looked only mildly surprised. "How long has it been since you've seen her?"

Leah hadn't been home since she left it fifteen years ago, and Wyatt had only ever known her by name. "Aunt Vivian and I visited her in Chicago three Christmases ago. A few other times too."

"And your other sister?"

Emma shrugged. Wyatt knew the bare details of her sisters' fallout. It was local lore, and besides, she couldn't exactly say that it was normal that her fractured family never came back to Fog's Landing.

"Sadie will do what Sadie wants. Doing the right thing isn't a pri-ority to her like it is to Leah or me." She heard the bitterness in her tone and forced a smile she didn't feel, thinking of all that she'd given up by staying here longer than she'd planned, that while Sadie was off living her carefree life in New York, Emma had done the right thing for Vivian, and now she was technically free—to do as she pleased, to go where she wanted. Only now, with Wyatt looking at her like that, she couldn't imagine being anywhere else.

The timer in the kitchen went off, dragging her attention away from that lazy smile and those cloudy blue eyes.

"I forgot that I had brownies in the oven!" She'd eat them even if they were dry if it meant she could spend a few extra minutes sitting this close to Wyatt.

But Wyatt was standing up now. "I wish I could stay. You know I can never resist your sweets."

Emma felt her cheeks flush, and she hoped he couldn't see the disappointment in her eyes. She couldn't even look at him as she walked to the kitchen and fumbled to turn off the egg timer—a birthday present from Viv last year.

The last one, Emma thought dully.

"Somewhere to be?" Her tone was strained, darn it.

"I'm short staffed at the pub tonight, but I ran into Linda at the market, and she insisted I make sure you eat something."

So it hadn't even been his idea.

If Viv were here right now, she'd have pursed her lips in that knowing way she tended to reserve for these types of disappointments that were inevitably caused by Wyatt. As it was, Emma had a difficult time looking little Sully in the eye. He knew. He saw it all.

And what was plain as day was that Wyatt wasn't here to keep her company, to make sure she wasn't alone, to lift her spirits or even make sure she ate. Wyatt was doing a favor for *Linda*.

Emma opened the oven door, nearly forgetting to grab a mitt before she reached for the pan, and luckily, stopped herself just in time. Wyatt always did this to her. Made her lose her good sense (and her dignity, as Vivian liked to tut).

He stared at the pan as she set it on the stove top to cool. The man obviously loved her baking more than he loved her.

"I'll cut you one," she said, even though they were too warm to eat. This was what she did. She fed people. Fed herself. Not proper food—even Linda knew she didn't have that instinct—but sweets. Solace. Comfort.

She'd eat the entire pan after Wyatt left. As for the pizza . . . well, she didn't even want to look at it now.

Wyatt made a grunting sound when he took the brownie wrapped in a paper towel from her hand, his fingers skimming hers long enough to cause a tingle to rush through her stomach.

"You're the best," he said, giving her one of those crinkly smiles that made every part of her, even the part of her that was pretty damn upset right now, go all soft.

She walked him to the door, feeling almost worse than she had before she'd called him. And what if she hadn't?

There begged the real question, of course.

"I'll call you tomorrow," he said casually as he stepped outside onto the porch. A cool evening breeze lingered in the hall for a few seconds after she finally closed the door, and only after she'd watched him retreat.

Tomorrow. Tomorrow Leah would be here. She'd make things better—she always did. Tomorrow Emma wouldn't be alone.

And as for tonight, she couldn't bear to be in this empty house a moment longer.

She grabbed Sully's collar and lead from the hook where she kept it and pulled one of Aunt Vivian's cashmere wraps from the hallway closet, and, tempting as it was to follow Wyatt down the lakefront path, she purposely took the opposite direction.

At the end of the day, there was only one thing keeping her in Fog's Landing now that Vivian was gone. And he had a girlfriend.

CHAPTER THREE

SADIE

Deep down, Sadie had always known that one day she would hear from one of her sisters. There would be a life event, something that would trigger news that had to be shared, even with her. Sometimes, she even imagined how it might go: there would be a wedding, perhaps, but then, there already had been a wedding, one that she had not been invited to but rather heard about in an awkward conversation with her aunt Vivian on one of their three calls per year.

There would be a birth, then. But that had happened too. Twice. Again, news got to her well after the fact and not from the source, making it impossible for her to send a card or a gift to Leah without adding to the strain that existed between them, reminding her that she had not been forgiven.

Still, she liked to think that someday, something would happen that would make Leah or Emma shake their heads and wonder how they had let one event change their family for good. That life experiences would give them perspective. That they'd yearn for the lost years nearly as much as she did. That they'd reach out and say hello. That was all she needed to hear. Hello.

Aunt Vivian died this morning. I thought you should know.

And *she* was the heartless sister?

The door to the kitchen swung open, and Sadie quickly stuffed the phone back into her pocket; she'd have to deal with Emma later. She had only two more tables, and they were both on dessert and coffee. Her shift was up in thirty minutes, and then she could go home, take a hot shower, and crawl into bed.

Oh, who was she kidding? If she went back to the Lower East Side five-hundred-square-foot walk-up that was considered a two-bedroom only because Sadie's room was just barely large enough for a double bed, she was bound to encounter one of two scenarios: either Jessie would be watching television with her boyfriend, annoyed at Sadie's arrival, or they'd already be in bed, leaving Sadie to smother her head with a pillow in the hopes of drowning out their whispers, laughter, and, well, everything else.

Usually, these nuisances didn't bother her, at least not greatly. Living in New York, she was out and about more often than she was at the apartment. It was a place to check in, change, crash for the night, and not much more. But right now, with her mind spinning and her heart pounding, she felt aggravated. By her longtime roommate's new and seemingly serious relationship, by the diners who had lingered far too long and were holding up her night. By the fact that her sister had reached out to her after all these years. More than anything, by the horrible, almost impossible fact that her aunt was gone. And she'd never even had a chance to say goodbye. To say so many things that she should have said years ago.

"Table three is ready for the check." Neil took one look at her no doubt shaky expression and gave a less than subtle arch of his eyebrow, one that said he was in boss mode now, and not just for the sake of appearances.

None of the staff knew about their relationship, and they'd both decided to keep it that way. It was a small restaurant—one of those basement places with cozy, candlelit tables and soft music. The staff was tight, like family, and as the owner, Neil, a hotheaded CIA grad who'd had a few stints on a popular cooking channel, liked to keep his private life to himself.

That was just fine with Sadie. She'd had her share of talk and gossip, thank you very much. Lying low was just one of the reasons she'd come to New York in the first place. In Manhattan, she blended in with the crowd. No one had to know her name, and no one bothered to discuss her life. The city couldn't have been more different from the small town in Door County where there was nowhere to hide and where everyone knew everything and liked to share what they'd heard.

Sadie delivered the check as told and processed the payment, all while keeping an eye on her last table, the occupants of which were lingering over the dregs of coffee that she wasn't going to offer to refill for a second time.

She discreetly placed the leather billfold on the table instead. "Whenever you're ready." Meaning the sooner the better, please.

She waited near the hostess stand, thinking of Emma's text, of the time it had been sent (late), of the delay in events. It had been an afterthought, perhaps. An obligation for sure. Maybe someone had suggested she send it. Linda, probably.

Still, she couldn't stop picturing her younger sister, just a teenager when Sadie had left town, pulling up her number and deliberately choosing to contact her. It felt like an olive branch. It felt like she still mattered.

She wondered if Emma was expecting a response. And how exactly was Sadie expected to respond to a text like that? She wondered if Aunt Vivian had been sick and no one had bothered to tell her.

Narrowing her eyes, she tried to concentrate on the last time she had spoken to Vivian and how she had sounded. It must have been April, around the time of Viv's birthday. They'd chatted briefly about Sadie's job, the weather in Door County, and of course, all the different happenings around town that kept Vivian busy.

They didn't talk about Emma. They certainly didn't talk about Leah.

And Viv had never so much as hinted that something might be wrong with her health.

Sadie chewed a fingernail and then dropped it, knowing that Neil would fire his waitstaff for such an offense, citing it as not just unseemly but unhygienic. She didn't know what she should do, but then, she never knew what she should do, from where she should live to what career she should follow to what men she should date. She doubted every choice, just like she'd doubted everything she'd ever said or hadn't said to her family in all these years.

Five minutes later, Sadie was shaken from her thoughts when the young couple (second date, by her guess; she'd learned to spot these things after observing people enough) finally looked around at the empty restaurant and took the hint. Sadie's feet were aching from a long shift by the time she made it back to the kitchen, and her stomach grumbled in hunger.

"You want to go out tonight?" It was Neil, his voice low, his eyes a little softer than they had been just a few minutes ago.

Sadie wavered. It was late—past ten—but the thought of going back to her apartment and thinking any more about her family was so unappealing that she was willing to postpone it for a little longer, even in these heels.

Avoiding the hard stuff had become second nature. It sure beat facing it head on.

She shook her hair free from its clip and grinned. "What did you have in mind?"

Ten minutes later, seated at the bar in a popular hotel lobby around the corner where they often met up after the restaurant closed (she arriving first, he usually a safe ten minutes later), she learned exactly what Neil had in mind.

"You're breaking up with me?" She stared at him, trying to read his expression, but he was a master of putting on a game face, and tonight was no exception. For a moment, she feared she might cry, and she steeled herself by taking a long sip of her glass of wine instead, telling herself that this day couldn't get much worse from here and that at least it would be over in less than an hour. It was an old trick she'd learned years back, and it worked, or at least helped. There was only so much one person could take. Sometimes, it was better to pile it on and get it over with all at once.

"There's been talk." He gave her a pointed look. "In the kitchen."

The implication took a second to set in. Sadie stiffened. "Oh." *Oh no* was more like it.

Neil pressed his hands flat against the marble bar top. "Look, you know I like you, Sadie, but I can't risk my career by tarnishing my reputation. I sank everything into that restaurant."

She narrowed her eyes at him. "You're saying that our relationship is . . . a liability." It wasn't a question, more like a need for confirmation.

He gave her a little smile. "It's not a relationship, though. We're just having a bit of fun. It's not like this was ever going to go anywhere."

Six months was enough time to classify as a relationship for most people, but Sadie didn't bother pointing that out. Neil was her boss, the relationship (or lack thereof) had always been on his terms, and that should have concerned her long before tonight, along with the fact that she had been sworn to secrecy about their . . . affair? Fling? Whatever it was.

He'd approached her at this very bar, right after her first shift. She'd been looking for a chance to unwind before heading home. He'd later admitted that he'd followed her. Creepy? Maybe. Instead, Sadie had been flattered. She'd heard the whispered conversation among the other staff, the long-harbored crushes, the comments on Neil's dark hair and eyes, his professionally whitened smile. He was a catch, and not just because he was the boss. He was arrogant, good looking, and good at what he did. Too good. And he knew it.

No, she supposed it had never been going anywhere, but she just hadn't thought about that until now. Since she'd first come to New York, she'd been hustling from one job to the next, always managing to get by but always living paycheck to paycheck. Bouncing from one boyfriend to the next, never stopping to think about marriage or family. She hadn't thought that far ahead; her sister Leah would say that she never did. She just knew that this was working—or had been, until now.

Once again, her lack of judgment had caught up with her.

"If word gets out that I date my waitstaff, I'll never be taken seriously. I can't put my career on the line."

"And *my* career?" She pursed her lips to underscore this blatant double standard.

He looked at her quizzically. "This is Manhattan. There are a thousand restaurants where you could work, but is that really what you want to do? Wait tables all your life?"

She opened her mouth to correct him—she hadn't waited tables until the past three or four years, and before that, she'd worked in retail, on commission—but she didn't want to argue.

Thinking of the future wasn't in her nature and never had been—at least not since she was a child and life as she knew it changed forever.

"You know I've been working on my novel," she reminded him. She'd offered to let him read a few chapters, but he'd always said he would wait until she had it finished. Now she wondered if he had never intended to stick around that long, or, worse, if he never believed she would complete it.

The truth was that there were days she thought she'd never finish, because when had she ever finished anything?

"I should go." She started to gather her bag to leave, wondering if he would try to stop her. He didn't.

"Hey, Sadie," Neil said as she fumbled to hook her bag on her shoulder.

She stopped, wondering if he had realized what a jerk he was being. If he'd take back his words, not that she particularly cared if he did.

She'd been played, or maybe she'd been a willing participant. Either way, she was better off alone.

Or so she'd been telling herself. She was still waiting to actually believe it, for the constant, restless ache of loneliness to leave the pit of her stomach.

"No need to come in for your final check. I'll mail it to you."

Or not.

Sadie could feel the disgust on her face before she turned and walked away from the table, weaving her way through the crowds of other, happier people. People who had their life together, their plans in place. People who didn't date their boss and expect to still have a job when things ended. People who had somewhere to go, something to fall back on, when times got tough. Someone waiting for them at the end of a long bad day.

A place like home, she realized. A place that hadn't existed to her in so long that it almost felt like it had never been real at all.

Her aunt had been the only string tying her to her sisters, however loosely. Now that she was gone, there was nothing left but the house connecting them, and that probably wouldn't be around much longer either.

The time had come to try one last time or to give up, forever.

And as with so many other things in her life, she'd have to make a decision. And live with the consequences.

There was no excuse not to go back for the funeral, not when she didn't have a job, not when she had nothing—and no one—keeping her here.

Tomorrow was suddenly wide open, and a more optimistic person might have said it was full of hours and minutes yet to be filled. A chance to start over.

Or maybe . . . a chance to make things right.

CHAPTER FOUR

LEAH

Door County was only a four-hour drive from the Chicago suburb where Leah had lived since Chloe was three months old—and less than five from the apartment in the city she and Ted had shared before that. Distance had never been the excuse for not coming back to the town where she'd spent her adolescent years, and now, as the miles ticked by in her rearview mirror, the memories she'd tried to keep firmly behind herself came rushing forward.

She'd been twelve when her parents lost their lives in a car accident. Sadie was nine, Emma not quite six. The authorities located a relative, an aunt their mother had never mentioned. Vivian had come to collect them that very day, holding a box of freshly made cookies that she had been baking when she'd gotten the call. It was only later, as an adult, that Leah wondered how Vivian must have felt when she heard the news. If she regretted the rift that would never have a chance to be repaired.

She'd stayed for the service and then helped them to pack their possessions. They drove all the way to Wisconsin in silence, aside from the radio and Vivian's soft voice singing the songs she knew. Had this been their mother, Leah or Sadie might have rolled their eyes, but their mother was gone, and they'd never hear her sing again, and somehow, they both knew to stay quiet. Secretly, they'd enjoyed it. Vivian's voice, like her wide smile, reminded them of their mother, but the only time they'd told their aunt that, she'd just given them a funny look and changed the subject.

It had been strange at first, living in that big white house across from the shimmering Green Bay, so different from the more modern house they'd lived in until then, but eventually, the house was filled with laughter. And for a little while at least, it had been home.

But they weren't all happy moments, and eventually, the bad overshadowed the good, making Fog's Landing—and every part of her that it held—something Leah wanted to forget.

Two days, she told herself. Three, tops. Emma had said that the funeral was tomorrow—and then there would be the house to consider. She'd honor Vivian, help Emma with the affairs, and then . . . then came the void. The same one she'd felt when Ted told her he was moving out and again this morning when she'd waved her children off at the airport terminal, blinking back tears while fighting to smile, telling them to have a good time, even if it would be without her.

The same one she'd felt all those years ago when she'd packed her bags and boarded the first bus out of Door County. Now, like then, she knew what she was leaving behind. But she didn't know what she was running to, and maybe she never had.

When she stopped to get gas at the halfway point, Leah checked her phone to see if Annie or Chloe had tried to call or text, but of course they were still on the plane, probably engrossed in a movie, each sipping a third can of soda since she wasn't there to stop them.

Her girls would have liked Door County: the eclectic shops in the towns that bordered Fog's Landing, the vintage ice cream parlors, and the fish boils that were quintessential to the area. Her aunt would have turned one of the rooms in her large house into a special place just for them, with twin beds and hand-sewn quilts in the soft cottage colors that filled the rest of the house. She would have given them empty jam jars to catch fireflies and let them walk barefoot back from the lakefront across the road. She would have wiped down the old bikes she kept in the shed, maybe even given them a fresh coat of paint. She would have taught them to bake sweets that would leave them happy and sticky and always wanting more.

Leah's throat closed up when she thought of how wrong it was to be finally coming back to town, now, when Vivian was no longer there.

By the time she crossed into Door County a couple of hours later and the farmland turned into a tree-lined winding road flanked by restaurants and shops, with the water visible behind the gaps in the pines, she was almost out of tears.

Coffee was what she needed to clear her head. Maybe she'd pick one up for Emma too. Remembering a family-run café in the town of Egg Harbor, she pulled off the main road and parked the car, knowing that she was a mere matter of minutes from home—though neither the big Queen Anne on the bay or the four-bedroom colonial in the bucolic Chicago suburb felt like home anymore; both bore the scars of good intentions turned bad.

She was stalling, perhaps, but she needed to gather her bearings and ease herself back into the reunion. She pushed through the screen door of the rustic little building off the side of Route 42, which ran all the way to the tip of the peninsula. The water glistened from the windows at the back of the café, just visible through the branches of the tall pines that shaded the establishment, leaving the room cozy and dark, causing her to lift her sunglasses for one brief moment.

Only to lock eyes with Carter Maxwell.

Her stomach dropped quickly; she knew with certainty that he'd seen the panic in her face. She fumbled for her sunglasses, pushed up on her head now, and contemplated pulling them back down, but that would have been even lamer than turning and walking right back out the door and hightailing it to her car, starting the engine and peeling off.

Which was what she wanted to do. Oh, so badly.

Instead, she pulled in a breath, reminded herself that she was, in fact, a thirty-six-year-old mother of two and that she had built an entire life for herself since leaving Door County behind—even if that life had started to crumble.

Carter's familiar eyes were dark and wary as he stared at her, as if he was just as unsure how to handle this reunion and possibly just as shocked at seeing her. To say that they hadn't parted on good terms would be almost laughable, if it didn't still make her want to cry all these years later. His brown hair was a little shorter than it had been the last time she'd seen him, his skin tanned from days out on his boat, no doubt. But when he lifted the corner of his mouth into a half smile, she knew that he hadn't changed at all.

And despite how much she'd tried, maybe neither had she.

"Leah." He hesitated for a moment before stepping toward her. "I heard about Vivian. I didn't . . ."

He didn't need to finish his sentence for her to know what he was thinking. You didn't date a man for five years and not know him—or so she'd thought.

She pursed her lips, refusing to let old hurts override the current ones. He hadn't thought she'd come back. Aunt Vivian was gone. Of course Leah would come back, even if she should have done just that a long time ago.

Instead, she'd let this man, their past, and all that heartache keep her away.

"How long are you in town?" he asked carefully.

She glanced at his hand that held his paper cup, the fingers that had once traced her skin closed around the stamped logo. No ring. She hated herself for even looking, blaming it on idle curiosity. In her conversations with Vivian and Emma over the years, she'd never inquired about Carter, and they'd never brought him up, knowing that such a topic would only sour the day. But she'd known that he was still around without them having to say anything. Carter had been born and raised in these parts. He was rooted to the water and trees in a way that Leah almost envied, because even though the big old house on Water Street had been in her mother's family for generations, Leah always felt like a visitor, especially now.

Except when she was in his arms, she thought. Except when they talked about the future. Their future. The one that had never happened.

She wasn't entirely surprised to see that Carter's hand was bare. Commitment had clearly never been his strong suit. Her own platinum bands were still intact on her left hand, even though she probably should have taken them off when Ted told her he was leaving her, and for sure when the divorce papers had been filed. She fingered them now with her thumb: a nervous tic.

"Just a few days. Maybe a week." At most. She might not have anything to rush home to at the moment, but running into Carter had been just the reminder she needed of why she'd stayed away all these years, and of why she wouldn't be sticking around very long.

"I'm sorry about your aunt. I know how close you were."

Were. A simple word was all it took to make her heart sink into her stomach, filling her with longing and regret for something that she could never have back.

Leah gave a little nod and then lifted her chin, hating the way the tenderness in his voice made her drop her guard. She would not cry. Not in front of Carter. Not again. She'd cried enough tears for that man and more than he deserved.

"Well, I should probably get going. Emma's waiting for me." She hitched her handbag straps higher on her shoulder and edged to the door.

Carter held up his paper cup. "You're not getting coffee?"

She stared at him for a moment. Time had been good to him, giving him laugh lines at the corners of those dark, deep-set eyes, filling out his tall frame in all the right places.

"Changed my mind," she said, lifting an eyebrow before pushing through the screen door.

After all, if anyone should know about that, it was Carter. He'd changed his mind about her a long time ago.

The Stewart family house, built by her mother's grandparents, was one of the prettiest in all Fog's Landing. Leah slowed her car when the trees parted and gave way to a wide view of the water and the town just across the inlet, its white inns, homes, and chapels peeking out from thick green leaves. She took her time rounding the sweeping bend that circled the bay, then pulled to a stop near one of the public beaches to have a proper look. The pebbled ground dug into her flip-flops as she walked toward the sand, searching across the soft waves to where the house was visible, even from this distance.

Vivian had made her mark on the house, but she'd made it clear from the start that it belonged to all of them, just as it had belonged to Leah's grandparents, whom she'd never met, and their parents before that, people she and her sisters knew only from the discolored black-and-white framed photos that Viv had kept on side tables and shelves, tucked in with antique vases that had been with the house for as long as it stood.

The unspoken words were that the house might have also belonged to Leah's mother, but she'd made other plans, ones that took her away from this little lake town. Ones that had eventually ended her life prematurely.

Ones that were never discussed, even once Leah and her sisters grew into adulthood. At the time, the mystery of the family fallout had made Leah curious; now, she understood how it could have happened. And how history could repeat itself.

She stood on the beach for a few more minutes, breathing in the fresh air, letting the wind rustle her hair, thinking it strange that she was so close to the place she'd once called home and yet she still felt so far away. From this distance, the house still felt far away and unreachable, even though she could be there in a matter of minutes. Even though, in many ways, it still felt as foreign as it had that first day when she and her sisters had arrived here, lost and heartbroken, scared and confused, and as familiar as it had as the years wore on, when it started to feel like the only home she'd ever known and the only place she'd ever want to be.

So much for that.

Life had a way of surprising you, right when you finally got comfortable.

Leah walked back to the car, knowing she couldn't avoid her circumstances forever. She shifted gears, merged back onto the road, and didn't stop again this time until she was sitting in the driveway outside the house. She might have stayed in the car for another half an hour if it weren't for the sight of her sister bursting out onto the front porch, smiling ear to ear in spite of the reasons for this reunion.

And despite all her trepidation, Leah smiled too. Seeing Emma, after so much time, was exactly what she needed to forget the reasons she'd left this town, and for a moment, question if she never should have.

"Emma!" Leah scrambled out of the car and hurried to meet her youngest sister at the base of the stairs, arms wide as she pulled her in for a hug. Tears prickled the backs of her eyes, matching the ones that shone in Emma's hazel gaze when they broke apart. She squeezed her arm for a moment, not quite ready to let go again.

"Thank you for coming. I wasn't sure if . . ." Emma shook her head, sending her long braid flying. "I'm just so glad you're here!"

Leave it to Emma to still find a way to smile so brightly. She'd bounced back the quickest when their parents had died, and at the time, Leah had attributed it to her age. Now, she wondered if it was Emma's spirit that kept her going.

"Of course I'm here," Leah said, but she knew that Emma was right to be hesitant. Nothing had ever lured Leah back before—not even after Sadie left and never returned.

She stopped just short of the porch steps to take in her surroundings. The roses that Viv had tended to with such care had grown over the years into hearty bushes in vibrant shades of pink, and Leah realized with a wave of sadness that Viv had lived to see them bloom one last time. There was small comfort in that.

"Need help with your luggage?" Emma asked, cutting into her thoughts.

"I overpacked since I didn't know what I'd need. It's heavy," Leah said, thinking that she could come back for it later. She longed to go inside the house nearly as much as she dreaded it, knowing that her aunt wouldn't be there to welcome her with one of her warm hugs.

Instead, a fluffy little dog greeted her in excitement, his mouth open in a sort of smile, his bark louder than his compact form would suggest.

"This your watch dog?" She laughed as she bent to let the little animal lick her face.

"His name is Sully," Emma said with pride in her voice. "He's still a puppy. Aunt Vivian gave him to me for my birthday last year."

A year. And somehow Leah hadn't known this. She frowned as she stroked the dog's fur.

"My girls would love him," Leah said, knowing that this was a gross understatement. They'd been begging her for a dog for years, but Ted had always given a firm no, claiming he didn't need any more responsibilities.

Leah could only roll her eyes now thinking of that. Another red flag. She should have seen this coming.

"I thought they might be with you," Emma said, looking a little disappointed when Leah stood, taking in the house. The long hallway with the stairs to the left, the ornate banister where they'd wrap garlands each December, the stain still worn from years of use. The front living room to the right with the big bay window looking out onto the water across the road, where today, like so many days, the sailboats could be seen coming into the harbor.

It was all the same. It was all exactly the same. The walls were brightly colored against the crisp white woodwork. And colorful candles, throw pillows, and artwork offset the antique brass and bronze candlesticks and fireplace grates. Viv had kept the house cheerful, as she said. But then, that was Viv, living life to its fullest. If Leah didn't know better, she might expect her aunt to come around the corner from the library or the den or the dining room, or the little sewing room under the staircase, where she liked to keep busy on rainy days, claiming that handiwork made the hours pass in the blink of an eye.

The blink of an eye. That's what it felt like now.

Leah pulled her attention back to the present, realizing that Emma was still waiting for an explanation. She thought of what her friend Gina had said and replied with a shrug. "Summer camp."

"Darn. I made brownies last night. Then I ate the whole pan," Emma added, looking only a little guilty. "So, I made more this morning, thinking they might like some . . ."

Leah's stomach grumbled loud enough to make Sully bark. Emma laughed out loud, and Leah joined her, but the moment was short lived, and soon Emma was wiping away tears, even as her smile remained.

"I can't believe you came! Well, I can, but . . ." She brushed at her cheeks. "It's so hard being in this house without her, even for one day."

"I'm here now." Leah set a hand on Emma's arm. "And in case you didn't already figure it out, I'd love a brownie. Maybe we'll finish another pan." It wouldn't be the first time. As girls they had huddled around the kitchen table, sharing secrets, giggling at anything and everything, finding pleasure in small creature comforts that slowly made their world feel whole again.

She smiled sadly now. Those days felt like a lifetime ago. Like a different family altogether.

They walked down the large hall, past the walls that bore framed photos of happier times, to the expansive sunny yellow kitchen that was almost more the center of the home than the big living room at the front was. All Vivian's cookbooks were still stacked on the baker's rack, dog eared and weathered, in no particular order. There had to be three dozen of them, certainly more than the last time Leah had been in the house.

She took her usual seat at the table, avoiding looking at the chair that Sadie once occupied.

"Tell me how I can help," she said, needing to keep busy, even as Emma set the pan of brownies down on the center of the table and handed her a fork, not bothering with plates. "You already coordinated the service for tomorrow. I assume that Viv had plenty to cover the cost."

Emma gave her a strange look and then said, "Actually, I just ended up paying for it with what I have in my account. She'll be buried in the family plot, so that was prearranged, but the rest . . ."

"Oh." Leah was startled for a moment but then realized that Emma probably didn't know how to access Viv's account yet. "Well, I can write a check for half the cost to cover you. It will all be reimbursed once the affairs are in order."

But when Emma told her the sum, she could only swallow hard. It was more than she'd planned to part with, especially when she still hadn't found a job yet, but rather than get into all that just now, she walked over to her handbag on the counter and briskly wrote out a check, which she tore from the book, her smile a little frozen when she handed it to her sister.

"I thought we could have a reception here at the house afterward with lots of food and flowers and music, all of Viv's favorites. I left it open for anyone to attend," she added, darting a glance at Leah.

In other words, Leah had just been warned that Carter could show up, and probably would. She pushed out a sigh as she settled back in her chair, knowing that she'd be in the wrong to protest.

"Of course. Vivian was such a pillar of the community. And the house is too. It makes sense for everyone to gather here to honor her."

She didn't want to think about what would happen to this house come next week, when they'd have some difficult decisions to make. Just thinking about it felt like another loss, and no doubt Emma agreed. It had been her home the longest, after all.

"Most people offered to bring a dish," Emma continued. "I'll bake some things anyway. It helps, being in the kitchen."

"I'm sorry you had to handle this all on your own," Leah said, setting down her fork.

Emma gave her a smile that brought the light back to her eyes. "I'm not alone now. I have you here."

Yes, Emma had her. Too bad the same couldn't be said for their other sister.

CHAPTER FIVE

EMMA

As wonderful as it was having Leah here, there was no denying the feeling that if Emma had to spend one more minute in this house, she didn't know what she'd do. This sensation had been creeping up long before now, making her feel itchy and restless, making her want to leave this house just as much as she wanted to stay put.

Guilt reared again, and Emma pushed back her chair, collecting the nearly empty brownie pan. "I have to order the flowers." She hesitated at the sink, unsure how much to push. "Do you want to come with me?"

"Of course!"

Leah looked a little injured, and since Emma wasn't sure how to respond without getting into a big discussion she didn't have energy for just now, she didn't say anything.

Instead, she locked Sully up in the back mudroom, where he wouldn't get into mischief, and grabbed her bag from its hook. "My car or yours?"

Technically, it was Viv's car. Or it had been. It was old and rusted in parts, but Viv had balked at the thought of trading it in, citing the prices of cars these days, as if gas wasn't bad enough. Emma didn't mind because her world was small and easy to get around on bicycle or foot, especially now that she had Sully. But sometimes, when the ignition didn't start right away, she worried about how long it would be until the old car finally kicked the bucket. And she worried even more about what would happen then. Viv might have been stubborn, but she'd had other reasons for not getting herself a new car. Reasons she'd tried to keep to herself, even though Emma saw the way she'd stash the bills and bank statements every time they arrived in the mail.

"I still have to get my luggage, so we may as well take mine."

Leah headed to the front hall, and Emma followed her, noticing the way her oldest sister moved slowly, taking in the house that she hadn't set foot in for over fifteen years, even though Emma had rarely left it for more than a few days at a time.

Sully whined and barked from the mudroom, pulling at Emma's heartstrings in the way that only he could (and he knew it, the little stinker). She locked the door to the house behind herself and followed Leah to her silver SUV, thinking it sad that up until today, she hadn't even known what color her sister's car was, let alone the make and model. The last time they'd visited, Leah had been driving a navy sedan, and she'd taken Emma and Viv down to the city, showing them all the tourist sites, like Navy Pier and Millennium Park, and then they'd gone shopping on the Magnificent Mile, leaving Emma with that growing sense of doubt and wonder, imagining what her life could be like outside this small town.

She felt the same way each time she visited Leah—which wasn't often. Leah's world was full of children and friends and new people and places. It was so different from her own quiet and simple routine that, in many ways, she felt like she didn't know her sister at all. Growing up, Sadie had been the bridge between their more-than-six-year age gap, while Leah had always been a bit of a mystery to Emma, maternal more than sisterly, protective and quiet more than a fun companion—disappearing with her sketchbook when Emma was still playing with dolls and, later, preferring the company of local boys to that of her sisters.

Make that one local boy. Carter's name hadn't been uttered in as many years as Sadie's name. Emma had been careful about that, and she knew her aunt had too. Even when Leah got quickly engaged to Ted after college and soon settled into domestic life with two little girls of her own, it was a subject that was too sore to mention.

Feeling a little skittish, Emma checked her phone for the umpteenth time since reaching out to Sadie yesterday. No reply. She didn't even know if Sadie still had the same number. It wasn't like she'd tried to reach out to her over the years. And it wasn't like Sadie had tried either. Emma had told herself she wasn't taking sides, but it wasn't exactly true. Over the years, she had often wondered just how different things might have been if Leah had never gone away to college, because that was when the trouble started.

Leah stopped to look at her before sliding into the front seat, and Emma stuffed the phone into her handbag, feeling guilty. Again.

She told herself she'd done her part. The best she could. Besides, neither of her sisters had ever bothered to think about the position they'd put *her* in—that because of their fallout, her family was fractured, and she had to suffer too. That while they'd gone off to Chicago and New York, she'd stayed behind—not unwillingly at first, because she'd always been a homebody and was content in Door County, but as the years dragged on, she hadn't been able to help but wonder what else life held for her, what might await her if she were to leave.

Now, she could find out. Only it didn't feel so sweet, only bitter.

"You tell me where to drive," Leah said as she slid her sunglasses onto her face.

Emma almost laughed and pointed out that Leah had grown up in these parts, too, but managed to stop herself. Things had changed—though not much. Of course Leah had forgotten. She had an entire life outside this county. This town, and everyone in it, was just a part of her past.

"The flower shop in Sister Bay is one of my favorites," Emma said, drawing no irony from the town's name. It was a bit farther than Fish Creek and in the opposite direction, but with fewer shops and restaurants, it would be easier to find parking. During summer, Door County was always crowded with tourists—something that most businesses relied on, even though, as a local, she yearned for the quiet winter months. "That's where I order the flowers for the front desk at the hotel, so I might be able to get a good deal." She didn't mention that Leah's best friend from childhood also ran the place now after having taken it over from her mother a couple of years back.

"You're still working at the Baybrook Inn?"

Emma stifled an eye roll behind her sunglasses. Of course she was still working there—nothing much changed in her life day after day or even year after year. She walked to work and back again unless the rain or snow was heavy, stood at the front desk with a smile on her face, sometimes enjoying her job, other times not. Happy to have a steady paycheck to bring home each month—one that she sometimes saved but usually put toward some of the bills that Viv didn't like to talk about.

They'd taken care of each other, she and Viv. But that was all about to change now, wasn't it? Or it could. At long last, the entire world was open to her, not just the daily routine of her small town.

For a moment, as Leah hit the brakes quickly to avoid a squirrel crossing the road, Emma feared she might be sick, and it wasn't on account of Leah's heavy foot or all those brownies either. It was the guilt. The endless guilt!

"Yep, still working there." With Sarah Maxwell, she almost said, but that would just get them onto topics that were probably best left alone. Besides, Leah would hear plenty for herself if she stuck around town long enough. Emma couldn't always play the messenger, not when it could backfire.

"I always loved that place, tucked right at the edge of town, with the trees to the back and the water to the front." Leah smiled at this, but Emma didn't.

Leah turned right, turning up the radio as the lakefront view disappeared for a few miles, hidden by tall trees as they climbed the bluff around the bay. They talked about the girls, who were away at summer camp, and the house, and Sully, of course, and all his antics. It wasn't until Leah had parked the car and they were walking down Water Street that she quietly said, "So Carter's still in town. Not that I'm surprised."

Oh. That. Emma stiffened until she realized that the only way Leah would have known this was if she had looked him up, which would be almost more shocking than her being back in town at all, or worse—had run into him.

"He left for a while." No sense getting into specifics, especially when Carter had sworn he would never leave Fog's Landing and that had been the start of all that tension between him and Leah. Emma hesitated, but Leah's silence told her she should continue. "I always thought Carter still living here was the reason you never visited."

"One of them," Leah said flatly.

They both knew the other one, though. Unlike Carter, Sadie hadn't been back to town since shortly after Leah left.

"He's working for his dad, at the bank," Emma continued, which pulled a frown from her sister.

She didn't mention that she was still friendly with him or that she saw him regularly, given that the town was small and she was still best friends with his sister, Sarah. He always asked about Leah, politely. How was she, how were her children, was she going to be visiting this summer? Emma would answer in her breezy way: Leah was fine, her children were adorable, and no, Leah didn't plan on visiting anytime soon. Carter would nod as he absorbed this information and then quickly change the topic.

She wondered if she should mention this to Leah, but she couldn't gauge her sister's mood when she was hiding her eyes behind those big sunglasses. Besides, she had enough to worry about today.

They walked by a few more shops, past a restaurant with its windows down, leaving the entire space exposed to the fresh air. There was always a lively, happy vibe to summertime in Door County, but today, Emma couldn't find a way to lift her spirits.

Of all the sisters, she'd been closest to their aunt. Vivian and she were, as they fondly called themselves, "kindred spirits." She'd known Vivian many years longer than she'd known her real mother, and though she'd never admitted it to Leah, in many ways Vivian felt like her mother, the only one she'd really known. The one who hugged her and laughed with her and who always lifted her eyebrow a little too high, saying nothing, when she saw Emma smiling at something Wyatt had said.

Swooning was probably a better descriptor.

Emma pushed open the door to the flower shop, the bell ringing their arrival. The owner of the store—Leslie Johnson—was busy with another customer, which suited Emma just fine. She wasn't up for an outpouring of condolences at the moment, and there would be plenty of those in the days to come. Vivian was popular in this town, having lived here all her life. She knew everyone by name, knew their families and their histories, knew their stories. And Emma knew that this was another reason that Leah had stayed away; she didn't like that everyone in the surrounding towns that made up this peninsula in Wisconsin knew all their history.

No doubt Sadie felt the same. Why else would she have vanished into the crowded streets of New York City?

Emma's chest felt so tight with sadness that she was almost relieved when Leah said, her tone ever so casual, even though she was unable to meet Emma's eyes, "Is he in a relationship?"

Emma looked up from an arrangement of mixed roses. "Is who in a relationship?" Surely, she couldn't still be talking about Carter! Leah had left town because she specifically didn't want to ever talk to or about Carter again. The man had broken her heart in two, for good.

Now Leah met her gaze, her look saying that she didn't want to have to say his name again.

"Oh." Emma wondered if it was worth mentioning that Carter had been known to casually date, sometimes the same woman for months on end, once even longer. But it was never serious. The only girl he'd ever been serious about was Leah. "I don't think so at the moment."

Leah nodded, her expression otherwise blank, and she stopped in front of a bouquet of lilies. "No lilies. Vivian hated lilies."

"Not as much as she hated daisies." Emma smiled fondly at the memory. Talking about her aunt like this made her feel like she was still with them.

"She loved roses. I can't imagine going with anything else."

"Although she did claim she grew the best ones." Another tug at Emma's heart. "But I agree. Roses. All the colors. The happier the better. She would have wanted that." She looked over to the counter, but Leslie had disappeared into the back room.

Leah sniffed a rose and gave Emma a coy smile. "What about you? Anyone sending you flowers these days?"

"Ha! I wish." Emma pursed her lips, thinking of how wonderful it would be to receive flowers from Wyatt, to have confirmation that what she felt for him wasn't one sided. She considered mentioning the confusing dynamic of their relationship to Leah but decided against it. Wyatt had a girlfriend. Emma was tucked firmly into the friend basket.

If that wasn't a reason to leave town, she didn't know what was.

Look at Leah, after all. She'd been devastated by Carter, but after she'd left Fog's Landing, she'd found lasting love, settled into a marriage, and had two beautiful children.

Surely there was hope for Emma too.

"It's too bad that Ted and the girls can't make it." Children were such a wonderful distraction in sad times, but even if the girls were at camp, surely Ted could have come for moral support?

Leah's hand stilled on a mixed bouquet, and then she waved her fingers through the air. "Oh, it's better this way. Girl time. You and me." They shared a smile, and Emma felt her chest bloom with love for her sister. She barely knew Ted, and, if she was being honest with herself, she barely knew her sister anymore. They needed this time. Just the two of them.

She chewed the corner of her lip as she walked around the store. Just the two of them. Really, that would be for the best.

She stole a peek at her phone again, happy for once to see that there weren't any texts. Normally, she'd be disappointed by this, hoping to see something from Wyatt, even if it was just an emoji. But no texts meant that Sadie hadn't responded. Maybe she hadn't even received Emma's message. Emma could live with the good conscience that she'd done the right thing, as Viv would have wished.

Sometimes, she was really tired of doing the right thing.

"Emma!" Now Leslie was coming toward her, arms extended, and Emma felt the tears threaten to return, warming her eyes as she let herself be squeezed.

"Leah's here, too," she said, a little awkwardly.

Leslie looked sharply at Leah, her expression one of such total shock that Leah had the decency to blush.

"It's good to see you again, Leslie," Leah said, giving her old friend a hesitant grin.

The two had once been good friends—not as close as Emma was to Sarah, but still, friends of the type that Leslie used to come over for sleepovers, join them on summer-afternoon bike rides and trips for ice cream down the road. Like she had with so many people in Door County, Leah had lost touch with her when she'd moved to Chicago. Sometimes, this reminded Emma not to take Leah's distance too personally, but other times, like now, it just made her feel sad for all that had happened.

"I hear you have two little girls! Did you bring them?" Leslie's big blue eyes were her best feature, and she opened them wide now.

Leah shook her head. "Not this time."

Now it was Emma's turn to frown. What could her sister mean by that? Did Leah intend to return? And to what? Vivian was gone; soon enough, the house would be, too, if her sisters had anything to do with it. They wouldn't want to keep it, not when they had fled far and fast and only now bothered to come back.

She couldn't afford to buy out their shares of the house. And did she even want to? That house had been a refuge, but at times, it had also felt like a gilded cage.

"Well, I'd love to catch up while you're in town. If you're up for it," Leslie added quickly, and Emma knew she was referring to more than just the circumstances that brought Leah back. She felt slighted, maybe even a little rejected. Emma understood. Leah's reasons for never visiting were clear, but it was hard not to take things personally after so much time.

Leah sighed into a smile, though, relaxing the mood in the room. "I would love that."

Leslie beamed and then turned to Emma. "You just missed Wyatt."

Emma wondered if Leah could see the burn that Emma felt rise up in her cheeks. Wyatt in a flower shop? She wasn't so sure she wanted to know. If he'd been buying something for his girlfriend, she wasn't sure she could bear to hear it, not today, when she was already struggling to brave a smile and keep going.

"He must have really loved your aunt Vivian. He ordered . . . well." Leslie gave a wink and flipped through an order form on her counter, turning it so Emma could see.

Emma's eyes popped at the sum. Wyatt hadn't just ordered a condolence bouquet. He'd footed the bill for most of the service flowers.

Did he know that times were tight? And if he did, then how many others knew? This town was small, as Sadie loved to point out, bitterly. But Emma saw it differently. She saw it as a community. And gestures like this—well, that's what made it easier to stay here.

And gestures like this from Wyatt? How could she even think of leaving?

She swallowed hard as Leah leaned in. "Who is this guy? I don't recognize the name."

"Just a friend," Emma said, even though he was so much more than that, and didn't this prove it? Her heart was beating so fast, she was sure that her sister and Leslie could hear it. What was Wyatt doing? What did he mean by such a gesture?

Surely, it couldn't be his way of saying he loved her.

Stop it, Emma! She blinked rapidly, trying to clear her mind of such totally inappropriate thoughts.

"Well, whoever he is, he's very generous," Leah remarked.

"He said he wanted you to pick everything out," Leslie assured Emma. "But my, he must have a soft spot for your family."

Emma nearly whimpered on a sigh. She could almost hear the rustling of Vivian's dangling earrings as she looked down on her, shaking her head with a vengeance. "You're wasting your time with that one, my dear" was all she'd ever said.

"We'll go with the roses. The mixed ones," Leah said. "Vivian wouldn't have wanted things to be too somber."

"With her laugh?" Leslie's smile was broad, but her eyes turned sad. "We're all going to miss that laugh."

Emma could still hear it when she closed her eyes. Vivian had a wonderful sense of humor, saying that if you couldn't laugh at life, then you had no business living it. She had been an eternal optimist. No doubt she would be shaking Emma by the shoulders right now over more than her three-year crush on Wyatt Bale. She'd want Emma to live a full life.

She'd died thinking that Emma was doing just that.

The guilt kicked in again. In all their time together, Emma had never complained. The way she saw it, she had no room to gripe about her circumstances. Leah and Sadie had left, and Viv had been the one who had not only taken Emma in, but stood by her, giving her love and consistency and a place she could always call home. Viv never knew about all that Emma longed for, the way she'd come home from her trips to Chicago thinking of all the sights and scenery, the restaurants and shops, the buzz of excitement, the feeling of possibility. How sometimes, after she'd turn off a late-night movie with Viv and announce she was going to bed, Emma would sit on her bed instead of turning down the covers, feeling as lost and lonely as she had when she'd first come to live in the big house. That sometimes, she wished Vivian would tell her to go, encourage her to move out—not just out of the house but out of Door County.

"I'll deliver everything tomorrow. I don't want you to worry about a thing." Leslie set a hand on Emma's shoulder. "You were so good to her."

Emma felt Leah's eyes on hers, and she looked down at the floor. She had been good to Vivian, she knew, because she loved her, yes, but also because she felt like she had no other choice.

Both sisters were quiet when they left the shop and walked back to the car.

"Anything in particular you want to do tonight?" Emma asked once they were nearly home. The thought of a quiet house, without Vivian's laughter filling the rooms, weighed on her. "Winston's for ice cream? A walk along the harbor?" Sully would enjoy it, and it would be good to get out of the house.

"Both sound good," Leah said, seeming in good spirits. But as they pulled up to the house, Leah's smile dropped. "Are you expecting anyone?"

There, on the porch, was a woman dressed in black jeans and a black tank top—an outsider, to all appearances, one with blonde hair the same shade as Leah's pulled back in a messy knot and oversize sunglasses shielding her eyes and obstructing her face, even as it grew clearer and more familiar as they approached.

A familiar knot of dread twisted Emma's stomach. It wasn't a neighbor or a friend looking to drop off a care package.

It was Sadie. And this could lead to only one thing. Trouble.

CHAPTER SIX

SADIE

Sadie knew better than to expect the welcome wagon, but jeez, couldn't they have at least feigned a little excitement? A part of her had dared to hope that when her sisters saw her again, in person, all those icky moments would be forgotten and all the good ones remembered and that maybe they'd actually hug, even cry, or at least crack a smile.

Instead, Emma looked alarmingly pale, and Leah . . . well, Leah's hardened expression said it all. All these years later, and nothing had changed. And clearly, nothing had been forgiven. Go figure.

It was Emma who, not surprisingly, finally collected herself, managing some sort of smile as she climbed the porch steps and gave Sadie a quick hug. "I'm happy you're here," she said when she pulled away.

Sadie lifted an eyebrow. She didn't know if she believed that, but then trust had long ago been broken.

"You texted. I came!"

Leah tossed Emma a sharp look, and Emma looked down at the floorboards, which were in need of a fresh coat of stain. Ah, so Emma hadn't even mentioned this little tidbit to Leah. Well, great. That would just add to the tension, and right about now, Sadie was regretting choosing diet soda over a glass of wine on the plane here, and she'd only done that because she couldn't justify the extra cost, not when she'd gone straight from the unemployment office to the airport.

Sadie waited to see if Leah would say anything, but as the silence stretched, it was clear that wasn't going to happen. Despite what most people in this town probably thought, Sadie had never been a fan of conflict, which was why she'd stayed away so long in the first place.

"Well, let's go inside," Emma eventually said. She eyed the luggage at Sadie's feet. Sadie decided not to bother explaining, instead swinging one bag over her shoulder and grabbing the other two with her hands. She was used to doing things on her own, not relying on anyone, not even her own family. She'd packed a lot, but only because she wasn't sure how long she'd be here. She wasn't in a rush to get back to New York—at least she hadn't been until now. There was no job waiting for her, and more and more the small apartment she'd shared with her roommate all these years made her feel more like a guest than a resident of what was technically her only home.

She looked around at the porch of this old house—no longer the home she had known the longest. Somehow, it felt the most familiar, even after all these years. When Emma opened the door, Sadie stepped over the threshold after only a brief hesitation. She pulled in a breath, feeling the sunlight that poured through the large window on the landing of the stairs warm her face. She didn't know what she'd been expecting, coming back here again after all this time, but seeing that nothing had changed, from the mismatched frames on the marble pedestal end table to the open music books that rested on the piano ledge, she longed for a past that she had tried to forget.

Emma muttered something as she disappeared into the back of the house, but Sadie couldn't hear because the sound of a dog barking drowned out her sister's words. Leah, she noticed, had decided not to join them just yet but instead remained at the base of the porch steps, visible only through the screen door.

Before she could contemplate how to handle her older sister, a ball of fur burst into the hall, yapping excitedly. For a moment, the awkwardness was gone, along with the sorrow that Vivian wasn't here, that Sadie had never said goodbye, that the words she'd said all those years ago when she left had never been meant to be the last. She smiled and laughed as the cute little dog jumped with contagious joy.

"Meet Sully," Emma said, her tone noticeably lighter.

"Yours?" Sadie looked up at her sister, who nodded, grinning with pride.

Sadie loved dogs. She'd always hoped for one of her own, but her roommate wouldn't stand for it, and besides, Sadie wasn't home enough hours to care for it. She could barely take care of herself, let alone another living creature. Somehow her younger sister had managed to do both, though. She'd taken care of this dog, this house, and Vivian.

Not for the first time, Sadie wondered how different her own life might have looked if she had stuck around, waited for the hard feelings to subside rather than reacted to them.

She scooped the little guy into her arms and stroked his fur fondly. "What a sweetheart. I bet Vivian just loved him."

Loved. It felt so wrong to say that word in the past tense, and from the startled look in Emma's gaze, she no doubt felt the same.

"I didn't think you would come," Emma said, seeming anxious as she glanced at the door. "You didn't reply to my message. I wasn't even sure you had received it."

Sadie pulled in a breath. She'd expected this. Maybe it was why she hadn't told Emma she was coming. Because she hadn't decided until the last minute. Because she didn't need any more excuses not to get on that plane. Because she was afraid of Emma telling her not to come at all.

But she had a right to be here, too, even if Leah probably didn't think so. But Emma had sent the text . . .

"It didn't feel right not to be here." Sadie glanced back over her shoulder at the screen door. "I guess Leah didn't expect me to come either?"

Emma chewed her lip. Clearly, the tension was mutual.

"What can I do to help?" Sadie felt so removed from everything. This house. Her sisters. Her family's lives. She knew the bare basics and nothing more. Vivian had kept their calls chatty and light, and Sadie knew that if Emma had wanted to talk to her, she could have at any time. The same, she knew, could be said for herself. All those times, she could have asked Viv to transfer her over; she could have tried to make peace, to explain. Instead, she'd let the years slip by until it felt like too much time had passed to suddenly reach out.

Now she saw that Emma was grown up. Her light-brown hair was longer than it used to be, tied back in a braid like she'd always fashioned it, and her eyes remained bright, along with her devilish smile, but her face had thinned out over the years, losing some of that adolescent baby fat, and despite her smile, she looked tired. Weary.

"The service is tomorrow morning," Emma said, pulling the dog up into her arms, reminding Sadie that he, like everything else in this house, was part of Emma's world, not hers. That she was a visitor in this house now, like always. "I'll have some desserts here for anyone who wants to come back to the house. Most people said they'd bring a dish."

Sadie gave a little snort. "I can see the community spirit hasn't faded."

Not that she'd ever really been a part of the community—at least, not in the end. Once, the close-knit town of Fog's Landing had pulled her in with open arms—she knew everyone's name, and they knew her; they knew her family, and they knew her story. People had waved when they saw her, exchanged brief conversations from where they'd left off just days before, and pulled together in small ways (like salting neighbors' sidewalks on particularly icy winter mornings) and big ones, like tomorrow.

A shuffle behind them made Emma's eyes widen, and without daring to turn around, Sadie knew that Leah had come inside when the screen door banged closed. Emma looked over her shoulder watchfully. Even Sully seemed to sense that something was brewing and stayed quiet, his round brown eyes alert.

Leah finally spoke. "You certainly packed a lot. I didn't realize you were so willing to spend time here."

"I could say the same about you." Sadie stared at her sister properly for the first time in fifteen years, since the last time they'd both been in this house together, when Sadie had been begging for forgiveness that never came.

"My roommate was eager for some of the extra space in my absence," Sadie explained, but all the while she was thinking that after fifteen years of silence, this was what they were talking about? Luggage?

She didn't feel welcome at her apartment in the city, but she could sense that she wasn't welcome here, either—that she was crazy to think about staying long, or even coming at all.

"I have an extra black dress if you need to borrow it."

Sadie narrowed her gaze suspiciously. She knew better than to think that Leah was just being nice. "Thanks, but I live in New York City. More than half my wardrobe is black." She gestured to her current attire, hoping to ease the tension.

Leah didn't take the bait. "Just making sure you weren't planning on wearing red. I know how much you like to be the center of attention."

"So, this is how it's going to be?"

"And why would you expect it to be any different?" Leah leveled her with a stony gaze.

"Oh, I don't know, because it's been fifteen years! We were young, Leah!"

She saw Emma wince as fresh anger bloomed in Leah's cheeks. "That hardly justifies sleeping with my boyfriend."

"I'm not . . ." Shoot. She hadn't even been here an hour, and she'd already made things worse. She sighed and softened her tone. "I'm just saying, look at you." She refrained from pointing out Leah's neat and tidy suburban-mom look, complete with a designer tote, white jeans, and name-brand flip-flops that were more for show than comfort, which was so different from her city-streetwear look purchased off the sale racks. "You have a husband, two kids, a house in the burbs, probably a white picket fence to boot." In other words, more than Sadie had ever had, or could even dream of having, at this rate.

Something in Leah's forehead pinched, but she shook it away, backing up into the kitchen. "You would see it that way."

"Please!" Emma all but shouted. "Viv hasn't even been buried yet. Can we at least get through the funeral in peace, out of respect?"

Sadie knew that she should apologize to Emma for upsetting her, to Leah for her part in bringing them to this point. But she wasn't so sure that Leah would believe it, or right now, with the way she was behaving, if she even deserved it.

"Are your girls here?" she asked suddenly, realizing that she hadn't heard any movement from upstairs. Maybe Leah's husband had taken them down the street for ice cream. She wondered what they would say when they saw her.

She wondered, a little uneasily, if they would even know who she was.

Leah stiffened, averting her gaze. "Just me."

"Just *us*," Emma said, giving a smile that did little to hide the strain in her eyes.

Oh no. The three of them. Alone in this house. No Aunt Viv as the buffer. No significant others to change up the dynamic.

Sadie really shouldn't have come.

"Well, seeing as we're all here, we should probably talk about what we'll do with the house," Leah said with a sigh.

Sadie glanced at Emma, who was staring at Leah the way she always had done—looking for guidance, for a solution. Maybe for assurance that everything would be all right.

But Leah seemed just as overwhelmed as Sadie felt, not that she'd be letting on. She wasn't here for a cut of the profits, even though of course this house was likely worth a pretty penny.

"Maybe there's something in the will . . . ," Leah started, but Emma shook her head.

"I doubt that Viv left me anything," Sadie said, getting right to what they were all thinking. "After what I did."

"How could you even say that?" Emma said, her eyes dark with hurt. "Aunt Vivian loved you, Sadie. She loved all of us."

Sadie felt a lump in her throat grow, and she couldn't respond. Couldn't speak. And even if she could, she didn't know what to say to that.

"Whatever Viv had left will be left to us three," Emma said.

"You sure of that?" Leah asked, not looking Sadie's way.

"Nice," Sadie said, shaking her head, but the hurt in her chest felt fresh and raw. And for today, she was a little tired of falling back on these old roles, especially as they'd left them.

"Besides," Emma said, "there's no will. Viv would never make one. She was too superstitious."

"Viv was a very fair person," Leah conceded. "I am sure Emma is right and that she wanted to split things evenly between us."

If only because the last thing she'd want was for the sisters to have another reason to resent each other.

"Well, the only thing of value is really this house." Emma was hugging her dog tight, looking uncomfortable with this conversation. "Viv didn't really work, just lived off the estate."

Leah nodded. "You've lived here the longest, Emma. This is your home. What are your thoughts about what we do with the house?"

Emma looked so torn that for a moment, Sadie feared she might cry, and Sadie really couldn't handle that. She was barely holding it together herself, with Leah harboring so much anger toward her still.

"I don't know. It's a big house. Too big for one, or so Viv always liked to say." Emma frowned and stared at the floor, as if she was thinking of something else, something in the past, not what they should do for the future.

"We'll need to have everything assessed before we decide anything," Leah said in her matter-of-fact way.

Sadie supposed that was a good idea. One she hadn't thought of, because she never did think two steps ahead, did she? She had never been practical. Never had to be, because they had Leah for that.

Maybe at least one of her problems would be solved by coming back here after all. If they could sell the house, then she could have a nice cushion, a safety net for the first time in her life.

But then, what were the chances of Emma wanting to move out of her own home?

"I'm going up to my room," Sadie announced, only then realizing that she wasn't even sure if her old bedroom was still intact or if it had been cleared out, transformed, or just forgotten when she left all those years ago.

Emma didn't try to stop her, and it was Emma who had remained here all these years and seemed to own the house, so Sadie continued her clumsy march up the half-turn staircase, pretending that her suitcase wasn't loaded to the point of possibly breaking the zipper at any moment, that most of her treasured possessions weren't tucked away under the canvas.

She reached the top stair and looked down the hallway lined with brass sconces that would lend a warm glow by dusk. The arched doors on each side were closed, but she knew the order. Her aunt's room was at the front of the house, with the stained glass windows that bordered the bigger picture window with the view of the lake, along with another small bedroom with a working fireplace that was being used as a sitting room, or had been, last time she was here. Then came the rooms by birth order: Leah, Sadie, Emma. They alternated sides of the house, leaving Sadie alone, on the opposite wall from her sisters. No irony in that.

Sadie pulled in a breath and turned the knob, pushing the door open into the room, which remained exactly as she'd left it. Sun filtered through the large window that faced the double bed, draped in a quilt that she knew Vivian had made. A row of stuffed animals was propped against the pillows, and at the desk, a collection of framed photos showed happier times, ones spent down at the sandy lakefront, mostly. A single bookshelf housed the paperbacks that she loved to read, curled up on the deep window ledges that Vivian anchored with pillows, down at the rocky shoreline, or sometimes up on the third-floor balcony, where the world below seemed so far away.

With an ache in her chest, she sat down on the bed, wondering what had made Vivian keep the room like this all these years. Had she been holding on to a memory, or worse—holding out hope?

Unable to bear the thought of her aunt waiting for a visit that came a day too late, she pulled her phone out of her bag, desperate for a connection to her city life. But the only text was from her roommate: Easier to say this now that you've gone home but Randy's moving in and we need the extra space. Let me know when you can swing by to get your things. I'll put your security deposit toward the last month's rent. Thanks!

Gone home. Contrary to the evidence surrounding her in these cozy four walls, this was not her home, and she was not welcome.

She should have seen it coming. Maybe she did, and maybe that was why she'd had the sense to pack up what little she did have and bring it with her. She'd never trusted that anything in her life could be permanent.

Still, with a meager unemployment check and no savings for a place in New York, she'd have no choice but to stay in Fog's Landing even longer than planned. Or at least until they sold this house.

CHAPTER SEVEN

EMMA

It was the kind of warm June day where the clouds never dared to appear in the clear blue sky. The kind of day where the sun held the promise of a long afternoon and a cool evening. The kind of day that most people never wanted to end—and the kind of day that Vivian deserved.

"It was a beautiful service," Linda Price murmured to her, once they were all gathered back at the house. Their next-door neighbor and Viv's closest friend, Linda was one of many people that Emma knew so well, she felt more like family than community. There was Fran, who had taught her piano every Monday evening in this very house, and Shelly Nelson, who always baked the best shortbread cookies and made the rounds every December. And the Maxwells, whom Leah and Sadie were probably avoiding as much as they were each other.

The house had filled up quickly, with most people crowded around the dining room table, which was covered in a spread of casseroles, sandwiches, and sweets, or sitting in the front living room, admiring the collection of framed photos of Vivian and some of Emma and her sisters during happier times.

But Emma didn't need to look at those photos that Viv had insisted on keeping, because just looking at them made her wonder what she would do with them, along with everything else in this house. Pack it up? And put it where?

She supposed Leah would have a solution for that. A solution she both craved and resented. It was so easy for her oldest sister to come back to town and just take charge.

Sometimes, Emma wished she could be so decisive.

Fighting off too many emotions, Emma excused herself to slip away. She needed fresh air and space to think. Viv was gone, and her once too-certain future now felt daunting.

Emma sat on the porch swing, looking out over the water and listening to the chains creak as she swayed back and forth. It was a spot she often came to when she needed to think—lately, about Wyatt, not that she was doing that today. Today she was thinking about all the times she'd sat on this very seat with her aunt at her side, sipping lemonade, looking out over the water, talking about nothing in particular but feeling satisfied all the same.

Her relationship with Vivian had evolved over the years after she was no longer a little girl in need of direction. Once it was just Emma and Viv, they made new traditions. On the first warm day of summer, they spent the day at the lakefront. On the first crisp day of fall, they went apple picking at Howard's Orchard and then came home to spend the entire day baking apple crisps, turnovers, and pies that they sometimes shared but often ate. Friday nights were spent at the pizza place over in Fish Creek if Emma wasn't out with Sarah; Saturday nights they alternated—Viv usually choosing to frequent one of the dining rooms of the many inns in Door County, while Emma opted for the newer establishments, eager for something fresh. Sundays they always had takeout, which they ate in front of a classic movie before returning to bed. As much as Emma sometimes felt restless, sometimes even bound by duty, she appreciated Viv's companionship.

Viv, she knew, probably counted on it. She had friends, a community, sure, but Emma was her only family once Sadie and Leah ran off to go live their own lives, leaving her behind. She could have followed in their paths, and Viv, being Viv, would have boasted a big smile and supported it. But she'd never suggested she leave, which told Emma what she already knew. Viv wanted her to stay.

And Emma decided a long time ago to pretend that it was her choice to do just that. It had been easier when Wyatt came along, until he became just one more reason to go.

The swing creaked under her weight as the chains shifted, pulling Emma's attention away from the water and onto the house itself. It was one of the prettiest homes on Water Street, maybe even one of the best in all Door County. A proper family home passed down through the generations, and Viv had liked to point out that they didn't make homes like this anymore. It wasn't just the gables and the wraparound porch or the picket fence with its climbing roses. Installing central air had been the only modern concession. Viv insisted that homes like this were meant to be maintained, not updated, preserving the past as she moved along through the future. It used to bug Emma when she longed for an updated kitchen or windows that didn't stick on the hotter days of summer.

But she knew better than to complain. And she suspected that Viv's reasons hadn't been based on stubbornness but on something else. Something that made Emma a little queasy every time she thought about it. Something that kept her here, handing over part of her paychecks each month, wanting to give back to the woman who had given her so much.

The screen door banged open, like it always did when it caught the slightest lakefront breeze. It had been one of Vivian's few complaints, especially when the girls were younger, leading her to call out from the kitchen, always a second too late. Later, after what happened between Leah and Sadie, and once they were gone, her aunt had confided to Emma that she longed for the sound of that door banging shut because the house felt too quiet now.

And comments like that . . . Well, how could Emma even think of leaving her?

She looked up to see Wyatt poking his head around the door, and immediately her stomach made a swooping sensation. And how could she ever think of leaving Wyatt? Even though she should. She really should. Because as Viv had liked to say, Wyatt was a "dead-end road."

He grinned at her, and darn it if her heart didn't flutter for a moment there. "I thought I'd find you out here."

He knew her so well. Too well, maybe, but also, maybe not as well as he thought. Did he know, for example, that she had been in love with him since the very first time he'd flashed her that smile and passed her that drink? That after they'd talked for most of the night while he tended the bar, about his business, about what brought him to Door County (a fresh start) and how long she'd lived here (most of her life; it was home by now), she'd felt like she was nearly floating when he informed her that he was closing up, and could he walk her out?

She didn't think he knew. If he did, he wouldn't hang around her so much, wouldn't get her hopes up, wouldn't keep her hanging on.

Unless . . . the hope bloomed in her chest like it always did, much as everyone in her life tried to tamp it down.

"Hiding out?"

"Caught red handed." She scooted down on the swing to make room for him. "Everyone means well, but it's a lot. Sometimes . . ." She stopped herself for a minute. "Sometimes I think about what it would be like to live somewhere else, where no one knows me."

"I rather like this small-town life myself," Wyatt said, coming to sit beside her.

Emma pulled Sully onto her lap. Her heart sped up a little when his leg skimmed hers. "But that's because it's a new place for you." Though not so new, not anymore.

He looked at her quizzically. "You wouldn't really leave, though?"

Was he asking her to stay? She was a little ashamed to admit that she had fantasized about this exact scenario far too many times, imagining him begging her to stay, coming to his senses, realizing that he couldn't live without her, that he'd loved her all along.

"This house is too big for one person. Aunt Viv always used to comment on how happy she was to have us three in her life, filling the walls with laughter and chatter." Emma felt her eyes well up, but she pushed her emotions back. "Besides, my sisters have as much right to this house as I do. They'll want to sell."

Though they hadn't directly said as much, it was obvious from their conversation yesterday. They were back, temporarily, to honor Viv and settle the estate. Only they didn't know what Emma knew: that the only thing Viv had to her name was this house and everything in it.

"But selling the house doesn't mean you have to move out of town." Again with the look. Again, her heart leaped with hope that she really should have let go of a long time ago, like the day she had learned he was unavailable.

"You saying you'd miss me?" It was bold of her, and her cheeks flushed from more than the summer heat.

"You and this guy," he said, giving Sully a scratch behind the ears. "Who else is going to make me those delicious brownies?"

Maybe it was a compliment, but it wasn't what she wanted to hear. She wanted him to beg, maybe even tear up. In her wildest daydreams, he even dropped to one knee in desperation.

"Doesn't your girlfriend bake?" Emma so rarely mentioned her existence that it felt awkward, even challenging. Judging by the lull in their conversation, she could only gather that Wyatt felt the same way. The fact that he had a girlfriend was well established. Mention of her was not. In all their years, Emma had managed to never meet her—the few opportunities that came along she made sure to avoid.

"I don't think there's anyone in the Great Lakes that can bake like you," he said.

She managed not to roll her eyes, instead smothering a smile. "Viv was the real baker in the family. She taught me everything I know."

She looked out onto the water, eager to get a little space from him. "It's weird not having any family left in town."

"You have your sisters," he pointed out.

She looked at him sharply. "You know they haven't been back in fifteen years."

"I met one, actually," he said.

"Which one?" She could only hope they didn't share any embarrassing stories about her, like the time she'd cried her eyes out on their first fishing trip with Viv, insisting on throwing the flailing thing back in the water so it would have a fighting chance.

He waggled his eyebrows. "The blonde."

"They're both blonde," Emma pointed out. She alone had inherited her mother's hair color.

"The one with the tight ponytail."

Given that Leah's curls rendered that impossible, that meant only one thing. "Sadie." She sighed. "Oh, brother. What did you think?"

"I think . . ." His mouth did that little thing when he was trying not to smile. "I think that she'd rather be anywhere but here."

"Ha! That obvious?" But it was, and it saddened her. Vivian had always hoped that Leah and Sadie would come back together, but she wouldn't have wanted it to be like this. Not today. Especially not today.

"I take it that this wasn't the reunion that you were hoping for?"

Everyone in Fog's Landing knew about how Carter and Sadie had slept together when Leah was in college, when she and Carter had apparently broken up, but maybe not, to hear Leah tell it. It had been a big old mess, big enough to drive all three parties from town at various points and for varying lengths of time. Big enough to leave Emma a casualty that none of the others seemed to consider, only Viv, who was equally impacted by the fallout.

"I suppose the circumstances didn't exactly lend themselves to a happy reunion," she said, giving a small smile.

"How long is everyone staying?"

That, she didn't know. She didn't dare ask Sadie—at least not in front of Leah. "I wouldn't be surprised if Sadie leaves tonight."

She fell quiet, unsure of how she felt about that. This was her opportunity to try to bring her sisters together, and with each minute that ticked by, the chances of that happening were slipping away.

She'd talk to Leah. After this. It's what Viv would want of her, and it was probably her last chance.

But for now . . . she looked up into Wyatt's eyes and wondered if he could tell that every part of her body had just gone to jelly.

She wondered—not for the first time, yet each time, she hoped, for the last time—if his girlfriend felt the same thrill every time she saw him walk into a room or smile, or stare at her the way Wyatt was staring at her now.

She wondered, like she always did, why Wyatt was spending this kind of time around her when he had a girlfriend at all.

But then . . . friends. They were friends. Very good friends. And she hated the thought of losing that, which was why she had never told him how she really felt. And maybe she never would. The way she saw it, she had a few choices. She could keep enjoying what they had. She could wait and hope that eventually he and his girlfriend would break up. Or she could get on with her life once and for all.

Emma sighed and looked up at the sky overhead. If she didn't know better, she'd say that Viv had up and left her just to make her thoughts on this matter abundantly clear.

"I wanted to thank you," she said. "For the flowers. You didn't have to do that."

"Sure, I did." He gave her a sad smile, one that toyed with her already heightened emotions, leaving her confused. Did he? And if so, why?

Again, friends, she reminded herself. Very good friends.

"I was going to pick up an arrangement for you, too, but I figured that you'd probably have so many after the service . . ."

It was true that the house seemed to be full of arrangements that they'd taken home this morning, filling the rooms with colors and fragrances but reminding her all the same that they were here only because Viv was gone.

"I want to do something to cheer you up," Wyatt said, grinning at her.

She managed a weak smile. Hated herself for gazing a little too long into those dusty-blue eyes. "I'm not sure anything could cheer me up right now, honestly. I felt a little better when Leah got here, but then, well, Sadie arrived."

"Then let me get you out of the house," Wyatt said. "The Founder's Day event is next weekend. You think you're up for it?"

She resisted the urge to agree right away, like she normally would. Things were different now. Her sisters were in town, she didn't know when they were leaving, and truth be told, she didn't know when she was leaving. The decision about the house would be settled within days, if not tomorrow, and then . . . then she'd have no reason to stay. And many, many reasons to go.

Even if the one reason she should leave was also the one keeping her.

She stared up at him, seeing the question in his eyes at her hesitation.

"Let me see what my sisters have planned," she said. And then, because she couldn't help herself, she added, "But I'd love to go."

Because I love you, she thought as she watched him grin and walk away, toward his car.

Home to his girlfriend.

CHAPTER EIGHT

SADIE

Sadie stood alone in the corner of her own childhood home, giving tight smiles to those who greeted her with condolences, keeping a watchful eye on the room, on her sisters' comings and goings, on their brief interactions: Leah had slipped upstairs the moment the Maxwells appeared on the front porch, and Emma was now out there talking with a handsome guy that must be new to town. Boyfriend, perhaps? Not like she and her sisters shared these types of things. Not like they'd had some cozy chat long into last night the way they'd once done, years ago.

She'd hoped today would be better. That she could keep some distance, that the crowd would dilute the tension. Instead, she couldn't help but feel like she had all those years ago. The talk of the town. Or in this case, the room.

Keeping her distance seemed like the best option, and if it hadn't been for the fact that she'd seen Leah slip up the stairs, Sadie would have done the same. She longed to be alone, behind a closed door, to lie on her childhood bed and pretend that there weren't a hundred people downstairs with opinions about her, that she hadn't royally screwed up all those years ago, that she could somehow go back in time and make it all right. That her family would be whole again, Vivian included.

But Leah was upstairs, and Sadie didn't want to risk running into her. She moved from the front living room to the safety of the dining room, where hopefully the large buffet of food would distract most people, leaving their mouths too full to talk. It wasn't in her head. She could see the way people were glancing at her, looking away when she met their eyes, no doubt whispering about her the moment she turned her back. She didn't have to listen to know what they were saying. She'd come back. Dared to show her face again after all this time.

They thought they knew her, but they didn't. They knew the girl she used to be—scrappy and bold because it was the only way not to break under the circumstances. She was untouchable; nothing could hurt her, even though everything hurt, so much and so deeply.

It was easier for Emma, who had bonded better with Aunt Vivian. Sadie would listen to their laughter and frown before turning a page in her book, hoping to find escape in the fictional world. Now, she knew that all she ever had to do was set down whatever novel she was reading at the moment and join them. Vivian would have welcomed her with a smile, and Emma was always eager to include her—but she'd never thought to do it, instead allowing herself to feel left out until she was eventually cast out.

It wasn't just Emma she envied—her youth, her ability to bounce back, her easy way of finding joy and happiness again. Leah, being older, being just as shaken as she was by the upheaval in their lives, was the one Sadie paid special attention to. Leah, with her quiet disposition and confidence. Leah, who didn't open up like Emma, but who instead slowly came around to their new life, eventually making a full life for herself in Fog's Landing, with friends, neighbors, and of course a boyfriend. She'd imagined what it would be like to be Leah, who had somewhere to go every weekend, something to dress up for and to look forward to, and most of all, someone to love her. She'd watch out the window as her sister ran down the porch steps to where Carter would be leaning against his car, grinning at her. She'd watch as they hugged, sometimes kissed, and she saw how her sister was still smiling after they pulled out of the driveway. She imagined what it would be like to have that feeling of belonging.

And one day, in her misguided youth, she'd acted on it.

Sadie sighed and looked around the room for a familiar face, but none of the kids she knew from school were here. That was for the best, perhaps. Fewer questions. Less explanation. Less pretending. Most, like her best friend, Jimmy, had probably moved away, maybe even gotten married by now, and settled in bigger, more cosmopolitan areas, returning only for a week each summer. Door County was a summer place for most.

Seeing Linda, she caught her eye, knowing that it would be rude to not walk over to her. She had been Aunt Vivian's closest friend, always letting herself in the back door without knocking first, which was the way both women had preferred it. And more than that, she was Sadie's best friend's mother.

"Sadie," Linda said now, reaching out to squeeze her hand. "It would have meant so much to your aunt to know you came."

She was right, Sadie knew, that Vivian would have been happy to know she had come home, and that was why she felt so uneasy.

"I feel bad for not coming back sooner." She swallowed hard, hoping her emotions wouldn't get the better of her. No good came from that. It wouldn't bring Viv back. It wouldn't change the past. It only made today worse, and today was already turning out to be a zero out of ten.

Linda nodded. She knew the whole sordid story, like the rest of them, of course. "You're here now. Focus on that." Her gaze flicked over Sadie's shoulder, searching the room. "And Leah's here too?"

If Linda was hoping this meant a reconciliation had happened, she could think again. "Yes. We're all here."

"Jimmy was so sorry he wasn't able to come today," Linda said with an apologetic smile. "One of these arrangements is from him, but there is such an outpouring, I'm sure it will take you a while to look through all the cards."

Sadie felt herself soften at the mention of Linda's son. Having Jimmy here would have made this day a little easier, or at least, less awkward. But like her, he'd moved on and away, and their conversations over the years had dwindled.

Just one more thing to regret.

"And how long do you plan to stay?" Linda asked when it was clear that there would be no discussion of how Leah and Sadie were getting along.

Wasn't that the $20,000 question? Not having an answer even for herself, she said, "As long as I'm needed."

She almost snorted. Like she was needed at all. Her sisters had made it clear this morning that everything was already handled: flowers, food, event plates, and napkins. Sadie's help wasn't wanted any more than her participation. She'd been cut out a long time ago.

"Well, hopefully, we'll have another opportunity to spend a little time together before you go back to New York." Linda smiled. "It must be exciting, living in such a big city!"

If by *exciting* she meant living paycheck to paycheck and sharing a minifridge with a roommate who preferred smelly cheese and a bathroom with her roommate's boyfriend, who liked to drain the hot water tank, then yes, it was exciting. About as exciting as the sirens that seemed to scream all night long.

"And what do you do there, in New York?"

Float around aimlessly from job to job, boyfriend to boyfriend, and sleep in what would pass for a walk-in closet around these parts when I'm not fiddling around with a novel that no one seems to believe I'll ever finish, including myself.

Sadie would have laughed at how the truth would go over if she hadn't felt like crying instead.

"Oh, I recently transitioned from high-end retail to the restaurant industry." That was a stretch, but it was better than admitting her waitressing job had fallen through because she'd been shagging the boss.

"Anyone special in your life?" Linda's eyes lit up with hope.

Sadie supposed that they would. If Sadie could have just found her own boyfriend years ago, maybe she wouldn't have tried to steal Leah's. That's what they all thought, wasn't it?

"I've been seeing a celebrity chef, actually." Slightly more honest, and hey, it beat the truth.

"Wow! It must feel so quiet here compared to all that action," Linda continued.

Sadie's smile felt thin. It did feel quiet. Lying in her bedroom last night, with the window cracked for a breeze, she'd slept better than she had in months, if not years, despite the circumstances. She'd forgotten what fresh air felt like in her lungs, what clear sunlight waking her could do for her mood.

She'd forgotten a lot of good things about this place. Survival mode. It was what she did.

"Come find me before you head out again," Linda said, giving her hand one more squeeze before moving into the next room.

Left alone again and not seeing any friendlier faces from her school days, Sadie decided to stand a little closer to a huddled group of women, pretending to be indecisive about which casserole to choose from, even though they all looked the same and she had no appetite. Well, she thought, glancing at the cake that Emma had baked that morning, maybe she had one for that.

"She was too generous for her own good!" The woman speaking clucked her tongue.

Well, they can't be talking about me, Sadie thought with a chuckle. She cut herself a thick slice of carrot cake and loaded it onto her plate as the women continued their conversation.

Cream cheese frosting and grated carrots—definitely fresh, definitely Emma's recipe. It was one of Viv's favorites, especially in the springtime. She helped herself to another bite, realizing how hungry she was, and leaned against the wall.

"She must have given away everything she owned over time," another voice said in a loud whisper. And then, after a pause, "I doubt there's anything left but this house."

Now Sadie inched a little closer, keeping her back to the women, hoping that they didn't hear the pounding of her heart. The fork was poised in her hand, but she didn't dare set the metal down against the plate. Emma's words from yesterday came back too clearly: "Whatever Viv had left."

Was this what she had meant?

"Oh, but that's the worst part!" the clucking woman said. "She mortgaged the house to fund all her good deeds."

"No!"

No! Sadie's mind raced nearly as fast as her heart, thinking of what this meant, what could be expected of her.

"Yes! You know how she was, always spearheading a committee or event. Everyone in this town knew her, and she was all too happy to offer personal loans to anyone who fell on hard times."

"But the house! It's been in the family for generations!"

"I know! And it's not like she put any money back into the place."

A murmur at that. Sadie realized she was clenching her teeth. Sure, the house was old, but that was part of its charm. Or so Viv had always said.

Now Sadie had the sickening sensation that maybe the reason Viv had kept everything the same for so long wasn't sentimentality but necessity. Sadie knew all too well what it meant to scrimp and save. To go without. To make do with what you had.

To hold on to it for dear life.

"Don't quote me on this, but I think she'd had some trouble with the recent payments," one of the women said.

Oh no. No. Sadie closed her eyes, wishing she could block her ears too.

"Sadie."

Sadie was so startled that she almost dropped her plate, and she blinked several times, barely registering Carter's face as she processed what she'd just heard. Were they talking about Vivian? They must have been. But Vivian never would have mortgaged this house! It had been in the family for generations, passed down to her from her parents, and their parents before that.

But it was like they said. The house was old. There hadn't been any improvements made over time. Vivian had never really worked outside the home, unless selling her quilts and pies at various fairs counted for income. She had been able to live here only because there was no monthly payment other than the usual bills that her inheritance must have covered.

Until maybe it no longer did.

"Carter." She didn't smile, and she didn't expect him to either. Their history was brief but loaded, and their relationship—if that was even a word she could use to describe the fleeting few months of friendship that had ended in one fat mistake—had abruptly transformed into nothing more than a terse nod of acknowledgment when they bumped into each other around town, until Carter finally left and then, soon after, she did too. She noticed that her hands were shaking, along with the plate. She set it on Aunt Vivian's favorite marble pedestal table, beside the framed photograph of all the girls under the Christmas tree when Sadie must have only been about eleven. It was hard to remember a time when they'd all been so happy together.

She hadn't ever spoken to him about what had happened, and she worried now that he'd bring it up, but the years had passed, experiences had changed them—at least some of them—and she saw evidence of that time in the corners of his eyes when he gave her a small smile. "I'm sorry about your aunt. I know how close you were."

They had been, once. Not like Emma or even Leah, but she had her own special bond with Vivian, one that she had never quite shared with anyone else. Vivian had always said that Sadie reminded her of herself when she was younger, and that was . . . well, loaded.

"Thank you." She swallowed back the lump in her throat. "And how are you? Still living in the area? Married? Kids? Work?"

She didn't really care beyond idle curiosity. Carter had been a teenage crush, nothing more. She had just failed at the time to realize how much more he meant to her sister. That maybe, had things not gone the way they did, Leah and Carter might have ended up together, made a life for themselves right here in Fog's Landing. That she, too, might have stayed, or at least visited. That today would still have been sad but not quite so lonely. That instead of hiding out in the corners of her own house, she could be gathered around the kitchen table, sharing one of Emma's desserts, wiping away tears as she and her sisters reminisced about a woman who had loved them as her own.

"Back in the area," he said. "No kids. Not married. I'm at the bank, but then you probably could have guessed that."

Huh. Carter had never wanted to follow in his father's footsteps, but then, he wasn't that twenty-one-year-old kid anymore.

And who was she to judge? Her life hadn't exactly gone as planned, either, had it?

Already she felt the attention in the room tilt toward them. She took one step back to create some distance, then broke off a decent-size chunk of cake. One thing certainly hadn't changed in all these years. Emma sure could bake.

"Listen, this may sound like a strange question, but have you heard of my aunt . . . lending money to people? Anything about a . . . mortgage?" As soon as she said the words, she wanted to take them back. It was wrong to be discussing Vivian like this, today of all days! She was being overly sensitive, assuming something based on a bit of gossip or half information, no different from most of the people in this room.

Carter, however, didn't look surprised, causing Sadie to stand a little straighter.

"She was very generous, your aunt. But you knew that already." He sighed. "It always worried me a bit that people were taking advantage or something, but she promised that it was her choice and that everyone would pay her back in good time."

Sadie already dreaded the answer to her next question. "And did they, do you know?"

He shrugged, but his expression told her what she already knew.

She closed her eyes. So, it was true then.

"Oh!" A smothered sound of surprise made Sadie turn to see Emma looking panicked, Leah close at her side.

"We were just talking," Sadie said mildly, mostly for Emma's sake but also for Leah. It was easy to feel annoyed, even angry over Leah's refusal to move past what had happened all those years ago, but it was also a reminder of how badly she had hurt her sister.

She glanced at Carter. How badly they both had.

"It's not what you're thinking," Carter said, his tone a little firmer, reminding her of where his loyalties lay, where they always were, even though she'd known all along.

"It's fine," Leah said with a shake of the head that sent her curls bouncing, but the look in her eyes told Sadie that it wasn't fine at all.

Sadie gave Carter a look, and he took his cue, leaving the sisters without a word.

"I can explain—" Sadie started to say, but Leah held up a hand.

"I'm here to honor Vivian. What you and Carter have to say to each other is none of my concern."

Only her expression said otherwise. Sadie glanced at Emma, who looked like she was about to make a runner, not that Sadie blamed her.

"Oh, it's absolutely your concern."

"What do you mean by that?"

Sadie took a big breath, resentful that she held the honor of delivering bad news. "It's the house. It's mortgaged to the hilt. And now that's our problem. *All* of ours."

For the first time since Sadie had arrived, Leah looked her square in the eye and didn't waver. And for the first time in fifteen years, something passed between them. A connection, perhaps.

Even if it was one built on fear. . .

CHAPTER NINE

LEAH

For a moment there, Leah had thought that Sadie knew—about her marriage, about the fact that she wasn't as blissfully happy as she'd pretended to be. That her life was a sham. That nothing had gone as planned, starting with her and Carter breaking up all those years ago.

But the house?

For the first time in days, Leah wasn't thinking about her daughters, her divorce, or even Aunt Viv. Armed with a bottle of wine and a platter of half-eaten cakes, brownies, and cookies, she sat beside Emma at the same old wicker table on the front porch, looking over the water, trying to make sense of it all.

Both of them were wearing pajamas; they had made an unspoken decision to change into something comfortable, out of the black dresses that seemed to confine their skin and make everything feel more official. Viv was gone; the house might be too. Once again, life was uncertain, and the only thing that she was sure of was that they had each other.

But now, unlike all those years ago, when they'd first climbed the steps to this very porch, that was a small comfort. They weren't so tight knit anymore, and it had been a long time since they'd drawn comfort from each other.

Leah tugged her lightweight cardigan tighter around her as a breeze blew in off the bay, ruffling one of Viv's wind chimes. She was grateful that she'd overpacked, knowing how the mornings and evenings could be cool this far north.

Emma pulled up the zipper on her gray hoodie and snuggled her dog closer onto her lap. The desserts sat before them, but neither one of them reached for anything.

"This reminds me of all the tea parties that we used to have out here, even on rainy days." Leah didn't know why she had suddenly thought of that, not when she hadn't properly thought of her childhood in years. She was too busy raising her own girls, focused on her new role, which seemed to define her, as if the younger version of herself had never existed, or was just biding time for this next phase.

Or maybe it was just easier to forget.

"I miss those days," Emma said sadly. She stroked her dog's head, over and over, something that Leah realized she probably did often, even though she hadn't been around to witness it.

Fighting back guilt because she knew so little about the details of her sister's and aunt's lives in recent years, Leah asked, "Did you and Viv still come out here?"

"Not for tea parties, obviously." Emma took a small sip of the wine. "But we came out here all the time, of course. We spent a lot of time together."

There was a strange pinch to Emma's forehead, but Leah didn't dig any deeper. This was the toughest on Emma for so many reasons, and admitting that only made her reflect on her part in that. Emma was an adult, but she was also the youngest and the closest to their aunt. And this house was her only home.

Probably the only one she even remembered.

Sadie burst outside in cutoff jean shorts and a threadbare tank top, leaving the screen door to bang shut in her wake, carrying a tumbler of something amber colored—whiskey, no doubt—filled a little higher than was probably socially appropriate, but then, nothing about this day felt appropriate. Or right.

And Sadie had never been one to follow the rules.

"I thought those people would never leave." Sadie dropped loudly onto a chair and took a sip of her drink, the ice rattling.

Leah gave her a cold stare. "Those people meant a lot to Viv. It would have made her happy to know that they cared about her enough to honor her today."

"Those people took advantage of her," Sadie said slowly and with force.

"I'm sure they intended to pay her back," Emma said, but her voice matched the uncertainty that Leah felt.

Sadie gave Emma a look of disbelief and then met Leah's eyes for a moment before perhaps remembering that she wasn't going to find support there. She clucked her tongue and shook her head as she leaned back in her chair, clutching the glass in her hand, bare legs curled up. "No good deed goes unpunished, as the saying goes."

"And you should know," Leah said. "Tell me, Sadie. What have you been up to for the past fifteen years?"

"I've been punished enough, if that's what you were hoping to hear," Sadie said, narrowing her gaze.

Leah shrugged. "We all make our choices."

"And some are made for us," Sadie said, her tone cutting straight to the heart of what they all shared, what had once united them and eventually drove them apart. What had ultimately led them here, to this porch, tonight. Loss.

"I'm sorry, but when did you become a victim in what happened with Carter?" Leah shook her head and poured herself a glass of wine with a heavy hand, then did the same for Emma, who showed no signs of reaching for it. "Besides, you don't know anything about my life."

"And whose fault is that?" Sadie shot back.

Leah raised her eyebrows. "Yours, if I'm not mistaken. Unless somehow you think this is my fault?"

She laughed, but there was no amusement in it. Emma, looking like she might cry, reached for the glass of wine.

Sadie shrugged. An infuriating gesture that was just . . . just . . . so Sadie! Leah was momentarily angered and stricken by the memory of her doing the very same all those years ago, when they'd first come to live here, when the anger and hurt in Sadie's eyes were dismissed with a simple shrug when Viv asked if she wanted to come down to the kitchen or out onto the patio, if there was anything that might cheer her up.

But they weren't kids anymore. And she was sick and tired of Sadie continuing to act like one.

"The phone works both ways," Sadie said archly. "And I apologized."

"Apologizing doesn't take back what you did," Leah said.

"Neither does holding a grudge for fifteen years and counting," Sadie said. "You broke Vivian's heart, you know."

"Guys—" came Emma's plea, but Leah couldn't deal with it, not now, not when her heart was racing and every emotion she had buried for so long was at the surface, bursting to come out.

"You're the one who slept with my boyfriend. You're the one who hurt me, hurt Aunt Vivian, and made yourself the talk of this small town."

"And you're the one who refused to let it go. Even after you'd moved on. You couldn't forgive me, couldn't put it behind us. You kept it alive, Leah."

Leah was momentarily silenced. She'd thought she'd killed it, banished the memory, put it to rest or at least put it behind herself. But maybe Sadie was right. Maybe she'd just kept it going, in another form, in a place where she wouldn't have to deal with it.

"Look, I don't like having to be here any more than you do. And as bad as you think you have it, I have it worse," Sadie said, rattling the ice in her glass.

"Is this some contest to see whose life sucks harder?" Leah asked.

"People around here welcomed you back with open arms, am I right?" Sadie gave a little shake of the head. "You know what people in town think of me. So yeah, I do think it's worse."

"Then why come?" It had been the question on Leah's mind ever since she'd first seen Sadie standing on that porch, hiding her eyes behind her giant sunglasses.

But the sun was setting. There was no place to hide now. Sadie had come back to the one place she claimed to not want to be. Why now?

"Because I should have come a long time ago. And you should've too."

Leah's heart was pounding against her rib cage, but she fought against it, hell bent on pretending that this night and the past fifteen years had never happened.

"Look," Sadie said, plunking her glass on the table. "Like it or not, you're stuck with me until we figure this mess out. So maybe until we do, we can put all this behind us and focus on what we need to do about the house."

Leah pursed her lips and slid her eyes to Emma, who was looking at her beseechingly, as if silently begging her to let it go, for now at least.

She gave a small nod, if only because she couldn't trust herself to speak. Viv was gone. She'd thought today would be her closure. That tomorrow she'd go home and put this house, and everything that had happened here, behind herself for good.

But that wasn't possible.

"I promised you that I'd be here for you, Emma, and I stand by that," she said.

Across the table, Sadie snorted. "Glad you care about one of your sisters."

"Again, I can say the same," Leah said evenly.

"Fine, then we're both here for Emma," Sadie said pertly.

"Sure took you guys long enough," Emma grumbled into her wineglass. Her little dog attempted to take a lick, but she set the glass on the table, no longer able to hide her frown.

"You had Viv," Sadie pointed out. "You weren't alone, Emma."

"It wasn't that simple," Emma shot back. "All you two cared about was your issue. But it wasn't mine. And you made it mine. And you made it Viv's."

The silence felt louder than any of their words. For a moment, all that could be heard were the chirping of the crickets, the soft lapping of the water against the rocks across the road. Leah had heard these words before—the accusation—from her daughter. Chloe, angry over the divorce, over the changes she'd been thrust into without any say. She was a casualty in Leah's divorce; much as Leah had tried to shield her children from it, it was inevitable. And all she'd wanted to do was protect them.

She looked at Emma now—her youngest sister, the girl she could still picture as young as her own children—and she felt the same need to do right by her. To take this problem off her shoulders. To undo whatever hurt she had caused.

"We'll work together for this, Emma." Leah glanced at Sadie, wondering if she'd dare to argue, but all she did was lower her eyes.

Feeling the need to brighten the mood, to lift at least Emma from the trenches of this difficult day, she reached out and squeezed her youngest sister's hand, pulling a small smile from her that was far from happy.

"Maybe it's not even true. Maybe there's a misunderstanding," Leah said. But in her heart, she knew that wasn't possible. You could wish and hope all you wanted that life would be different, but it didn't change the cold, hard facts. It didn't make someone still love you. It didn't make someone who was gone suddenly appear. It didn't turn back time.

"You heard what Carter said. He wouldn't lie," Emma said. Then, catching Leah's expression, her eyes widened, and she quickly added, "I mean about this. He wouldn't lie about . . . this."

Emma snatched a brownie from the plate, shoving it in almost its entirety into her mouth. Leah couldn't even look at Sadie.

Instead, she looked back out onto the water. No, Carter wouldn't lie about the house. He had no reason to, and worse was that he had information. Information that he hadn't shared with Emma, until now.

"Just when was he planning to tell us?" Leah said, suddenly angry. She looked at Sadie, who seemed to shrink from her stare. "If you hadn't said anything? When would we have found out?"

"I'm sure we'd have found out something this week. Or, rather, I would have," Emma said miserably.

Long after Leah had left town, in other words. Sadie, too, no doubt.

"She never complained about money being tight?" Leah pressed. Certainly, there had to have been some clue along the way.

"No." Emma's gaze searched the table, but she was looking for something else. An answer that couldn't be found, not here, not anywhere. Her smile lifted when she looked up. "I had my suspicions. She'd always hide the bills. But you know Viv. She was always so upbeat, so positive. Nothing got her down. She never let it."

Leah sipped her wine thoughtfully. It was true, and in all her conversations with Viv in recent years, they'd kept things light, focusing on the girls, their activities, or the happenings in Fog's Landing, always careful to omit anything that might open old wounds. A few times after Leah first left town, her aunt tried to convince her to talk to Sadie, but Leah shot her down quickly, and eventually, Viv stopped pressing the topic.

"We're all here, so it makes sense that we do this . . . together." Leah caught the hope in Emma's expression and felt a pang of guilt. "I'll stay on and help you get everything sorted out."

"But what about the girls? And Ted?" Emma asked.

Leah almost let herself slip but caught herself in time. "The girls are at camp," she said lightly.

"I guess that means that I'll stay on longer too." Sadie added quickly, "To help."

"But what about your job?" Emma looked at Sadie, asking the very question Leah was thinking.

Sadie shrugged. "It was just a waitressing gig, and it didn't work out. It's no big deal," she added, catching their looks. "I always find another."

Across the table, Leah met Emma's gaze, but neither of them argued. Leah held in a sigh. She'd half expected Sadie to bolt at the first sign of responsibility, and now she wasn't sure whether to be impressed with Sadie's decision or agitated by the thought of having to spend more time with her.

They couldn't run this time. Tempting as it was. They couldn't do that to Emma. Not again.

"Viv always had a way of bringing us together," Emma said quietly. "I can almost feel her smiling down on us."

"Or laughing," Sadie said through a mouthful of food. When she didn't get the reaction she wanted, she dropped her fork, letting it clank against the plate. "Oh, come on. You know that Viv always hoped that we'd all come back together again, at this house. Now she's succeeded. You can't tell me she wouldn't be a little satisfied right now, knowing that she was the one who made it happen."

"In a twisted way," Leah said, but there was truth in the statement. Viv would be pleased knowing that her death had brought about her greatest wish, even if it had become an unspoken one in recent years. Even if she hadn't lived to see it happen.

"We can't let her down," Emma said, giving Leah a warning look. One that said very clearly, *Be nice.*

"Viv's gone, honey," Leah said gently.

"But she's not. Not really," Emma insisted. "This house. It still smells like her. Like Earl Grey tea." She grinned. "And this table. She sat right there, every morning and evening, from March through mid-November, so long as it didn't dip below forty degrees." She pointed to the fourth, empty chair that sat between Leah and Sadie, facing the water. "This was her home. And we were her family. And we can't let it all go just because she's not physically here."

"What are you saying?" Leah asked.

Emma swallowed hard. "I guess I'm saying that we have to do right by this house."

Leah nodded thoughtfully. They owed Viv that much. Whatever *do right* meant.

CHAPTER TEN

EMMA

Maybe it wasn't exactly safe to leave Leah and Sadie alone together, but by the next morning, Emma was too eager for a distraction to give it much thought.

She fastened the collar around Sully's neck and hurried to the front door, eager to slip away before one of her sisters stopped her. Technically, she wasn't working today—or anytime soon. But she knew that her boss wouldn't send her away if she stopped by the inn, and she also knew that her friend Sarah would be all too happy to have Sully in her office for a few hours.

After all, she could barely trust her sisters with each other. She sure as hell didn't trust them with her fur baby.

Yesterday evening, the sisters had been quiet. Each disappeared to her corner of the house, which wasn't completely unusual. Back when they were little, Sadie was usually off in a corner reading, Leah would be drawing, and Emma would be following Viv around, and her aunt used to say that she'd have it no other way.

But those days were over, and unlike before, when they'd all reconvene for a meal, Emma had stayed up late, in front of the television, watching one of those old black-and-white movies that Viv loved and that she'd learned to enjoy, or at least take comfort in. Eventually, the clouds had rolled in over the bay, and the rain started to fall, and all Emma could think was that of course it would rain on the day of Viv's funeral. It was like the entire sky felt her sadness and was crying with her. As if the elements—of Viv, perhaps—had conspired to keep them all in this house together.

She knew her sisters thought she was being silly for thinking that Viv was somehow still a part of them, but wasn't she? That house was her home. Still contained her belongings, however tattered or treasured. Still held every memory.

But today the sun was shining high above the lake, and the water glistened in the distance. The sweet smell of grass and flowers cleared her head, replacing the icky memories of last night with renewed hope. In the distance, the soft purr of a lawn mower reminded her that life went on as usual. And for this moment, at least, she felt okay. Even content. Her skin was warm from the sun; the sky was a brilliant, cloudless teal blue; and she'd dare to say that her future felt almost bright. That as much as she didn't want to lose the house, the reality of their financial straits felt like a sign.

Like maybe Viv had set this up. It was her way of pushing Emma along. Telling her what to do.

Emma took her usual path to the inn, enjoying the walk and the distance it put between her and that house that now held so much conflict. As expected, Sarah was so busy setting up the patio breakfast buffet that she didn't even notice Emma until Sully barked.

"Hey! What are you doing here? I thought you were taking some time off."

"I've had enough time off. It's tourist season, and I know full well that we're booked through August."

"I felt terrible about not being able to slip away for the service," Sarah lamented.

Emma set a hand on her shoulder. "You're short staffed, and it's summer. I know you would have been there if you could."

"Carter told me about it," Sarah said, flicking a nervous glance at her as she pulled the plastic wrap back from a bowl of ripe berries, which always went quickly with the guests unless an ornery child decided to put their hands in the bowl first.

Emma smiled now when she thought of Pamela's silent fury when a little boy last week had proudly held up two hands, displaying all ten digits topped with raspberry "hats," as he called them.

No one had eaten the raspberries that day.

"Which part did he mention?" Emma tethered Sully's leash to one of the sturdy patio-umbrella stands and started adding the appropriate serving utensils to each bowl or basket. "The part about us losing our ancestral home, or the part about him seeing Leah? Or the part about him seeing Leah while talking to Sadie?"

"Yikes." Sarah winced. "The part about the house. Carter doesn't like to talk about Leah to me."

"Then we have something in common. Leah doesn't ever mention Carter to me either."

"It's sad, isn't it?" Sarah shook her head. "They were so in love once."

"Well, that was a long time ago," Emma said, rising to her sister's defense. It wasn't always easy, because the situation had been complicated, to say the least, but Carter and Sadie had hurt Leah, and that part of things was irrefutable.

"And Sadie?" Sarah's eyes widened. "How's that going? I was a little surprised to hear that she came back to town."

"That makes two of us." Emma glanced toward the doors to the lobby, knowing that guests would start to rouse at any moment. "Leah and Sadie together again. Honestly, I'm not sure there will even be a house to return to when I leave here today."

She looked at Sarah, and the pair burst out laughing.

"I needed that," Emma said. All these years, she'd thought she needed her sisters. Her family. Lost for what felt like the second time.

But now that they were all together again, it was just a reminder of the strain. And all that might have been.

"Good. And I needed you here." Sarah looked relieved as she set the last basket of croissants on the long table just as the first couple came through the door. She greeted them with a smile and started pushing the cart back toward the lobby. Emma scooped up Sully and followed Sarah into the service hallway that led to the small offices that Pamela had carved out years back, when she'd started the inn. Emma knew that her position at the front desk gave no hope of ever having an office of any size, and even Sarah's pantry turned office felt like a refuge on a long day with difficult guests.

"So, you haven't told me if another person was there yesterday," Sarah said coyly as she slipped behind her small desk and dropped onto the swivel chair.

Emma didn't bother playing along. Instead, her heart swooped when she remembered how she'd left things off with Wyatt yesterday. Just thinking about it now made her smile. It was the bright spot in an otherwise pretty grim time in her life.

"Wyatt invited me to the festival," she said, trying not to show too much enthusiasm, even if she had to focus on her dog rather than look Sarah in the eye.

Emma didn't want to see it. The skepticism that her aunt had shared. Sometimes, even the dismay.

Sarah reserved her opinion on the matter, but from the pinch of her lips, it was clear that she had one.

Emma had already started thinking about what she might wear, what she and Wyatt might do, and how long they might stay. Whether the day would turn into the evening and whether this year she would finally have someone to dance with when the sun set and the strings of lights flicked on and the band started to play in the gazebo on the town green.

"Well, that's something to look forward to," Sarah said with a hopeful smile.

"If my sisters and I survive that long." Emma sighed.

"Think of it as long-overdue quality time." Sarah gave her a knowing look as she pulled a dog treat from her stash in the top drawer. Sully immediately scampered over to her and collected his reward for simply being cute. No tricks necessary, not even a sit.

Emma could practically hear Viv's cluck of her tongue now.

Emma dropped into the visitors' chair. Scooping Sully up, she rested him on her lap and stroked his soft fur. "What have I missed?"

"You've barely missed any shifts," Sarah reminded her with a smile. She started shuffling papers—likely for the many upcoming weddings that she helped organize. It was a job that would have interested Emma, but Pamela required only Sarah's help for special events, stating that Emma was most helpful at the front desk because she was a "people person."

A trained one. You didn't grow up with the likes of her sisters without learning how to keep the peace and stay chipper in the face of adversity.

"Oh, come on now. I missed an entire weekend in June. There had to be a few complainers."

Sarah glanced toward the hallway and then closed the door, even though her office was at the back of the large home that served as the main space on the property. The thirty guest rooms had been built separately, extended on either side of the home, each with a private balcony and a view of Green Bay—albeit some partially obstructed by the trees.

"You know how Pamela switched shampoo vendors?"

Emma knew. It was a cost decision, one that Emma hadn't given much thought to, except for the new shipment of orders she'd had to place and the boxes she'd had to sign off on when they arrived early last week. Was that only a week ago? She frowned at that, thinking of how much her life had changed since then, when so little had changed here, at her place of employment.

"You remember the Whitakers, right? From Illinois?"

"Of course," Emma said. "They come every June."

"And this time, Mrs. Whitaker was very vocal about the change in toiletries. Said that she doesn't like the smell or the packaging."

"Well, she could bring shampoo from home, then. Or buy some at the grocery store." It was only a mile away, and anyone who came to Door County came by car.

"It's not that," Sarah explained. "She said that she likes to bring a bunch of it home every year. Gives it as stocking stuffers to her grandkids!"

Emma always thought she'd heard it all when it came to guest stories, but this one made her laugh, not because it was unusual for a guest to pocket some of the amenities but because they'd dared to admit it.

"The best is that she made this complaint to Pamela since you weren't here."

"Oh, I would have loved to have seen her expression." This business wasn't easy, Emma knew, mostly because Pamela relied so much on the warmer months. The winters were quiet, almost pleasantly so, and Emma personally enjoyed the stillness of the lobby, and the crackling of the logs in the fireplace near where an odd couple or two might sit sipping coffee from the station that she oversaw, or reading a book from the shelves that Pamela kept stocked. The snow falling softly at the window made everyone, including her, appreciate the coziness inside the quaint inn all the more.

"Needless to say, she struggled for composure."

"If I were to run this place, I'd make the soaps and shampoos available for purchase. That way if the guests enjoyed them during their stay, they'd have the option to bring them home. As a proper paid-for souvenir."

But then, if she were running this place, she would do quite a number of things differently.

"Maybe you should start your own inn," Sarah teased. "There's more than enough business. I've had to turn away no less than fifteen couples hoping to stay any weekend in July. Don't people know that you have to book four months out minimum if you want a decent room around here in the summertime?"

Emma chewed her lip. Her mind was racing, but she was only half listening. There were many inns in Door County, Fog's Landing included. They ranged from large homes that hosted guests in the upstairs rooms to larger resort-like accommodations with pools for the warmer months. Most matched the general feel of the area—white, wood-sided structures with overgrown hydrangeas edging their porch rails. Several had landmark status. And all were booked solid through fall.

Confirming this, Emma asked, "Were you able to guide them anywhere else?"

Sarah snorted and set some papers in a file folder. "Maybe Michigan. But good luck there too."

Emma nodded along as Sarah told a story of another problematic guest, but an idea was taking shape. It was true that the Great Lakes were the summer playground for people in the Midwest—an easy escape from the hassle of city or suburban life. An escape from the daily stressors.

Now, Emma thought of her own stressor—or at least one of them. Viv's home was large, at least as large as some of the inns on Main Street. The inns that were booked summer after summer, often spring and fall, too, usually months in advance.

The house would need work, she thought, sobering her excitement, but not too much. People liked things quaint around here. And they were willing to pay a premium price for it too.

She thought of what the going rate was, and what they could charge for the waterfront rooms, especially during the busy months. The house could literally pay for itself. Sadie could run it—she'd made it clear that she had no job at the moment. It might give her the sense of purpose that she was looking for.

And Emma . . . she would have one less thing to worry about.

One less thing to hold her back.

CHAPTER ELEVEN

SADIE

Sadie had managed to avoid Leah all morning, but luck had never been on her side, and she wasn't about to push it now. Last she'd checked, when she'd dared to sneak out of her bedroom like a burglar in her own childhood home, Leah had been on the phone, presumably with her daughters.

She all but tiptoed into the kitchen; she plucked a few pieces of fruit from the bowl on the counter and pondered Emma's whereabouts. She'd left early, without informing anyone, but then why should she? It wasn't like Sadie needed a breakdown of her itinerary or daily routine, but a little warning about being left all on her own with their eldest sister might have been nice.

At least with Emma around, there was a buffer. Another dynamic to the conversation. Even a bit of a peacekeeper. But she couldn't expect Emma to stay here indefinitely.

Heck, none of them could stay indefinitely, not with the house in dire straits. Which invited the question she was doing her best not to think about: Where would she go?

Since she couldn't possibly answer that today and just thinking about it made her stomach literally hurt, she rummaged through the closet near the mudroom until she found one of Viv's many faded canvas beach totes, along with one of the threadbare towels that had seen many afternoons along the shoreline.

She started filling it for a long day with leftovers from the fridge and a large bottle of water. She opened each drawer and cabinet quietly, freezing when the floorboards creaked upstairs, in the distance, only exhaling when she heard Leah's peal of laughter, meaning she was still on the phone.

Sadie thought it strange that she was calling her kids at camp so much—shouldn't the girls be busy swimming or making necklaces out of dried pasta or shooting arrows? Or catching poison ivy? That was one thing she did not miss about this place, she thought as she sneaked out the back door and inhaled the fresh scent of Viv's prized flowers coming into bloom. New York was a great place to hide, but there was something special about getting lost in nature. She felt like herself for the first time in days. Alone was how she was most comfortable.

Or at least, what she was most used to. At least when she was alone, no one could accuse her of not living up to their standards, messing something up, or letting them down.

At least when she was alone, nothing more could be taken from her. She was in control. Of her thoughts. Her choices. She could go wherever she wanted, no compromise required.

The backyard was sheltered by a tall hedge of arborvitae; Viv always liked to say that people were too friendly in these parts for an actual fence unless it was of the picket variety, but the wall of greenery spoke otherwise. It fortressed this old house off, giving Viv a safe place to live. And the girls, for a while at least.

Sadie walked through the sliver of yard dividing the side of the house from the great hedge, the path made narrower by Viv's aggressive gardening, which had grown larger in scale in the years since Sadie had been back. A rustling in the plants didn't particularly bother her at first—well, other than the first jump, until she remembered that this was Wisconsin, not Manhattan, and that she was sharing the yard with squirrels, birds, maybe even the occasional chipmunk.

And someone else too.

This time, seeing the figure standing at the opening to the front yard, she did let out a yelp, but she laughed when she realized that it was just her next-door neighbor.

"Jimmy Price!" she said in a mock-scolding tone. "You scared the dickens out of me."

His mouth quirked into one of the many smiles he owned that she loved. "The *dickens*? I can see that New York hasn't changed you too much."

It was a saying of Viv's. Antiquated and somehow unique to her. Now it was Sadie's turn to grin as she grew closer to him and leaned in for a long, hard hug. For one daring second she closed her eyes, breathed in the familiar scent of his hair, and felt the warmth of his lean torso close against her body.

It was the first proper hug she'd had since coming back here. The first good reminder of her childhood. The only good thing to ever come out of this place.

She pulled back, and he looked at her properly with those greenish eyes that were framed by enviably thick and dark lashes that used to make his mother wonder if she should have tried for a second child, a girl, if she hadn't had Jimmy so late in life.

He was her miracle, Linda used to say. Her best surprise. Her pride and joy.

And he had been Sadie's best friend in Fog's Landing. Maybe her only friend.

"How long has it been?" he asked now.

She shrugged, knowing just how long even though she didn't want to admit it. "About a minute. Or two." Because even though it had been years, it didn't feel like any time had passed at all.

"I've missed you," Jimmy said, his smile slipping a little to show the hurt in his eyes.

Sadie stared at him for a moment and then cleared her throat. She'd missed him too. They'd kept in touch at first, on a regular basis. Jimmy had even visited her in New York a few times before he'd gone on to law school and life grew too busy. But their talks had become fewer and further between, and now she couldn't remember the last time she'd heard his voice, much less seen his face.

She began walking toward the road, the bay in full view now. Jimmy was close at her side, falling in step with her like no time had passed.

"I didn't realize you were back. Weren't you off in Los Angeles or something?" Opposite sides of the country. That was the last they'd left off, a long, long time ago.

"Moved to San Diego. Then Seattle. Then back here."

She stopped walking to give him a gawking stare. "You moved back? You have got to be kidding me."

"You say it like it's something bad." He gave an easy laugh and waited for a passing car before they moved onto the road.

Sadie was still trying to make sense of this as they fell into a single file line, she going first, passing between the same two boulders that had always provided a clearing to the lakefront.

"Well, it's just . . . not what I expected." She set her bag and towel down on the sand. "You weren't at the house this weekend."

"I was out of town for a wedding." The sympathy in his face made her instantly uncomfortable. "I'm sorry about Viv."

Sadie swallowed hard. The pity wasn't hers to own. She hadn't seen Viv in years—too many years to be rightfully grieving a loss. She busied herself with her towel, but the wind kept blowing it away. Jimmy reached out for the opposite end and tugged it taut, securing it with two nearby rocks.

"She had a big heart." Sadie sighed. Too big, came the darker thought. She glanced at Jimmy, wondering if his mother was one of the many who had taken a handout and never repaid it, but then she felt ashamed for even thinking such a thing. Linda Price would never take advantage of Viv like that. Besides, she was too proud. A widow who worked hard to keep a clean house and raise her only son, she was honest and charitable, and all her good traits had been passed down to the man—a man!—now sitting beside her.

Sadie shook her head. "I still can't believe you're here."

He grinned at her, and a hundred memories of childhood that she'd managed to forget came clear as the blue sky overhead.

She'd forgotten that smile, but more than that, she'd forgotten how it made her feel.

Like she wasn't alone in the world. Like she didn't want to be either.

"More like I can't believe you're here. But I'm glad you are." He turned so he was properly facing her instead of the water. "Tell me you aren't running off anytime soon."

She almost barked out a laugh at that. Even if she wanted to— and a part of her did—it wasn't an option. But now, sitting here with Jimmy, she realized that staying might not be so bad. It could certainly be worse.

"I'm here for a while at least." Now she grinned, and she wasn't even sure when the last time that had happened was. At the restaurant? Out with her sleazy boss she'd once considered something more?

New York felt a million miles away. Like a different person's life.

And sitting here, with the water lapping at her feet, Jimmy at her side, she almost remembered what it felt like to be herself again.

"So you're still in New York?"

She nodded because it was the closest thing to an honest answer she could give. Technically, some of her stuff was still in New York, if her old roommate hadn't boxed it up and put it on the curb by now.

"You still writing?" he asked as she bit into an apple.

Another topic she didn't want to discuss. She chewed thoughtfully. "When I get the chance," she said, not looking to talk about her life in New York just now. "How about you? Still lawyering?"

"Yep. It's not glamorous, but I don't mind."

A sudden thought took hold. "Don't tell me you're Viv's lawyer."

"Of course I am," he said cheekily. "Or . . . was. Man, that feels weird."

"Not as weird as it feels to be here. I suppose you're aware of Viv's . . . situation."

"That's more of the bank's business, but yes. Things were lean for a while. I . . . I know she was worried the bank might seize the house, but the bank structured a payment plan, and she kept insisting that people would pay her back."

Sadie bit back a snort. Jimmy gave her a hooded look. They'd seen enough of the world to know how this story would end.

"Viv never got around to making an official will, but she did make it clear that she wanted you girls to have the house. All three of you," he added, answering the question that he knew would be on her mind.

"Emma said as much. Right now, I'm almost wishing Viv had cut me out."

"You don't really mean that," he said gently.

Sadie shrugged. No, she didn't, not really. And Viv never would have done it either. And not just because it would have caused more conflict between them all. But it certainly would have made it easier for Sadie to walk away now.

Maybe that's what Viv had been trying to stop from happening.

Jimmy was giving her a small smile. "Your aunt loved you, Sadie. I hope you know that. It . . . it would mean a lot to her that you came back."

Sadie's eyes prickled, but she shook all those emotions free and instead nudged Jimmy playfully with her elbow. "Look at us. Together again after all these years."

He locked eyes with her for a moment, and she studied the freckles that were dusted over his nose. Then he snatched the apple from her hand and took a big bite.

She laughed. "Not much has changed."

And right now, she wasn't sure if that was such a bad thing after all.

After Jimmy left to go to work—at a proper office in the neighboring town, which made Sadie feel both old and like a complete failure—she spent as many hours as she could watching the water and making her way through Emma's leftovers, thinking that her sister might even be a better baker than their aunt, which was high praise indeed.

Finally, when she grew bored and the beach area grew too busy with tourists and townies that she thankfully didn't recognize—young children who were loud and splashed too much—she decided to brave the house once again.

It wasn't like she could stay away forever, after all.

Leah was in the kitchen when Sadie appeared at the back door, having hoped to slip in quietly. Sully greeted her with a bark, announcing her arrival, which meant that Emma was back, too—sweet relief.

Leah gave her a quick glance and then went back to slicing vegetables on the thick cutting board. Was it just her, or was she cutting them with more force than necessary?

Feeling uncomfortable as she hung the canvas tote in the mudroom, then seeing no sign of Emma when she reemerged, Sadie asked the obvious: "Emma back?"

"Just now," Leah said flatly.

Sadie nodded as she approached the island. It would be so much easier to walk away, up the stairs. But she was tired of hiding in her room, and besides, they still had the issue of the house to consider.

"You were on the phone when I left," Sadie said.

Leah paused for so long that Sadie wasn't even sure she'd ever respond. "I was talking to my daughters."

"And how are my nieces?" Sadie asked.

Now Leah looked at her sharply. "You've never even met them."

Sadie closed her mouth before she said something that would make this all worse. It was true; she hadn't. But that didn't mean she didn't care about them. Or want to know them. It was Leah who had made it clear that she wasn't wanted in their lives—or hers.

She was relieved when Emma walked into the kitchen, pushing her long braid off her shoulder, all her attention on Sully, who was all but dancing at her feet.

"Why didn't you mention that Jimmy was back in town?" Sadie asked her.

Emma gave her a funny look as she filled Sully's water bowl. "I don't know. Maybe because this is the first time we've talked in years."

Sadie watched as her sister set the bowl down and the little dog began lapping up the water. He dipped his entire face into the dish, even getting the tips of his ears wet. When his thirst was finally quenched, he looked up at her with big brown eyes, a sopping-wet mouth, and if she didn't know better, she'd say a smile on his face.

Despite the sting of Emma's statement, she couldn't help but grin.

"He moved back, oh, three years ago, I think. It was after Wyatt moved here, I know that much."

"Wyatt, huh? Was he that good-looking guy you were talking to out on the porch at the reception?" Sadie asked.

"You think he's good looking?" Emma appeared either flattered or panicked; Sadie couldn't be sure. Either way, she had a definite reaction to the guy. Clearly, there was more to that story, but instead of elaborating, Emma said, "Anyway, enough about this. I had an idea."

"Don't tell us that you plan to lock us in the house for the rest of the night," Leah said cheekily. "And don't think we didn't notice that you slipped away for hours today without so much as a warning."

"I had to go into work!" But Emma didn't meet their eyes, instead scooping up her dog. "It's tourist season, and I left them in a lurch. And I rushed straight home too."

"Thank you," Leah said with a smile. "Now, what did you have in mind? Dinner in town tonight? Is the Old Creek Restaurant still in business?"

Sadie's stomach almost grumbled at the thought of the first restaurant Viv had brought them to when they'd moved here. Their whitefish sandwich had been one of her favorites growing up—and it wasn't something you could find in New York either.

But then she realized she might not exactly be part of those plans. That Leah wouldn't want her there.

"Forget dinner. I think I know a way to save the house," Emma said breathlessly. Her eyes bounced from Sadie to Leah, whose opinion always mattered the most, even to Sadie. Even now.

"Well? Spit it out!" Sadie was not one for surprises. She'd had enough unexpected twists in her life, thank you very much.

"You know what summer is like here," Emma said, and Sadie and Leah both nodded along. They did. Summers here were full of flowers and sunshine, long hot afternoons and cool, breezy evenings. Nights spent chasing fireflies and collecting them in glass jars, and the best sleep of Sadie's life because of the energy spent running wild all day, stopping only to eat fresh slices of watermelon or berry pies from the farm stand, or to drop into bed, satisfied with another day well spent and the promise of another one in the morning.

"The best," Sadie whispered. She caught Leah looking strangely at her and cleared her throat.

"They are the best," Emma agreed. "Which is why everyone flocks here, from all the surrounding states. The inns and hotels are booked out months in advance, and not just for weekends. And people return, year after year, usually for the same weeks. It's their family tradition."

Family tradition. Something in the wording stung, hitting Sadie in a place she didn't like to admit existed, not even to herself.

"I'm sorry, but what does this have to do with saving the house?" Leah asked impatiently. "Do you think we should try to rent it out? It's sort of big . . ."

"Exactly! It is big. Big enough to be a bed-and-breakfast. Or some sort of inn."

Silence fell over the room for a moment as Emma let her words sink in, but Sadie didn't need much time to think about this, and not just because she was prone to snap decisions. For once, she knew she wasn't demonstrating poor judgment.

Because she couldn't resist, and because she sort of felt compelled, Sadie darted a glance at Leah but saw no obvious sign of disagreement in her expression. "The house is huge, and we can convert the attic to more bedrooms if needed. But there are six bedrooms upstairs. Seven if you count Viv's sitting room."

One-third of the revenue would be hers to keep. And if they couldn't sell the house, at least this would cover the bills. Because it wasn't like Sadie could take another financial hit.

"Or five if we made hers a suite." Emma looked at Leah. "You have the vision for this type of thing, Leah."

It was true, and already Sadie could see Leah's mouth pinched in thought.

"It would require some minor construction . . ."

"How are we going to pay for that?" Sadie interjected, because if they thought she could fork over some cash right now, they could think again. "It's not like Viv had savings if she had to mortgage this house."

Now both Leah and Emma looked a little uncomfortable. "I have some savings, but I was hoping to use that money for something down the road," Emma said vaguely.

"If we're successful, then it's just an investment," Leah countered. "We'd get it back once this place started turning a profit."

The way she chewed her lip made Sadie realize that she was considering the idea. That she might even think it was a good one.

So Leah was thinking they'd keep it, not sell it. Probably what Viv would have wanted.

She looked around the room, filled with Viv's touch, from the mixing bowls that she'd used for as long as Sadie could remember to the window that looked out onto her prized garden.

Definitely what Viv would have wanted.

"But it would take some money up front," Leah said, shaking her head. "And we can't expect you to hand over all your savings, Emma. We . . . can't expect that from any of us."

The frown between her brows told Sadie that Leah was thinking of her own children. Her husband. Her responsibilities at home. Like Sadie, she'd walked away from this house years ago.

But one glance at Emma confirmed what Sadie also knew. They couldn't just walk away again now. Not without all solving this problem. Together.

"I'm between jobs, so don't look at me," Sadie said. "And New York is expensive. I live paycheck to paycheck."

She expected a sharp comment from Leah, but instead all she saw was resignation. For once, her sister was out of ideas, when in the past they'd always turned to her to guide their way.

To tell them that everything would be okay.

"Can't we try to get a loan?" Sadie asked. She hesitated to even say his name, but desperate times called for it. "You can talk to Carter, Leah. He owes you," she added, giving her older sister a hard stare.

Leah pinched her mouth but then nodded. "It's worth trying. And I suppose I am the one who should go." She said this without much enthusiasm, and Sadie wondered just how much it still bothered her to have to interact with the man, now, after all these years. After she'd met another man, married, had a family.

"He might not be able to give us a loan," Emma pointed out. "Then we're back at having to sell. Probably not making much of a profit, depending on the size of the mortgage. Then we lose the house and money."

"But if it works out, then it's all thanks to you for thinking of turning this house into an inn, Emma," Leah said. "And you're the perfect person to run it."

"Oh." Emma's mouth opened, but she seemed to freeze. "Unless Sadie—"

Now Sadie barked out a laugh. "With my reputation in this town? Besides, you know I'm not here to stay. But I'll help get things set up and in order. It's only fair since I have a third of the share in things."

And it wasn't like she had anywhere else to go at the moment.

"With your experience at the inn, it makes complete sense," Leah assured Emma. "You'll be paid whatever you're used to at the inn."

Even Leah was smiling now, and Sadie basked in the feeling that for a moment at least, all their problems were solved. It wasn't until she saw the way that Emma's brow pinched that she wondered if there was something she had missed. Some part of this plan that she'd misunderstood.

Like the possibility that it could all go very wrong.

CHAPTER TWELVE

LEAH

Leah didn't know much about running a business, but one thing she did know was that if they were going to clean up this house and bring in new furniture, at least in all the bedrooms, then they'd need money.

In other words, they'd need a loan.

They were gathered in the kitchen, the morning sunlight filtering through the parted linen curtains, the coffee percolating, and one of Emma's fresh coffee cakes cooling on the counter. They'd been quiet all morning coming off Emma's big idea the night before.

"You really think that the bank will give us a loan, given the mortgage on this house?" Emma asked.

Leah wasn't sure of anything, but she still took her role as the eldest seriously.

"We know the family. Besides, it doesn't hurt to ask, does it?" As much as Leah dreaded the thought of another conversation with Carter, she also knew that he was inclined to help. Whatever their history, he'd cared about Viv. And at one point in time, he'd cared about her too.

"Maybe we should see what Jimmy has to say," Sadie offered, which seemed remarkably mature of her until Leah realized it wasn't maturity at all. It was cautiousness. Fear, even. A sentiment that had become prevalent at a young age for them all, when their carefree childhoods were interrupted, their innocence lost. "I saw him yesterday, and he said that he was Viv's attorney."

"Yes, well, we already know what Jimmy will say," Emma told them. "Viv didn't keep a will. Thought it would tempt fate. And I doubt that Viv had any hidden secrets we didn't know about."

Leah just raised an eyebrow to that, and all the sisters fell silent. Viv had been full of secrets, and not just about her finances. For years she refused to discuss the falling-out she'd had with their mother, instead deflecting every time it was mentioned. "That was a long time ago" was her favorite excuse, and later, as she aged, "I don't even remember."

Eventually, the girls had stopped asking, but now, Leah idly wondered just how much there was about Viv that they didn't know.

And now never would.

"And what are we going to do if we don't get a loan?" Sadie asked, ever the pessimist. Though in this case, she voiced Leah's own concerns. "I'm not in a position to be contributing financially."

None of them were, even though both her sisters seemed to look a little hopefully toward her. If they only knew, she thought. But now wasn't the time to get into that, and it certainly wasn't something she felt like discussing in front of Sadie either.

"Let's take it one step at a time," Leah said. She pulled out a list she'd made, some initial ideas that had kept her up long into the night, not that she would have gotten much sleep anyway. It wasn't easy, being back here, sleeping in her childhood bed, which felt as foreign as it had the first time she'd lain down in it, yet as familiar as the last time, when she'd cried into her pillow. And it wasn't easy being away from the girls either.

But once she'd gotten started on the list of things they needed to do to the house, the hours ticked by quickly. She hadn't felt this focused or energized in a long time. Or this optimistic, and not just because turning the house into a business might be the answer they were looking for.

She'd tapped into a part of herself that had long been buried by car pools and after-school activities, grocery store runs, and, lately, marital troubles.

She passed the list across the counter to Emma, then turned to open the upper cabinet for a mug, only to reach for the handle at the same time as Sadie. They locked eyes for a beat, Leah thinking how awkward and, at the same time, awful it was to be engaged in such a power struggle, but here it was.

She tried to imagine her own girls like this down the line, thinking just how much it must have hurt Viv to witness it. With that, she dropped her hand.

"Thanks," Sadie muttered before quickly grabbing a mug and scooting to the side to lift the coffeepot.

Leah saw Emma raise an eyebrow when Leah handed her a mug and then took one down for herself. She told herself that she'd feel better after her first cup. Adding an extra splash of cream and a heavy helping of sugar was necessary on days like this. Required, even.

A few minutes later, she sat at the table near the window, feeling at least warmer, if not slightly clearer headed.

"So, what do you think?" she asked, feeling suddenly nervous at having her ideas on display. "Feel free to give your thoughts." She directed her attention to Emma, and not just because she'd be running the business and had the most experience. Talking to Sadie was difficult at best. It felt forced and unnatural, and every topic seemed to make the unspoken one more obvious. "You're the expert."

Emma's cheeks flushed, but she didn't seem to give the list much attention. "Oh, I don't know about that. I've just worked the front desk. Dealt with guests . . ."

"That's more experience than either of us has!" Sadie pointed out.

It was assumed that Leah was not an option, not just because of Emma's work at the Baybrook Inn but because Leah had two children and a house in the Chicago suburbs. An entire life that couldn't be easily changed, even though it already had been in many ways, snatched out from under her, forcing her to adapt.

"We need to talk about the off months," Leah said, daring to voice her biggest concern. She looked at Emma. "How slow are things in the winter?"

"Slow," Emma admitted. She pushed out a breath. "But you can't find a vacancy anywhere in the summer. We could charge a premium to offset the winter months."

They could. They'd have to. And they'd have to be smart if they were going to get through the lean months.

"Maybe we could do some specials during the winter, to bring people up for a weekend. Themes, or packages." Again, she turned to Emma. It felt weird, looking for guidance from her youngest sister, when it was always the other way around. "We could go all out for the holidays, create activities, indoors and out."

Already Leah was thinking of the Christmas tree that the guests could decorate, the stockings they could hang from the mantel in the front living room, which would serve as a lobby. She grabbed the pen and paper and jotted a few things down.

"That could work," Emma agreed, but she didn't sound enthusiastic.

"The house has good bones; it just needs some freshening up," Leah said, getting back to the issues that she could actually control. She felt her heart race with excitement when she envisioned how the house could look. It was the same way she'd felt when she and Ted had been house hunting in the early years of their marriage. When she could walk into a room and reimagine it another way. A better way. "We'd need new beds, mattresses, and linens for all the guest rooms. The dressers and desks are antiques, so we could probably get away with keeping a few. New towels, of course. And for the first floor, we'd probably want to change things a bit, create more seating in the front room, maybe with armchairs instead of the couches?"

"Those lamps are pretty old," Sadie added.

Ah, ever the pessimist. Still, they were pretty shabby, and they wouldn't be expensive to replace. And small details like fixtures were exactly what were needed to elevate this old house.

Leah noted it on the list. The changes didn't look like much, but she knew they would add up, and more ideas would pop up once they got started. Then there was the painting to factor in, maybe refinishing the floors, too, or at least replacing some of the area rugs. They'd want to reupholster the patio furniture and give more outdoor seating options to the guests.

"We'll want to decide what to do with the first floor. We never used half the rooms growing up, and it doesn't look like much has changed. Emma, you could probably move down to the back sunroom; that way, you're near the kitchen. There's a full bathroom down here. Maybe you can take that little sitting room you like to watch movies in too. I doubt that den would be much use to the guests if they have the front living room as the lobby space. Since there are already French doors in place, it won't take any real work to seal off the back of the house."

"You'll be like a servant in your own home," Sadie said, more than a little sarcastically.

Leah glared at her. "That's not what I'm saying. But the guests will enter into the hall, and it's plenty wide for a check-in desk. And that front room is huge by any standard. The dining room can easily fit eighteen, and maybe the large table could be replaced with smaller ones, not that I imagine much beyond a continental breakfast would be served. The rest of the downstairs can be for family use only. Emma will have plenty of space to still live and work here."

Emma's hand stilled over the coffee cake, but she just blinked a few times and then nodded. "That makes sense." She smiled, but the expression didn't quite meet her eyes.

But then, change was difficult. And Viv hadn't been gone for even a week.

Sully barked, and Emma stood up. "I should take him for a walk."

"I'll join you," Sadie said, pushing back her chair.

It might have been nice to sit and discuss the changes to the house some more, to get her sisters' input and enthusiasm. Instead, she couldn't fight the nagging sense that once again, all responsibility fell on her. She was the oldest. She was a mother. She solved problems, and she made everything right.

But her sisters didn't know the half of it.

The bank where Carter worked was in the center of town, in a quaint brick building with a glass-paned front door flanked by two planters bursting with blue hydrangea. By all accounts, it was a friendly place, but standing against the cloudless blue sky, it felt as foreboding as the courtroom that Leah had visited in her custody agreement. Only today, instead of having a lawyer at her side whom she barely knew and was paying way too much, she was on her own.

Behind the front desk was a young receptionist, pretty, with blonde hair that fell at her shoulders and an eager smile. "Can I help you?"

Leah stared at the woman, unable to stop herself from wondering if she and Carter had ever been a thing, but then her attention was snagged by Carter himself, coming down the back hall in long strides. The gray suit and tie made him look as out of place as he'd seemed at the service.

The Carter she knew had other plans in life. Plans to become a teacher, travel, make an impact in the world. But then, she supposed she didn't know Carter anymore and hadn't in some time.

Maybe she had never really known him at all.

The Carter she'd thought she'd known was gentle and sweet. Had given her the type of security that she'd never thought she'd find again after her parents' deaths. Had offered her a glimpse of a future that was so much better than her past.

A future that she'd thought would be shared.

"Leah." His gaze flicked to the door. "Are your sisters here?"

Leah hooded her eyes and decided not to go there. Now wasn't the time for snide remarks about Sadie. "Just me."

He ushered her into a nearby office and closed the door. Leah took in the space. A large wooden desk sat before a wall of bookshelves that housed framed photos and books that looked like antiques. Her heart hitched when she considered that he might have a girlfriend, or more, and she discreetly looked a little closer, seeing that the photos were all of the Maxwell clan, snapshots taken over time. There was one of his father, his hair thinning more than she remembered, standing on his boat, a large fish in his hands, a proud grin on his mouth. One of his mother, still with her lovely smile, sitting on the bench in their garden with his sister, Sarah. Carter's parents had been at Vivian's service, but so many people had filled the house that she hadn't had a chance to properly greet them.

With a little shame, she knew that she'd purposely kept her distance.

Leah pushed back a longing for a time gone by and sat in one of the visitors' chairs while Carter settled behind the desk. Suddenly, she felt like bursting out laughing. They were two adults, in a bank, on official business. And it felt like they were playing house.

Perhaps feeling as uncomfortable as she did, Carter said, "I was just about to grab a coffee. Care to join me?"

She nodded, not because she cared to join him anywhere but because she needed to get out of this office. Away from the photos. The past and the present were at odds, reminding her of time lost.

"Coffee works. But my reasons for meeting are professional."

"I wouldn't expect anything else," he said with a strange smile that made her feel almost foolish for needing to clarify her request to see him. She was, to him at least, a married woman. And despite his other shortcomings, he'd never been prone to self-flattery.

Besides, what they'd shared had ended years ago. It was kid stuff. Certainly not worth still thinking about now.

Even if, as they fell into step and began walking down the sidewalk toward the Harborview Café, where they'd once spent many lazy

Sunday afternoons, pretending to do homework while fantasizing about the future, it was all she could think about.

Back then, the future had seemed so broad and open, like a blank notebook, its pages just waiting to be filled.

They'd talked about where they'd travel, how Carter might teach abroad, how Leah could join him, take some extra classes, and hone her design skills, which she could apply back stateside. They imagined the city, the excitement, new faces, and fresh experiences.

Instead, Carter was working for his father at the very building they used to pass. She wondered when he'd changed. Given up or just readjusted that vision he saw for himself.

She wondered if he was happy.

Carter pushed the door to the café open, and it jingled their arrival. Inside, the space was exactly like Leah remembered. The walls were still the same shade of buttery yellow, the counter at the back of the room was still covered with jars of coffee beans, and the chalkboard sign overhead listed the roasts and seasonal drinks. The food offerings were limited to cookies, muffins, and scones.

Outside, the tables facing the lakefront were filled with tourists laughing happily while they relaxed. Leah watched them through the window and then turned to see Carter pointing at a table in the corner instead.

Their usual spot.

She flicked a glance to him, wondering if he remembered, and then casually said, "Some fresh air might be nice."

His gaze seemed to challenge hers for a moment, but before he could speak, there was a rustling behind the counter, and Sandra O'Connor appeared in a faded apron bearing the logo of the shop she owned and operated.

"Well, I'll be! Carter and Leah! Together again!"

Leah's smile felt like more of a grimace, even though she was happy to see the familiar face. "Sandra. It's so nice to see you again."

"You, too, dear. Though I'm sorry for the reason that brought you back to town." Sandra's wrinkles deepened when she frowned. All too quickly, though, her smile turned coy. "But I'm sure your aunt would be thrilled to know that her sad news brought about *this* reunion."

Carter cleared his throat, but before he could order, Sandra started chuckling.

"I remember you two lovebirds like it was yesterday. You'd come here three, four days a week and sit over there in that corner. I swear I never saw a cuter sight. Thought for sure that I'd still see you two sitting there when you were old and gray."

Leah couldn't even look at Carter, even though she had the distinct sense of his body stiffening beside her.

She wondered if she should mention that she was married and decided not to bother. Or maybe she should offer up that she had children. But that might be just as awkward.

Instead, Sandra went on, saying, "But then that would have been impossible, wouldn't it?"

"Absolutely," Leah said, louder and firmer than she'd planned, given the way Carter looked at her so sharply, his brows drawing into a line, his jaw tense under the firm press of his mouth.

"I mean, by the time you two are that old, I'll have been long gone . . ."

"Just the usual, Sandra," Carter said, pleasantly but firmly.

Leah wondered idly if this was his grown-up voice. The voice he used when he had to call a client at the bank, tell them they had an overdraft or that their application for a mortgage had been declined. It was so strange to see Carter, the same boy whose hair was always a tad too long and used to flop over his brow, standing here in this suit and tie.

Just as strange, she supposed, as the wedding ring that still slid around on her ring finger because she'd never made the time to get it adjusted, and now there would be no point.

"A black coffee for you, Carter, and . . ." Sandra held a fist to her mouth, showing that she'd forgotten what Leah's preferred beverage was.

"A vanilla latte with skim milk and a sprinkle of cinnamon," Carter said.

Now it was Leah's turn to look at him sharply. He remembered. After all these years.

Only unlike her, he'd faced these memories every day for years until they probably lost their meaning. The places in this town couldn't hold the same meaning, not when they were commonplace, replaced, no doubt, by new experiences.

Glancing through the window and seeing that the last remaining seats on the patio had been taken, she grudgingly walked to the table in the corner and settled herself into a chair while Carter waited for their drinks. She tried her best not to let her gaze linger too long in his direction, and not just because Sandra kept casting suggestive glances her way. Carter looked good in a suit, and the way he filled it out reminded her in more ways than one that he wasn't a teenager anymore.

"So," he said when he eventually joined her. "You and me. Together again."

The corner of his mouth lifted, and despite herself, Leah couldn't help but laugh.

"It's funny how people hold on to the past." She took a sip of her coffee and then sat up a little straighter. "But then, that's why I wanted to meet with you today. I need to understand my aunt's financial position."

"Well, it wasn't great." Carter gave her a long look. "I tried to help her, Leah. I set aside enough to make sure her property taxes would be covered for the next couple of years, so that money can be kept in place or reallocated depending on what you want to do. I assume she wanted everything to be split evenly."

Leah nodded. Viv was fair like that.

"There's not much left, Leah," he said matter-of-factly. "The house is worth a lot, but she took out a sizable mortgage, kept insisting one day she'd waltz in and pay it all back, and maybe she would have done."

He gave a sad smile at some distant memory. "From what I gather, Emma's contributions have been footing the monthly payment."

Now Leah's eyes widened. And it was all the more reason that she'd have to take matters into her own hands now, do right by the family.

"I wasn't in a position to share any details of Viv's personal finances with anyone before now," he added.

"Emma is invested in the house," she said. And more than just emotionally, it would appear. "And I don't think my aunt's goal was for us to sell it."

Carter's eyes drooped. "Probably not. That house has been in your family for generations. Any sale price would have to cover the mortgage to make it worth it for you. And then you have all the fees that go along with that too."

Leah understood. She wasn't new to homeownership. Her sisters, however, were probably clueless.

It was time to level with Carter. "We have an idea for how to save the house."

"Oh?" Carter looked interested but not exactly hopeful, and for a moment, Leah wavered, wondering if she was being foolish, if she was refusing to accept the reality of their circumstances.

But no, she'd always been a realist. Life had hit her too hard at too early an age for her to dare to dream too much. Except with him.

"We're thinking of turning it into an inn." She searched his eyes for any hint into his opinion, but he kept his expression remarkably neutral. Maybe this was his professional face.

Or maybe she no longer knew him at all.

He nodded as he leaned back in his chair. "There's certainly never a shortage of demand during the high season. But I assume that there's more to this plan, or you wouldn't have sought me out."

She pulled in a breath, wondering why she suddenly felt so nervous. Maybe it was Carter's company, the fact that he was sitting so close that she could smell the soap on his skin from his morning shower, the glint in his soft gaze where the light filtered through the windows. That she was sitting here with him at all, after all these years.

"We'd need to make some changes to the house. Spruce it up. Buy new furniture." Among other things. She leaned into the table, knowing he already knew what she was going to say.

"If anyone could make that house even more beautiful than it already is, you could."

Maybe he was flattering her, or maybe he was just remembering the girl she used to be, back when they knew each other. Back when her ideas were as big as her dreams. Before she wished she'd never gone to design school.

"Well, it's been a long time." Since she'd followed her passion. Since he'd spoken to her.

"I have no doubt that you can make that house into a showstopper," he said, grinning at her.

She lowered her eyes. She needed his support, but not in the emotional sense. Those days were long gone.

"We'd need a loan." She held her breath, waiting for his response.

"The interest rate would be steep, all things considered," he warned her after a brief hesitation. "Loans don't work without collateral."

"I have a house." It had already been agreed that she would keep it. But could she really mortgage her own home, risk her own children's future, for a house that she hadn't returned to in over a decade? A house they'd never visited, a family they'd never really known?

Prepared for this, she pulled out her phone and showed him the current value.

Carter stared at the screen for a moment before glancing up at her. "I'm glad that things worked out for you, Leah."

Nothing in life had worked out for her—other than her two girls. But everything that had happened had led to them being in her life. And that was something she would never take back.

"Things worked out the way they were supposed to," she said firmly. Even when they didn't feel like it.

She tried to tell herself this now, thinking of what she stood to lose if things didn't work out. If she sank all her money into this house, into the business, only to have it all go wrong.

"I think we could make this work," Leah said with more confidence than she felt. They had no choice but to make it work.

Carter was silent for a moment. Finally, he leaned back in his chair and gave her a long look. "Let me talk to my dad."

Leah tried not to show her excitement, but there was little worry of that when Carter added, "But no promises."

"Of course not," she said, a little bitterly. After all, any promises Carter had made to her had been broken, and maybe she'd do best to remember that.

His gaze lingered on her for a moment before he gave her a sad smile. "So I guess this means that you're sticking around for a while?"

She nodded as she slid her phone back into her bag. "My daughters are away, and it's a convenient time for me to help my—" She stopped before she mentioned Sadie. "Emma could use the help."

"As I said, I'll see what I can do." Carter glanced to the door and jutted his chin. "Shall we?"

Leah was a little surprised at how quickly he was ending their conversation, and she wondered why she didn't feel more relieved. It was strange, being here, with Carter again. Pretending like nothing had happened. Convincing herself that it didn't matter anymore, not when, as she'd said, things had worked out the way they were supposed to.

Even if it had hurt along the way.

The sun felt bright in contrast to the darker lighting of the café when they stepped outside. She shielded her eyes, prepared to make her excuses, or maybe one final plea, when Carter hesitated on the sidewalk.

"The Founder's Day Festival is this weekend," Carter said, thrusting his hands into his pockets. He hesitated for a moment and then said, "We used to really like that pie stand."

Despite herself, she felt a fond memory resurface. "Well, we had to. Viv entered the contest every year, and we had to support her."

"The samples didn't hurt either," Carter said with a grin.

A part of her was unwilling to open that door to her heart again. It was so much easier to keep things distant, to leave off right where they'd parted. With all the anger and hurt that had lived somewhere below the surface all these years. She'd worked hard to bury that pain, but seeing him again had brought it all back.

It had also brought back other feelings. Memories of laughter and excitement, of her stomach swooping with anticipation every time he leaned in for a kiss, of the look in his eyes every time she ran down the porch to meet him on the gravel drive, the way his arm felt around her shoulder, the way her hand felt in his.

He was doing her a favor. The more cynical side of her might have considered that he was doing her family a favor, and Sadie was part of that family. But she knew that there was nothing going on between the two of them. No, whatever had transpired had been quick, like a bomb that exploded and broke everything around it.

A hint of a grin lifted one corner of his mouth. "So maybe I'll see you there? Maybe sometime after lunch? Somewhere near the pie stand?"

"Maybe," she said, pausing at the corner to let him cross the road back toward the bank, because just like Carter, she wasn't sure she could really keep a promise when it came to them. To what they might still have. Or what they might have been.

CHAPTER THIRTEEN

EMMA

By Thursday, the only thing the sisters were talking about was the plan for the house—but at least they were talking. The meeting between Leah and Carter had apparently been "hopeful," though what her eldest sister meant by that, Emma was unable to determine. She didn't want to ask for details, not when she was torn between hoping that the house could be saved and hoping that there was no chance of qualifying for a business loan.

And certainly not when that involved discussing Carter Maxwell.

The man's name was rarely mentioned in Sadie's company, which was probably for the best. They had far bigger things to worry about at the moment than a romantic tryst that had happened more than a decade ago.

At least Emma did.

After a breakfast of leftover coffee cake and slightly bitter coffee made by Sadie, whose time in the restaurant industry clearly hadn't involved barista duties, Emma left Sully in his room, thinking with a bitter snort that she was surprised Leah hadn't considered the mudroom for her quarters, or the carriage house out back! Yes, she could sleep with Viv's old car, next to the bikes and cobwebs and gardening equipment. She could cross the lawn each morning to the house she'd grown up in, where she could wait on guests, her sisters nowhere to be seen. She'd be like Cinderella, cleaning and cooking and listening to the endless string of complaints in the house that had once been her home, dreaming of a better life all the while.

She asked herself for the hundredth time how she had gotten it so wrong. How one suggestion had spiraled into this plan while she kept opening her mouth to explain or protest, yet no sound ever came out.

Gone was the dream of a big city, or culinary school. Of a bakery all her own, a kitchen with sunlight pouring in, and a display case overflowing with her creations.

Gone was the dream of traveling the world, savoring the offerings of each country, honing her skills, and learning new recipes that she could take back and share.

All her money was going to be sunk into the house—at least what she hadn't already put into it. At best, she'd have a roof over her head, trapped in this house for the rest of her life.

It wasn't a fresh notion, but now it had taken an especially unappealing turn. She was used to working at an inn—but at least she could leave the Baybrook Inn at the end of a long, busy day. Now there would be no break. It would be work, work, work, all day and night. Leah would be living her picket fence suburban dream with her two beautiful children. Sadie would be living on the edge in Manhattan.

And she would end up just like Aunt Viv. Serving others with a smile on her face.

Blinking back tears, Emma hurried out the front door, taking the porch steps as fast as her legs would carry her, grateful that she wasn't going to work today because she wasn't sure how she would be able to keep a smile plastered on her face. It had been difficult enough to do that all through breakfast.

More than once she'd considered just slamming down her coffee mug and saying that she'd made a mistake. To forget what she'd said about the inn—it was a crazy idea, truly. Crazy because it meant that she was cementing herself to this house, as surely as if she'd poured concrete right into her shoes and melded into the foundation. Because, really, what had she been thinking?

She'd gotten swept away, excited by the idea of saving the house. Because unless one of her sisters came up with a better idea, there would be no way they could keep this place. It would be sold. They'd all go to their separate corners again—Sadie to New York, Leah to Chicago, and Emma . . . she didn't know where.

And that was why she'd said nothing. Because she had no plan, not really. And the inn was as close to one as she could get.

And the only possible way of keeping this house in the family. Of having anything left of a family at all.

Her sisters were both out and about—where, she didn't care. She no longer took comfort in them being here, and not just because they were hell bent on holding a grudge about something that should have been long forgotten. Now their presence was another reminder of her place in the pecking order, her birth order, and her role in life.

Emma had stayed behind and taken care of Viv. It was expected because both her sisters had fled the responsibility.

And now she was expected to stay behind and take care of the house.

Her mind went to Wyatt, as it usually did at least once a day (oh, who was she kidding?—more like ten times a day), drifting into the heart-thumping place when she pulled up his image. Maybe he and his girlfriend would break up. It wasn't like he ever talked about her. Maybe he'd realize that she was the one he loved, the one he was meant to be with. Maybe he'd move into the house with her.

That was a lot of maybes.

Already the wonderful view of Wyatt's smiling face faded, only to be replaced by one of Viv with pinched lips, echoing Emma's innermost thoughts: How exactly could Wyatt move into the house if it was meant to be turned into an inn? If her living quarters would be reduced to the back two rooms off the kitchen?

She realized with a rush of panic that she had no future here, not at all, just like she'd always thought and always feared. But moving on had felt scarier. And staying had been safe.

And she hadn't been given much choice.

And Wyatt sure as heck wasn't making things any easier. An invitation to the Founder's Day Festival wasn't something she could exactly overlook.

Maybe things would work out in the end. Maybe it was a sign that she was meant to stay here in Fog's Landing, embrace her lot, and make this her permanent home.

Her task for the day was to contact a handyman and get a quote for all the repairs that she and her sisters couldn't handle for themselves. Leah had assigned it to her—probably because she didn't trust Sadie, even though Sadie probably could have hustled a better rate. She probably thought Emma would have contacts, but Viv had never bothered with a handyman before. When the old wiring got fickle and a fan stopped working, she'd cracked a window. Now, Emma realized that it wasn't just because it was Viv's way to be content with what she had.

It was because Viv had been broke, and she knew it.

Emma could have argued, she supposed. Or spoken up. Said that they had it all wrong. Set them straight. But it wasn't like she had a hard plan to fall back on. Just . . . a fantasy.

First, Emma needed coffee, as in good coffee, not Sadie's brew that she'd only sipped and then poured out this morning, watching the bits of grounds wash away down the drain. She marched past the tourists enjoying their lattes and (she knew from experience) dry scones at the wrought iron tables on the patio of the Harborview Café, the water nearly within arm's reach. Inside, the small space revealed a long line, reminding her that even at midmorning, there was never a shortage of patronage in the warmer months.

"Ah, Emma." Sandra smiled as she approached. "Your sister was just in here the day before yesterday. With Carter Maxwell." She gave Emma a highly suggestive look, but Emma knew better.

Still . . . Leah had left out that part of the story, instead returning to the house looking flushed with satisfaction, saying that she was certain that she and Carter would be able to work something out and she should know more soon.

Now, Emma wondered if more than a conversation about the loan had transpired.

Just as quickly, she stopped herself. What was she thinking? Leah was a married mother of two. And Carter was . . .

Well, it didn't matter what Carter was or ever had been. Right now, all that Carter was good for was pulling out a loan to cover the cost of repairs.

And staying clear of Sadie until she left town for good. And when exactly would that be? Emma was starting to wonder if it might be better if Sadie left rather than stuck around to help so at least there would be less tension. But then that would be just like Sadie, wouldn't it? To run at the first sign of trouble? To leave Emma to clean up the mess.

No, the fair thing was for them to all stay until the house was in order.

Sandra was still talking about Leah and Carter, shaking her head fondly. "It was like old times, seeing them together again . . ."

Emma registered the suggestive gleam in Sandra's gray eyes and decided to set her straight, lest more gossip about their family start to fly. The saga of Leah and Carter and Sadie had been the talk of the town for a solid three months, and the return of the elder Burke sisters had clearly stirred things up again.

"Oh, I think they're just settling more of my aunt's affairs," Emma replied.

That did the trick, even though it was sad that Viv's passing had to be used in this manner.

Sandra's smile drooped. "It won't be the same without her. I swear, I get weepy every time I see my tin of Earl Grey. But we'll still see you, right? You aren't going anywhere?"

Emma's stomach felt like a lead ball, and it took everything in her to lift her mouth into a vague but stiff smile. "No. I'm not going anywhere."

It was the first time she had said it out loud, putting it out into the universe. The declaration of a decision made, even if it had been made for her. It was as overwhelming and terrifying as if she'd announced that actually, she'd be moving out of state next week, maybe crashing at Sadie's apartment in New York for a while before opening her own bakery.

Instead, she had confirmed that she'd never get a chance to say those words.

And that she'd probably be better off never thinking about them again either.

A line had started to form behind her, and Sandra went back to the business at hand. "Now, what can I get for you?"

"An iced latte," Emma said, thinking that it would be a hot day. Maybe later she'd go down to the waterfront, even take a dip. Swimming always calmed her and made her present rather than caught up in the past or worried about the future.

Today, she wasn't so sure it would do the trick.

She paid for the drink, added a few bills to the tip jar, and walked over to the neighborhood bulletin board, wondering if there were any new happenings in town that she wasn't already aware of, though this place was so predictable she couldn't imagine that would be the case. Immediately, her attention was snagged by the listing for next month's knitting club, something that Viv looked forward to, even if she preferred to crochet.

Looking away before her emotions got the better of her, Emma saw the listing she was hoping for. Under the Services section were painters (though her sisters had established they could handle that on their own), landscapers, and—aha—handymen.

She had three choices and decided to go for the one with the nicest flyer. The one that had only two flags left at the bottom of the sheet.

She went to rip one off but was interrupted by the clearing of a throat behind her.

"I wouldn't go with him if I were you," a deep voice said.

She turned, surprised, and saw a youngish guy with deep-brown eyes and a nice smile looking back at her.

"Why not?" She was happy for a recommendation—or a warning. She knew from working at the hotel that some tradespeople could take advantage or walk out on a job without finishing it, leaving the owner in a lurch.

Instead of answering her question, the guy pointed to another flyer. One that bore all its flags containing the contact number and the name Brody.

She didn't see anything particularly special about this flyer. If anything, it was a bit minimalistic, even too clean, meaning that maybe it had just been put up recently.

She turned back to him, narrowing her eyes in suspicion. "Don't tell me you're Brody."

His grin was bashful. "I am. And I come with the promise of a fair wage and excellent service."

If Emma didn't know better, she'd swear that Viv came up from behind her and whispered, "It helps that he's easy on the eye too."

She blinked, shaking off that completely inappropriate thought.

"I'm—"

But before she could speak, he said, "Emma Burke." Now his cheeks grew a little pink. "I've seen you around. It's a small town."

It was. But she was a little embarrassed to admit that she hadn't seen him before.

"Are you new around here?" she asked instead.

"Moved here around this time last year. My grandparents used to have a weekend home near here, and when they passed away, I took it over. Technically, it went to my four brothers, too, but I was the only one willing to look past the leaky faucets and mold, not to mention the wood rot."

"Yikes." She grinned, then, decisively, ripped one of his flags from his flyer. "If you can handle that, then I'm guessing you can handle some odd jobs at my aunt's house. We live just up the road—"

"I know where you live." He grinned again. "I promise I'm not a stalker. I actually knew your aunt."

"You did?" Emma blinked, trying to place him. "Were you at the service over the weekend?" If he had been, she hadn't seen him, but then, half the town had turned out for Viv.

He shook his head. "I didn't know her that well. She was friends with my grandmother, though. Or friendly, I should say. You might have known her. Her name was Shirley Hudson."

"Shirley!" Emma smiled fondly when she thought of the woman with the big smile and enviable garden that Viv must have driven Emma by at least once a week from May through August, her foot off the gas pedal, always disguised by her ancient oversize sunglasses, her eyes on the road while Emma was instructed to all but press her nose against the glass and report every last petal and new addition. The year that Shirley had added a rare nostalgie rosebush the same week that Viv had planted one in the backyard still stuck out in Emma's mind. "She was Viv's nemesis in the flower competition every year."

Emma didn't mention that Viv had finally won when the poor woman passed away.

Now Brody shared her smile, his gaze turning a little wistful. "That's her. Unfortunately, I don't have the same skill set when it comes to gardening as I do when it comes to construction."

"Don't tell me the roses—"

"I don't think they'll be blooming this year." Brody cringed, and Emma couldn't help but laugh.

"Well, I'll give you a call," she said, realizing that they were lingering and that the man probably had somewhere to be.

"Or you could just tell me what day works for you, and I'll stop by," he suggested.

A savvy businessman, not willing to let her off the hook so easily. She didn't mind. She needed a handyman, and it looked like she'd found one.

"Does Monday work?" That would give her and her sisters more time to think through the plans.

Or, in her case, digest them.

"Monday works." He reached out a hand, and after a beat, she took it, her body tensing at how warm and smooth his palm was, how small her own hand felt in his. "Afternoon okay?"

"I'll be there," Emma said, releasing her hand to give a little wave.

Because where else would she be?

CHAPTER FOURTEEN

SADIE

Carter called the house the next morning. Sadie hadn't meant to answer it, but the concept of a landline was a little foreign to her, and Emma was nowhere to be found. The dog was also missing, meaning that she'd probably taken him for a walk, and a long one, if her sudden and indefinite disappearances from the house were any indication.

Carter seemed just as confounded as she was when he identified himself. "Sadie. I wasn't expecting you to answer. I . . . thought I'd be speaking to Leah."

Sadie leaned against the kitchen island and kept one eye on the doorway to the hall. "Should I hang up and let you try again? Maybe you'll get the sister you prefer next time."

It was childish, she knew, but she couldn't help it. She'd never loved Carter, not like Leah had. And she'd certainly never known him like her sister either. What they shared was contained to one event. An event he had promptly told her he regretted.

And that was the part that stung. It didn't matter that she didn't plan to repeat it or pursue him, that she regretted it just as much as he did—if not more so.

It was the fact that he had said it. That she was a mistake. Second best.

And even now, after all this time, she was coming up behind Leah. Leah, who had a comfortable house (at least from what she could glean), two healthy and beautiful daughters, and a husband. She had a family. And Sadie didn't even have an apartment to return to, much less a husband, kid, dog, or job.

Her heart started to drum quickly and heavily in her chest just thinking about it. "We can talk," Carter said evenly. "I mean, what I have to say to Leah could be said to you or Emma."

Strictly business, then, which was just as well. Contrary to what Leah might think, Sadie had no interest in reliving a mistake she'd made half a lifetime ago. What was done was done, and now here they were. Adults, handling adult matters. Like finances and mortgages and possibly bankruptcy. Really, it was all fine. Dandy, actually.

At least for Leah. She might have suffered the most at first, but like always, she came out on top. It was no different from after their parents had died and they'd moved here. Leah had easily found friends, a community, and a boyfriend. An entire life and a future that was once again crystal clear.

Now, like always, Sadie's horizon felt blurry, not bright.

"I managed to pull some strings here and get you guys a small business loan," Carter said.

Sadie stood a little straighter, suddenly filled with hope, even though she wasn't exactly sure where she fit into things with this house. But it was good news, at least, and that was certainly better than her recent trend line. And didn't good things usually come in threes? If so, then maybe two more were waiting for her, ones that she could benefit from a little more directly.

For now, she was just relieved to know that they could keep the house, Emma and Leah would be happy, and by extension, that would make life a little easier for her in the short term.

As for the long run, she never really thought that far out, did she?

And how could she? She couldn't count on tomorrow, so how could she really plan for next week?

"Leah mentioned pulling from her personal finances, but I think we can avoid that for now," Carter continued.

Now Sadie frowned. Leah had done that? But why?

Maybe it was this house, the one part of their family that was still standing. Or maybe it was guilt. Either way, she felt her heart soften a bit toward her sister.

"But do you mind me asking how?" She might not be the most responsible person around, but she was certainly no dummy. "Viv had nothing left; she'd mortgaged the house."

"Viv isn't here anymore," Carter said, not unkindly. "The house has been passed down to the three of you, and I think—or rather I *know*—that you're all good for it."

Well, that silenced her. No one had ever put that kind of trust in her before, especially not since she'd gone and betrayed the person she loved the most, and definitely never since.

But she wasn't in New York anymore, where she knew almost no one and had, at best, fleeting and superficial relationships with those she did.

People in Fog's Landing knew each other. Knew each other a little too well at times, but other times, like this . . .

She blinked quickly. "Well, thank you. I'll let my sisters know."

She hung up the phone and walked down the hall with a newfound sense of purpose. She paused halfway up the stairs, wondering if she should break the news to Leah, who was upstairs in her room, or if she should wait until Emma was home.

Wait, she told herself, coming back down the steps. A conversation with Leah could take an unexpected turn, however good her intention. And when Carter was involved, it was better to say nothing.

Armed with a list of rooms Leah had said they would need to paint—either for aesthetic reasons or for maintenance—Sadie instead walked out the front door. Leah would, of course, decide on the final paint colors, but Sadie could be useful by providing some options. And it sure beat sitting around the house wondering just what she was going to do with her life.

She took her time walking toward the hardware store. It wasn't a familiar route, because the shops they had usually frequented when she was growing up were more of the food or clothing or craft variety, but she remembered where it was located, and she presumed that it was still there. Like many shops in town, it was owned by a local family, passed down through the generations much like the big, rambling house. There was always at least one person willing to carry on the business or name. In their family, that was Emma.

Sadie knew that it made sense, of course. And it wasn't like she could have offered to take over the inn. She didn't have the experience, and she wasn't especially good with people.

She could just imagine what kind of reaction that would have been met with. Emma might have cried. Leah would have laughed, and not from amusement. No, no, Emma was the right person for it. She'd lived here the longest, knew the house best. And she had industry experience, of course.

And Sadie, well, Sadie didn't really have any reason to volunteer, did she? It was Emma's home, really. And it had never especially felt like home to Sadie.

The sidewalks grew more crowded the closer she got to town, and Sadie was grateful for the oversize sunglasses she wore, even if they did make her stick out nearly as much as her head-to-toe black clothing. Could she help it if it was the only color she owned, other than denim and the occasional burst of camel? She didn't want to look anyone in the eye, feel their stares or their judgment.

She was relieved when she pushed through the door of AJ's Hardware, happy to see that she didn't recognize the boy behind the counter. Old AJ's grandson, perhaps? Or maybe just a local kid, earning money for a down payment on a used car.

Sadie took her time walking the aisles, even though they didn't exactly pull her attention the way a bookstore might. Nails, screws, and an entire row of bolts in all different sizes. Finally, she found the paint chips glowing under their fluorescent lights. The only burst of color in the entire space, otherwise reserved for gray and metal. And she thought she was monochromatic.

Naturally, her hand went to the shades of gray, but a little voice beside her said, "Too dreary."

She turned, happy to see Jimmy standing there, holding a bag of gardening soil.

"How do you even know what this is for?" she asked.

"I don't care what it's for," he said. "It's too dreary." He came to stand beside her, studying the chips for a moment before tapping on the blues. "I prefer these myself."

"What are we doing, designing our dream house?"

"Would that be so bad?"

His crooked grin sparked a memory in her. One of them side by side on the lawn out back, dusk settling in and crickets chirping. A cool breeze coming in off the bay, but she hadn't wanted to go inside. She'd been too content right there, in her best friend's company.

"Wouldn't it be nice if we could stay like this forever?" she'd asked.

"We could" was all he'd said, as if it were that simple, as if there weren't choices that would have to be made, options considered.

"Life isn't that straightforward," she'd said, and he'd fallen silent because he'd known he'd hit a nerve.

After a few moments, he'd said, "But it could be. You and me. Forever. Doesn't that sound nice?"

"It sounds . . ."

"Wonderful," she whispered now. Feeling his frown on her, she shook her head, forcing a smile. "Sorry, you're right. It's, uh, a wonderful color." She grabbed the nearest blue chip and then considered her list. Six bedrooms to paint. Bathrooms too. The front hall, front parlor, and dining room. She felt a flinch of panic.

"What is this?" He snatched it from her hand before she had a chance to stop him and then looked at her with something close to surprise but more like fear. "You're not fixing up the house to sell, are you?"

Wouldn't that be easier? Maybe, but maybe not.

Sadie huffed out a breath, unsure if she could tell him but then thinking that of course she could. This was Jimmy. They might not have seen each other or spoken in years, but he was still her person. Still someone she could trust.

And there weren't many people she could.

Besides, he was practically family. Emma wouldn't mind. Surely Leah wouldn't, either, but then, maybe she would . . . it didn't take much to set her off where Sadie was concerned.

"We're thinking of turning it into an inn, actually. More like planning to," she corrected, thinking of her call with Carter.

A plan. The concept was so foreign to her, but the future felt just as murky as it always did. Once the house was finished, her purpose here would be spent. And that was where the plan ended, for her at least.

"Really?" He grinned widely, looking pleased. "That's a great idea."

"You don't think your mom would mind, then? The people coming in and out?"

Jimmy shook his head firmly. "Not at all. She's always complained about how quiet it's been over there in recent years. Like before you all moved in. It was . . . well, it was better when you were all there. Giving life to the place. Viv felt the same."

Viv. Sadie hadn't even given much thought to what her aunt would have thought of their plans, but hearing this filled her with both sadness and relief.

"I guess Viv would like it, then. Knowing the old house would be filled with more people."

"I'm sure of it. But I know one thing she wouldn't like."

"What's that?" Sadie asked, her heart thumping with worry.

Jimmy's mouth slid into a grin. "That gray paint chip you selected."

Sadie's smile was slow to develop, but then she laughed. Viv's house was bright and cheerful and filled with colors like the flowers she grew in her prized garden. "You're right."

Besides, it wasn't like she was going to live there. What difference did it make if she preferred the soft, subtle shades of dove to the moody blues?

With Jimmy's help, Sadie only somewhat reluctantly decided on a palette of colors and purchased sample-size cans of the bolder choices so her sisters could see if they worked. She had to brace herself when the kid behind the counter swiped her credit card, hoping the charge would go through, telling herself that in a matter of days, her unemployment check would hit her bank account. And after today, they'd have the loan.

The loan! Finally, she could be the bearer of good news.

Ever the gentleman that his mother had raised him to be, Jimmy insisted on carrying the heavy bag home for her.

"Doesn't hurt that I'm walking that way anyway," he added with a grin.

"How is it that a man like you hasn't been swept up yet?" Sadie marveled as they walked out of town, the congested storefronts changing into homes on one side, the bay on the other.

"You sound like my mother." Jimmy laughed. "What can I say? I was married to my work. Then, when I moved back, I was busy setting up my practice."

Seemed like a simple enough reason, and she didn't have a good one for herself either. But then, she wasn't Jimmy. She didn't have a fancy degree or respectable job. She didn't have any job at all.

She swallowed that little factoid along with the bubble of panic that always accompanied it. She'd always landed on her feet, and she would again. If she could show up in a strange city at the age of eighteen with a duffel bag and a meager savings account, then she could certainly do it again now, in her thirties.

"What about you? Anyone special in your life?"

"I'm looking at him," she joked, giving him a playful nudge in the ribs. She sighed deeply as they walked. "But no. I had a recent breakup. Lost my job too. And before you ask, yes, it was related."

"Yikes." Jimmy always knew when not to press.

Sadie sighed heavily. "I think I'm cursed when it comes to love and romance and all that."

"Cursed? You believe in all that now?"

Cursed. Karma. It had a name, even if she didn't know what to call it.

"Some people just easily slide into relationships and jobs and a routine life. That was never me." Still wasn't. The difference was that now, she had started to crave it. Started to envy the certainty that her sister Leah had, knowing that she had a home to return to, two daughters to manage, and responsibilities that no longer seemed so overwhelming, even if they did feel just as daunting.

"That's because you take risks," Jimmy countered, giving her a look of appreciation. "Take this house, for example."

They stared up the road for a moment as the big old Victorian came into closer view. Even from this distance, it stood out over the nearby homes, its gables and turret peeking out over the dense foliage, the sparkling water across the road seeming to shine just for it.

"Lots of people would have just sold the thing, gotten what they could out of it."

"Oh, well, that wouldn't be right," Sadie said quickly. "I mean, it's not really our house to sell. It's our family's house. Viv's house."

"Well, it legally belongs to all three of you now."

"I'm not so sure that's a good thing." Sadie pulled a face. "It's a lot of responsibility."

Jimmy looked at her, and in the late afternoon sunlight, the copper highlights in his hair brought out the freckles on his nose.

"True. It's a risk."

It was. The loan would have to be paid back, of course. And she still hadn't yet shared the news with her sisters.

The house was quiet when they let themselves in the back door. No Sully to greet them with his big bark and wagging tail, and the light in the kitchen was off. One glance into the front hall confirmed that Leah's sandals that had been near the closet earlier were now missing, which was just as well.

As much as she yearned to tell them the good news, she also worried that they might change their minds when presented with the fact that an idea could now be a reality.

Or maybe she was just projecting her own thoughts onto them.

Because like Jimmy pointed out, this was a big risk. And there was no guarantee things would work out.

"Why don't you come in and stay for dinner?" Sadie's tone was hopeful, not just because she wasn't ready to part with his company yet but because she needed a buffer. Her sisters would be equally grateful for a guest, someone to talk to other than themselves. Someone whose mere presence might keep things lighthearted. Even . . . fun.

"Only if you're cooking," Jimmy replied.

"Actually, that's a good idea. I'll cook tonight. Give my sisters one less reason to hate me."

"They don't hate you," Jimmy said softly.

Sadie gave him a look that said she wasn't so sure she agreed. "Maybe not Emma. But Leah . . ."

"Just give her time," Jimmy said.

Sadie gave a snort to that comment. "I've given her fifteen years. You'd think she'd be over it by now. A husband. Two kids. A big house and a nice car. What more can she want? It's not like she's still hung up on Carter."

Jimmy, who had been unloading the bag of sample paint cans, stopped to raise an eyebrow.

Sadie frowned at him for a moment and then swatted his arm. "Impossible. She's just determined to stay mad at me."

"And you?"

Sadie didn't know what she was. One moment she was determined to make things right, the next angry over the fact that all the blame had been placed on her. That Leah wouldn't hear her out or understand her part in it all.

That Leah couldn't just move on.

"I'm determined to have a nice dinner," Sadie replied. "And you're going to help me."

"Good, I like to cook." Jimmy walked over to the baker's rack, which was bursting with cookbooks in no particular order. Some were shiny and new, others faded from the sun pouring in through the large windows.

"I didn't know you liked to cook," Sadie said, coming to stand beside him. She pulled a book free, glanced at it, and returned it to its slot.

"There's a lot you don't know about me. I'm not a kid anymore."

"Neither of us is." Sadie sighed. "Besides," she said, nudging him with her elbow. "I know you better than anyone else. And you haven't changed *that* much."

"No? Well, neither have you," Jimmy said fondly.

Sadie knew it was meant to be a compliment, except that she wasn't sure if it was true. She had changed, or tried to, at least. Tried to run far and fast, away from her troubles, eager to shed her skin and start fresh in a city where no one knew her story or even her name. She could be anyone she wanted, but somehow, she had ended up being the same lost girl who had first stepped off that bus. The same girl who had once stood in this kitchen with Jimmy Price, the best next-door neighbor a girl could ask for.

Not wanting to keep going with this conversation, Sadie stooped to her haunches and weeded through the forgotten books at the very bottom, selecting one that she'd never seen, one that was slim, with no markings on the spine.

She was about to slip it back in place when a piece of paper slipped out. Upon closer inspection, it was a photograph.

"What's that?" Jimmy asked, leaning in as she stood.

"I don't know." Sadie picked it up and scanned it carefully, taking in the image of the two girls, their age gap made noticeable by their size difference. The older girl had shoulder-length blonde hair, the younger one darker long braids. The photo had been taken in this very kitchen, there at the table behind her. "It's a photo. It looks like Leah and Emma . . ." She squinted, turning it over to see if there was a date stamp on the back. "But it looks too old to be one of them."

"It's faded, and not from the sun, if you found it in that old book." Jimmy held out a hand. "Can I see?"

Like her, he gingerly took the photo and studied it closely. "It does look like Leah, though. But Emma would have been younger, wouldn't she? And how old was she when she moved to this house?"

Sadie stared at Jimmy with a pounding heart. He was pointing out all the facts she already knew but hadn't even considered, because they didn't matter. She knew who was in the photo, and it wasn't Emma. "I think this is my mother. And Vivian."

"Are you going to tell your sisters?"

"Tell us what?" Leah walked into the room, startling Sadie, who quickly thrust the photo back into the book and set it on the shelf.

Sadie swallowed hard, her heart hammering as she tried to digest the image that was at complete odds with the expression on Leah's face.

"Hello, Leah," Jimmy said, saving her. He smiled gallantly and walked across the kitchen to greet Leah with a hug.

Sadie couldn't help but feel irked at the way her sister's face lit up for him. It seemed Leah's good nature was reserved for everyone but her.

"I was going to tell you and Emma both," Sadie said, glancing at Jimmy. "Over dinner. To celebrate."

"I might see if my friend Leslie is free for dinner," Leah said, not looking her in the eye as she opened a cabinet and took down a mug and then began filling the kettle.

This wasn't how Sadie had envisioned the day, but it was probably what she should have expected. Hope was a funny thing. It still sneaked up on her at times, until she remembered that it had no place in her life.

"Well, the loan came through," she said flatly. So much for a big celebration.

Now Leah turned from the sink with large eyes. "For the business? For the inn?" Realizing her words, she glanced at Jimmy, but he just shrugged.

"I heard about your plans," he said. "Brilliant idea."

Sadie stiffened, wondering if Leah would take more issue with her over confiding in Jimmy, but luckily she was too caught up in the news.

An actual smile broke over her face for a moment, and even though it wasn't directed at Sadie, Sadie still felt some of the tension ease off her shoulders.

Until Leah said, "Who told you?"

Sadie hesitated. "Carter called. I happened to answer," she added.

Leah nodded, her smile gone as she set the kettle on the stove and flicked on the burner. "Did he give any more details?"

"No. Why, is there more I should know about?" Her mind went to a dark place, imagining credit card debt, or other secrets Viv had never shared.

Leah looked at Jimmy and then seemed to decide that he was practically family, someone she could speak freely in front of. And they were all adults. Technically.

"Just that it's a big risk. And I stand to lose the most."

Sadie stifled a sigh. "We're all on the hook for this house."

"Yes, but if the business falls through and we can't pay off the loan, they'll be coming for money, Sadie, and I'm the only one with property. I'm the only one with something to take."

Sadie was momentarily silenced. Beside her, Jimmy just raised his eyebrows. It was true, then. Leah was going to bat for them.

Or rather, for Emma.

Sadie was torn between gratitude and a deep, uneasy thought that this could be just one more thing Leah might use against her.

"Thank you," Sadie managed, her voice catching in her throat.

She expected Leah to mutter something, leave the room, or just cut her with a steely look.

Instead, Leah just nodded her head and managed—wait. Was that a hint of a smile?

"Well, this is the best news we could have hoped for. Emma will be thrilled," Leah said.

Sadie nodded, but for some reason, she wasn't so sure about that. It might have been Emma who had broached the idea and Emma who loved this house as much as Viv did, but her youngest sister was strangely quiet every time they discussed the plan for the inn.

But then maybe, like usual, she was just trying to stay out of the conflict that lived between her two older sisters. Their tension was almost a bigger problem than the fate of this house.

And the house looked like it was being resolved. As for Sadie and Leah, there was probably no chance of that.

CHAPTER FIFTEEN

LEAH

Leah was relieved when her old friend Leslie stopped by the house just moments after she'd hung up with her daughters—or rather, Chloe had all but hung up on her.

"Gotta go, Mom!" was the sign-off, the rush to get on with their day, to have the fun that didn't include her.

She told herself to get used to it. Like her friend Gina would say, *Make the most of it.*

But was spending time at the festival with her old flame making the most of her time? Gina would certainly say so. She'd be making a pitcher of margaritas and inviting Leah onto her back deck to dish every detail.

But Leah wasn't so sure there were any details worth dishing. She'd put Fog's Landing and everything that happened here in a neat little box, tucked away where it couldn't touch the life she'd built for herself, much like she'd tucked away the life before she'd moved here, which was just as well, given that Viv had never wanted to discuss it anyway.

She was just about to convince herself that a juicy phone call with Gina was not worth the complication it would cause her and that her time would be much better spent online shopping for new bed linens for the guest rooms when the doorbell rang.

Seeing the familiar face behind the screen door was just the distraction she needed. She needed to see someone other than one of her sisters. Needed to talk about something other than this house.

"I was wondering if you were heading over to the festival today?" Leslie said, breezing inside as if fifteen years hadn't passed and she still stopped by at random throughout the week.

Now, Leah wondered if Leslie had purposely held off this week, knowing that she and her sisters might need some space, when really, what they needed was space from each other.

"I was planning on it," Leah said slowly. More than planning on it, really. She'd been thinking about it ever since Carter mentioned it at the café, wondering if he really meant what he said and why.

And the bigger question was why she gave it a second thought, much less a third, much less a thought pretty much anytime she wasn't thinking about her daughters, her empty house, this house, or what she was going to do when she finally went back home.

The festival was just what she needed for a little break from all that worrying. And having Leslie show up was a sign—not that she tended to look for those things, but being around Emma so much was taking its toll.

She would go to the festival, with Leslie. If she happened to see Carter there, she'd be pleasant. Simple enough. And . . . it was the adult thing to do. She could be civil. Neighborly even. The man had pulled through for her, after all.

Even if it was fifteen years too late.

"I was just heading out, actually," she told Leslie. "My sisters already left." Technically, Emma was out for a walk with Sully and said she wasn't heading over to the town green until later in the day, and Leah couldn't be sure where Sadie had gone. A community event was hardly her type of thing.

She locked the door behind herself, and they headed out together, the sun warming their skin as they followed the crowd around the bay and toward the center of town.

On the walk, they caught up on all their news: Leslie's family flower shop, her two dogs, her lackluster dating life, and of course, Leah's girls.

"And your husband?" Leslie asked pleasantly.

Even though they hadn't seen each other since she'd left town, there was still a connection that Leah felt with Leslie, one that tied her to her childhood, one that made her remember the best parts of it.

"My ex-husband, actually," she said. "Or . . . soon-to-be ex."

"Oh, Leah!" Leslie looked understandably surprised. "I'm sorry. Emma never told me."

"That's because she doesn't know," Leah said. "It wasn't the right time to bring it up."

"I won't tell anyone," Leslie promised, and Leah knew that she wouldn't.

"Thanks. It's fine, really. I'm fine. Or . . . I will be." It was the same thing she'd told herself all those years ago, the same thing she'd promised her sisters after their parents had died. They'd be fine. Eventually.

Now, she wasn't so sure. Now, she wished that Viv were here, reassuring her. Reassuring all of them.

"This is about as crowded as it gets for summer," Leslie remarked as they approached town. "Makes me almost feel bad about closing the store for the day, but I doubt many people are thinking about flowers, and no bride would even consider having a wedding this weekend. Every inn in the county is probably booked solid."

Leah wondered if she was ready to share their plan with her friend and then questioned her own hesitation. It wasn't a secret, and everyone would be bound to find out soon enough. It was more that she was afraid of jinxing it. Afraid that somehow the dream would burst and what hope there was for holding on to the old house would be lost.

She realized that she was afraid of failing. Again.

"We're actually going to be turning the house into an inn," she said, holding her breath.

There was only a small pause before Leslie exclaimed, "What an excellent idea!"

Leah felt her shoulders relax. Every time she dared to think of how beautiful this inn could be, another part of her was busy thinking of everything that could go wrong. It wasn't like she had a great track record of life going according to plan.

For the moment, her friend's enthusiasm was contagious. She explained their plans in detail as they approached the festival, the music from the band growing louder with each step.

"You sound like you did fifteen years ago, when you were in design school," Leslie said fondly. "Like the old you."

Leah frowned a little. The old her. Meaning before Carter and Sadie. After that day, her design classes had felt tainted. The dream she'd had for her life gone.

"Who else knows?" Leslie asked.

"It's not a secret, if that's what you're worried about. But the Prices know. And . . . Carter. I'm not sure that Emma's told Sarah or her boss at the inn yet, though," she added, frowning a little.

"Don't worry about that. I'm sure she'll be thrilled for you guys. You know how tight everyone is around here."

Yes, Leah certainly did, and that brought her back to a thought that had been nagging her all week. "Do you know who might have borrowed money from Viv? Not that I'm surprised, but from what I hear, she was pretty generous."

"She was." Leslie nodded. "And as for who might have borrowed money, well, probably everyone at some point in time. Some surely paid her back. Others . . . well, I'm sure they planned to. They probably still do."

"With Viv gone? Maybe they think they're off the hook."

Leslie gave a weary laugh. "You really have moved to the big city."

"I happen to live in the suburbs," she clarified, but a wry smile pulled at her mouth. "You're right. It's just difficult to think that the very people Viv tried to help didn't help her in the end."

"They will in good time," Leslie said firmly.

Leah wanted to believe that, and a part of her did, but she also wasn't about to go knocking on doors, demanding payback. Viv had lent the money with a good heart and even better intentions.

"I hope so. Carter managed to get us a loan to spruce up the house, but we'll need to pay that back, of course, and I don't expect to get much business our first year, especially when we'll be lucky to open before the end of summer and most people would have already made their plans by then."

Just thinking about that loan made her anxious, but there wasn't another choice unless they wanted to sell their family home.

"So, Carter . . ." Leslie paused before they entered the green.

Leah groaned. "Before you say anything, remember, I'm technically still a married woman." For a few weeks at least. When Leslie raised an eyebrow, she corrected herself. "I'm a mother. I have kids to think about and an entire life back in Chicago."

"But you're here now. And are you two . . . getting along better? I mean, he knows about your plans—"

"Only because he works at the bank," Leah replied. She huffed out a sigh, almost reluctant to say anything more. "But, yes, I think we're getting along. Making peace. Putting the past in the past, or at least keeping it there."

It was easier that way, and nothing they said could change what had happened. Carter had apologized, Sadie too. Now they'd moved on. Technically, Leah had too.

Leslie looked like she wanted to say more but chose not to, which was just as well. Any follow-up question to the subject of Carter usually meant a conversation about Sadie, and that was one thing that was just too complicated and painful to think about. Maybe it wasn't fair of her, but it wasn't as easy to move past the betrayal with Sadie. Maybe because she'd expected more from her.

Besides, it was a sunny day, things were coming together for the house, her daughters were safe and having fun (if not a little too much fun without her), and she was going to have a nice day no matter what. Even around Carter.

She glanced toward the area where the pies were usually sold, not sure if she was more surprised to see that nothing had changed about the layout of the festival in all these years or that Carter was leaning against a tree, waiting for her, given the way he raised a hand when he spotted her.

"Looks like you and Carter might have more *business* to discuss." Leslie couldn't fight her smile as she started to back away. "Come find me at some point. I'll be here all day."

Leah waved and then made her way across the grass to where Carter stood, under the shade of a monstrous maple tree that Leah knew boasted the brightest leaves come October.

"You came," he said, giving her one of those slow grins that used to make her stomach roll over.

She was a little surprised that it still did. A little angry too.

She pinched her lips, steadying herself, and gave a nod. "You didn't think I would?"

"Would you blame me?"

Darn it, he had to go and grin again, this time with that boyish charm that made it impossible not to let him off the hook—at least most of the time.

"Leah, look—" he started to say, but she shook her head firmly, stopping him.

"Let's just have a nice time today, Carter. It's been a tough time lately. No need to pile on more."

"Fair enough." They began slowly walking around the perimeter of the festival, where booths were set up showcasing everything from local art to libations. "Wine?"

He stopped near the beverage stand, and Leah wavered. She needed to keep a cool head, but she also needed to relax.

"Why not?" she said, feeling like a rebel. "I'm not on duty at the moment."

He gave her a strange look and then said, "Right. Mom duty."

It hung in the air between them, and she wondered if he was think-ing what she was—that once, they'd talked about having kids. At least two, probably three. They'd have a summerhouse in town, near the bay so the kids could splash around like they used to—they'd always had an eye on that sweet little cottage right next to the beach. Or eventually, they'd move back here permanently; their plans hadn't been set in stone, but there was always the underlying belief that somehow they'd work out. Together.

She'd made a point not to think of those dreams. Chalked them up to childhood fantasies. She glanced at him, thinking it likely that he'd done the same.

That just like every other thing they'd shared, it had been brushed aside.

Carter handed over some money and took two plastic cups from the young woman behind the stand—no doubt one of the many sum-mer interns who flocked to the area for a seasonal job with plenty of perks.

"Should we toast?" He looked at her for direction for a moment and then said, "Or am I pushing it?"

"Let's toast," Leah said firmly, holding up her cup. "To the inn. We both need it to succeed."

He clinked her glass, if one could call it that with plastic, and they each stopped talking to take a small sip.

"I didn't get a chance to thank you for approving the loan yet," she said, trying to avoid mentioning Sadie. "I don't know how you pulled it off, but . . . thank you."

"No thank-you needed. I'm just glad I could help."

"I suppose I need to come in and sign some things. My sister didn't mention anything about my house in Chicago—"

Carter shook his head. "I got the loan through without that. Knowing you have assets helps. I'll talk to Jim Price this week and get things squared away. If we can tie it all with the estate, it might make things simpler."

She met his eye and understood his meaning. Simpler between her and her sisters.

"Well, thank you. Without that loan, well, I don't think we would have been able to keep the house."

Carter nodded. Of course he knew. "That house means a lot to me. To a lot of people. And . . . well, I hope I'm not crossing a line by saying that you mean a lot to me too. You always did." He stopped walking to give her a long look, and for a moment, she dared to see the emotion that filled his eyes. Dared to think that there might be regret shining through, and there probably was.

It wasn't like he'd run off with Sadie. Lived happily ever after together. Instead, he was single. Living here, working at his father's bank.

She was the one who had landed on her feet. For a little while at least.

"So, tell me about your kids."

"Chloe and Annie." Leah's heart swelled just saying their names, and she was as grateful for the chance to talk about them as she was for the change in topic. "It's too bad they're not here today. They would have loved this festival."

She could imagine Annie being first in line to get her face painted, even if by the end of the hot day, the exertion from all the games would have made the design drip and distort. Chloe would pretend to be bored, no doubt, but that wouldn't stop her from trying to win every prize, collecting her penny candy in a paper bag to enjoy at home on her bed like Leah used to.

Home. She frowned at that, wondering why she would have thought of Viv's house that way. Home was the suburban house on the cul-de-sac on the North Shore of Chicago. Home wasn't here. At least it hadn't been for a very long time.

"And your husband? Would he have found this small-town life charming?"

Carter's tone was polite, but there was a guarded interest there too. Leah hesitated and took another sip of her wine. She sidestepped an overexcited little boy who zoomed between them, his face painted like a dragonfly.

"Ex-husband, actually," she said, stealing a glance at him. "Or soon to be." She didn't know why she'd said it any more than why she should keep it from him. Maybe it was because, after everything, Carter was the one who knew her best.

And like her, his life hadn't turned out the way he'd once hoped. Or planned. Or dreamed.

His expression seemed to register this information for a split second. "Sorry. I didn't know."

"No one does," she said, sighing as they settled onto a bench in the shade, far enough away from the crowd that she could talk freely. "Well, other than Leslie. Viv's funeral didn't exactly seem like the best place to make an announcement. Emma's had enough to worry about." And Sadie had lost the right to know anything about her a long time ago, she finished silently.

"And the girls?"

"They're with him right now." She nodded. "I told everyone that they were at camp because . . . it was easier that way."

"No harm in that. But you know that your sisters would be there for you if you told them what you've been going through."

Leah gave him a look that showed she wasn't buying it, but to her surprise, Carter held steady.

"I mean it, Leah."

"Maybe Emma," Leah conceded. But Emma had been through enough, and besides, Leah was starting to pick up on something more than grief in her youngest sister lately. "And Sadie—"

Just saying her name to Carter made her feel edgy and uncomfortable. She wanted to shut this conversation down, and she was starting to regret ever saying anything at all.

"Sadie cares about you, Leah. I know you don't believe it, but she does."

"Oh, and you know my sister so well, do you?"

"The one thing I know about Sadie is that she always looked up to you. I think that's part of the reason why things happened the way they did."

Why things happened the way they did. Leah tried to process this with fresh perspective that only the passing of time could bring, but she still came up blank. Sadie had slept with her boyfriend. Ex-boyfriend, maybe, but still, it was fresh. Cutting. And it still hurt, even now.

"That was a long time ago," Leah said, feeling her jaw tighten.

"It was. And from where I'm sitting, Sadie's still probably looking up to you. Looking to you."

"To forgive her?" Leah looked at him, astonished.

He gave a little shrug. "Sadie probably sees you as this accomplished woman, with a husband, a house, two kids—"

Leah was beginning to think that this had been a bad idea, agreeing to meet, believing that she could put the past behind her and move on.

"Hey, until a few moments ago, that's what I thought too." His eyes looked sad when they met hers.

Leah conceded that point with a nod. It was what she'd wanted him to think. All of them.

"You have an amazing life, Leah."

She nodded again. Against all odds, she'd ended up with two good things. Her daughters. "And I wouldn't trade it for the world."

He gave her a sad smile. "There you go, then."

"So how about you?" she asked, half regretting it as she said it. As eager as she was to get off the topic of her own setbacks, she wasn't exactly eager to hear how Carter had been spending his time since they'd broken up.

"Anyone in my life, you mean? Or how did I end up working at the bank?"

He was poking fun at himself and managed to pull a smile from her. "Both."

Really, she might have been fine just hearing about how he ended up at the bank.

"I've dated, of course. No one special. There was one relationship that I thought might go somewhere, but what can I say, not everything works out. Sometimes you see it coming, sometimes you don't."

"You can say that again." Leah sipped her drink, thinking of all the twists and turns her life had taken, most abruptly, without any warning.

A memory of coming home to Fog's Landing, a smile on her face, a fullness in her heart, flashed to mind just as quickly as that awful image of her sister and Carter stepping out of his house. Together. Their faces as stricken as her own.

"My dad got sick," Carter added.

She turned to him sharply. "I'm sorry. I had no idea."

Mr. Maxwell, as she still thought of him, was a kind man, a little quiet, and a proud member of the community. He was happy to put in an honest day's work that served his neighbors and to donate his time to various board positions. He'd even run for mayor once but lost to AJ Benson. That was the only time that Leah had seen the man frown.

She'd asked if he'd run again, and he'd said he couldn't rule anything out. That sometimes life was all about timing. Sometimes it was about luck. And sometimes it was just plain unfair.

What Carter had just told her seemed to fall into the latter category.

"Is he . . . okay?" She swallowed hard against the shame and fear, thinking that Mr. Maxwell was about the closest thing she'd known to a father figure after losing her dad. He'd been an important person in her life, and she'd just moved away and moved on—purposely putting him out of her mind.

Just like she'd done with Carter. And everyone else in Fog's Landing.

Even Viv, she thought, looking down.

But Carter nodded. "He is now. We didn't really tell anyone. He didn't want it spread around." Carter gave her a look that told her he understood firsthand how gossip could fly in this town. "He didn't want the pity, and he didn't think it would be good optics for the bank either. People put their trust in my dad."

"And he put his trust in you." Leah let out a pent-up breath, thinking of all that Carter had given up, the dreams he'd once had for himself. The ones they'd had for each other. "You're a good guy, Carter."

He looked at her in surprise. "Those are words I never thought I'd hear you say again."

She managed a small laugh. "Well, I should maybe say that you're not all bad."

They locked gazes for a beat. "I'm sorry, Leah," he said softly. "I don't expect you to ever forgive me, but I mean it. I was sorry then, and I'm sorry now. We were broken up—"

"We were on a break," she corrected. Her heart was hammering with fresh anger, and she steadied herself, taking a sip of her wine with a shaking hand, looking around to make sure that no one was eavesdropping.

"A break that you asked for," he reminded her.

She said nothing because what she'd said had already been said, and what hadn't been said, he knew. Or at least, she'd thought he did.

"It was a confusing time. We weren't together. We started having different lives," he added.

Carter had stayed back, gone to a local college, and she'd gone off, to Chicago, to a school with a design program. And she hadn't known anymore if coming back to Fog's Landing was what she wanted, not when she'd had a taste of something else. Another possibility.

And it wasn't until she'd told him, heard the pain in his voice, the silence instead of a goodbye, that she'd known she'd made a horrible mistake.

"I made a horrible mistake," she said now because she'd never gotten a chance to say it then, when she'd boarded the bus that weekend and come back to town, knowing what she wanted more than ever. Sorry for ever doubting it.

He looked at her now, his eyes flat, his frown one of shared regrets. "I did too."

She swallowed back the rest of her drink, letting the silence stretch between them, the memories filling the space. She knew that he was thinking about that day as much as she was. The way her smile had slipped. The way she'd stared first at him, then Sadie, in confusion, until everything came clear. How he'd chased after her, apologizing to her, but she hadn't wanted to hear it any more than she had later, back at the house, from Sadie, when she was packing the bags she hadn't even ever really unpacked—just adding more, knowing she wouldn't come back. That she had a new life now. Even if she didn't want it.

"Like we both said. It was a long time ago. I don't want to go back there, Carter. There's no point."

And every time she thought of it, she felt the same old hurt. And regret. For her part in it.

"But there is a point, Leah. I never got a chance to make things right before. And I'm not going to stop now."

She looked at him for a long moment, not sure if she wanted to take him up on that challenge or push him away.

"Maybe we'll bump into each other again," he said, raising his eyebrows in question.

"Around the festival?" It was probably unavoidable, given that the town green wasn't large, but the crowds were thick.

"Or around town." He shrugged. "Another day."

She chewed the inside of her lip, thinking that was probably unavoidable too. That it was why she'd stayed away for so long. Never come back until now.

But she wasn't that twenty-one-year-old girl anymore. And neither of their lives had gone to plan.

But one thing could still be certain. Especially in Fog's Landing.

"I'm sure we will," she said. And for reasons she couldn't quite understand, she was almost looking forward to it.

CHAPTER SIXTEEN

EMMA

For the first time since Viv had died, Emma had something to look forward to. She took her time selecting the right outfit to wear to the festival today, her excitement growing when she thought of the invitation Wyatt had extended last weekend.

Last weekend. It was hard to believe how much could happen in a week's time. Plans were underway for more changes when not so long ago, life had plodded along, the same routine most days, day after day, week after week.

She didn't know whether to laugh or cry.

Smile, she thought as she held a dress up to herself in the full-length mirror and then discarded it for being too formal. Today she had something to smile about, and this was one smile she wasn't going to be putting on for show.

Her heart sped up when she checked the clock on her bedside table and saw that it was already past noon. She'd have to hurry at this point if she didn't want to leave Wyatt wondering where she was. She'd already gone through half her drawers and then her closet, but no outfit felt right for the day. It was sunny and warm, with the promise of a cool breeze by this evening, when she planned to still be out, enjoying Wyatt's company, maybe even a dance.

Jean shorts and a T-shirt might be too casual, giving the impression that she didn't care, but a dress might look like she cared too much.

The cluck of Viv's tongue seemed to echo through the room. Emma turned to Sully, who had been dozing on the bed, high up on the pile of pillows for the ultimate softness, having grown bored of the endless scrutiny and decision-making. Now he opened a lazy eye and then, suddenly alert, sat upright, cocking his head to one side, looking at her with those perfectly round and dark eyes that made everything else in the world seem to disappear.

"Wish I could take you with me, little guy, but Mommy has a big date today."

Sully's eyes seemed to light up for a moment before taking on a suspicious cast. He watched her carefully from his perch on the bed, as if he knew something she didn't, having been witness to so many of her exchanges with Wyatt.

And, of course, present when Viv gave her unwavering opinions on him.

What would Viv have to say to this? A date at the Founder's Day Festival? At least Emma thought it was a date. It sure had seemed like one when Wyatt suggested it. At the very least it was more time together, just the two of them, at one of the best attractions the summer offered. Sure, they would run into people; it was bound to happen with something like this. But ultimately, it would be the two of them, having a few drinks. A few laughs.

He'd known she needed this. And she did. It would be a good day. Even her sisters couldn't dampen it for her with their silent tension, passive-aggressive comments, and assumption that they could still decide the outcome of her life, just like they had all those years ago, when they'd both bailed on her, leaving her to be the responsible one, to hold what remained of their family together.

Finally, when the clock had ticked away another minute, she grabbed her most casual sundress and tossed it over her head. With some simple flip-flops, her favorite cross-body bag, and a jean jacket to tie around her waist for now and wear later on when the sun went down, she saw no excuse to linger.

Sully had been fed and walked. Her hair was brushed, her makeup perfectly applied. And she was ready.

Maybe it would all be okay, she told herself when she hurried down the front porch steps five minutes later. Maybe this had been Viv's plan for her all along. Maybe there was a reason why she would be tied to this town forever, to this house, now left to run it as an inn.

Maybe that reason was waiting for her. Right now. At the Founder's Day Festival.

The perimeter of the town square was lined with food and drink stands, and over near the gazebo, a band was already playing. Children ran with balloon animals, their faces painted, eager to get to the carnival that had been set up on the nearby school parking lot.

Emma smiled with contentment, thinking of how much she had always loved this weekend. When she was little, she and her sisters would save up their money, eager to buy cotton candy or take an extra ride on the Ferris wheel, even if Emma did always feel a little queasy when Sadie purposely rocked their compartment, even though the rules explicitly said not to do that.

When she was older and Leah and Sadie had already left, she and Viv would go together, always meeting Sarah or some of the other neighbors and friends in town. Since Emma had met Wyatt, she'd always kept an eye out for him, which was a force of habit when she was out in public, even though he'd always said he had to work at the pub, that his watering hole didn't dry up on festival days.

But this year, he'd made a change of plans. Now, she looked through the thick crowd for Wyatt, near the fountain where people sat on the encircled benches, enjoying a snack, resting their legs.

Her heart leaped when she spotted the back of his head, that dark hair that curled a little at the nape of his neck, and she didn't even mind that he was talking to Sarah. She didn't need to spend the entire day with him by herself. But a little alone time would certainly be welcome.

Sarah looked over and caught her eye as she approached, and Emma sensed something pass through her usual pleasant gaze. Apprehension, perhaps? But then, maybe they were talking about Viv. Or the situation with the house. Emma wasn't alone in worrying about its fate. She just didn't want to be tied to it forever.

And neither of them knew about the plan to save it. She'd have to break that news to Sarah gently, around the time she gave notice to Pamela.

A little bubble of anxiety threatened to overshadow what was turning out to be a very nice day, but before it could burst her optimism, Wyatt turned to give her a wide smile, one that just made everything else around her fade away, like it always did. She grinned, resisting the urge to fling her arms around his neck, and instead basked in the beauty of those sea blue eyes, the way they seemed to glimmer with every lift of his smile. It was an image that she could take in forever. Who needed the lake when you had Wyatt Price to gaze at?

"I was wondering if you were going to show!" His grin reached all the way up to his eyes, which crinkled as she approached.

Like she'd ever let him down! "I had to take Sully out before I left." And change my outfit about eleven times, she added to herself.

Fool's errand, Vivian seemed to whisper. Emma shook it off, chalking it up to the lake breeze and her overactive imagination.

She glanced at Sarah, who looked like she had swallowed something bitter and was too polite to admit it. As subtly as she could, Emma gave her a little wiggle of her eyebrows, girl code for, *What the heck is going on?*

"Have you two met yet?" Wyatt suddenly said.

For a moment, Emma almost laughed, thinking he was referring to Sarah, who had been her best friend since the first grade, but then she realized that there was another member in their fold. A woman not much older than herself. She was standing silently beside Wyatt, sipping lemonade in a plastic cup from a straw, looking a cross between bored and placated.

It was a face that Emma didn't recognize. Possibly the only person that she had never seen around town.

Someone she had hoped to never meet.

And even though Wyatt had never described her physically, never described her much at all other than a passing comment about her profession, Emma knew exactly who this stranger was.

Everything seemed to move into slow motion as she processed what was happening, realizing she couldn't avoid it any longer.

"Emma, this is Allie. Allie, Emma."

The woman smiled and gave a little wave, almost shyly. "Hi. Nice to meet you."

"Nice to get out, right?" Wyatt grinned at Allie and then back at Emma, but Emma's own smile had frozen.

Somewhere deep down, she'd denied his girlfriend was real. Other times, she'd seen her in complete clarity: an image that was self-created. She'd imagined model-good looks. Long, silky blonde hair and sparkling blue eyes. An upturned nose and a full mouth. Toothpaste-commercial smile. A laugh that sounded like bells ringing. A figure that would make Emma want to quit baking for good.

Someone Emma could never compete with; someone who might make it almost okay.

But Allie was none of those things. In place of the shampoo-ad sleekness, she had frizzy hair in a bland shade of brown. No professional highlights. No shine. Her face, while pretty, was plain, her eyes a little tired, her smile pleasant but hardly dazzling. Her clothes weren't designer. Her figure wasn't much different from Emma's, either, meaning that she wasn't a gym junkie.

She was perfectly nice. And perfectly ordinary.

This was a perfect nightmare.

Emma's mouth felt dry when she muttered some pleasantries and then managed to say something about needing to hit the bar stand—even though all she really wanted to do was leave. Run, really.

Sarah was quick on her heels as she cut across the grass, her vision blinded by hot tears.

"Oh no," Sarah said when Emma finally slowed down long enough for her friend to catch up. They were at the back of a long line, mercifully hidden by a tall tree with a fat trunk.

"I don't understand," Emma said, carefully catching her tears with her fingertips before they could fall. The entire county was out and about, and even though the tourists made everyone sort of meld together, it was inevitable that she'd see someone she knew and soon.

"You mean why she was here?"

"She's never been anywhere before," Emma pointed out. "And . . . he asked if I was coming. He knew I was coming. He wanted me to come."

Sarah gave her a pained look. "Because he's your friend."

The word had never hurt so much. Emma nodded because she knew Sarah was right, just like Viv had known Sarah was right.

But it still didn't add up.

"I guess I just don't understand," she whispered, reining in her emotions.

"Why he brought her?" Sarah was still not catching on, but then, Sarah didn't understand. If Wyatt cared about her so much, why did she have to be defined as a friend only? Emma had thought there would be a reason for it. A crystal clear one. But now nothing was clear at all.

"I guess I just don't understand why he isn't attracted to me." There. It was out. As lame as it sounded, the darkest and most vulnerable part of her was exposed.

"Oh, honey. Look at you! You're gorgeous. And I'm sure it's not that. Nothing is ever that simple in life, is it?"

Emma chanced a glimpse back to where Wyatt was standing, almost relieved to see the thick crowd that shielded her view but more disappointed, in a way, that he had stayed behind. With his first-choice girl. With his girlfriend. Not his friend.

No, she thought as they moved forward in line. Nothing in life was simple at all.

The way Emma saw it, she had two choices. She could send Sarah over to tell Wyatt that something had come up (but what, pray tell?) and she had to leave, or she could stick it out, face her fears, endure the misery of a long afternoon spent with Wyatt and his girlfriend.

Just thinking the word made tears well up, prickling her eyes, causing her to blink rapidly for fear they'd fall and every neighbor with good intentions would come running over to set a hand on her arm and ask her if she was okay.

She'd have to blame her grief. And that would be really, really shameful.

Neither seemed like a good option, but she was leaning toward the former. She could say that she had a sudden migraine, not that she'd ever had one before, but hey, there was a first time for everything, wasn't there? Like bringing your girlfriend of four years out in public? She blinked back tears. The migraine would be too sudden and suspicious. She'd just say that she forgot to fill up Sully's water dish. Or . . . she was spending time with Sadie before she left town. After all, there was no way that her middle sister was going to show her face at this or any other town event. Yes, that excuse might just be believable.

"There's my brother," Sarah said from their hiding station behind the tree. "Oh. And he's with Leah!"

Sarah looked at her with interest, but even this bit of gossip couldn't pull Emma from her misery. Besides, Leah was a married woman. If she and Carter were finally getting along, then great. If they were over there arguing over the past, then she really didn't want to be involved.

Sarah's expression turned worried by her nonreaction. "Will you be okay if I go over and say hello?"

"It's fine." Emma sipped her sangria miserably. So long as Wyatt didn't come over and expect her to engage with his girlfriend, she would at least make it through the day. She'd hide out, make the rounds, maybe even cling to Leah and Carter if Sarah felt out the temperature first and made sure it was safe.

Because there was no way that Emma was walking into an unknown situation for the second time in one day.

"It looks like they're getting along . . ." Sarah shielded her eyes from the sun with her hand and then shrugged. "I'll let you know!"

Emma watched her go and then darted a glance back in Wyatt's direction, relieved when she couldn't see him through the crowd.

A tap on her shoulder made her jump so hard that she almost sloshed her drink over her hand. With a pounding heart, she looked up to see the man from the coffee shop smiling back at her. The handyman.

"Brody, right?"

There was a flicker of surprise in his eyes. "Sorry, I didn't mean to startle you."

"It's okay," she said, taking another sip of her drink. "I'm just a little jumpy these days."

He leaned in and whispered, "I was worried that you were hiding from someone or something."

Emma's smile was wan, and she tried to picture herself from an outsider's view: furtive glances around the tree base, sucking down a sangria at rapid speed at high noon, eyes no doubt bloodshot from holding back burning tears.

If only she'd taken a page out of Sadie's book and thought to wear a pair of oversize sunglasses. Viv had had a pair tucked into her purse, ancient things that Sadie used to borrow for fashion long before she used them for privacy.

"That obvious?" Emma grimaced.

"An ex-boyfriend?" Brody grinned as he rolled back on his heels. "Don't worry, you don't need to tell me if you don't want to talk about it. But I can get you another sangria if you'd like; that way you don't have to leave your post."

Emma laughed. "Actually, I should probably slow down on the drinks, but I would love an excuse to move from this spot."

"You can join me over at the pie judging. I might even let you sneak a taste." His grin was friendly, and Emma wasn't sure which would be harder to say no to. The hopeful look in his eyes or the thought of comfort food.

Emma realized that a third option had presented itself. She could stay at the festival. Enjoy someone else's company. Correction: another *man's* company.

"Okay," she said, seeming to surprise Brody nearly as much as herself.

Without a glance back to where Wyatt stood, she cut across the square with Brody, giving a little wave to Sarah, who looked up in confusion from her conversation with Carter and Leah, who seemed to be getting along just fine.

"My aunt used to enter this competition," Emma said a little wistfully. Sometimes Viv would invite Emma to help her, but usually, Emma liked to sit back and let Viv take the lead, knowing how much the tradition meant to her. And knowing how upset Viv would be if she didn't win the blue ribbon, which paled against the bragging rights she enjoyed in the weeks that followed at her various club and committee meetings. Viv might have batted away their compliments with a demure smile, but there was no doubt in Emma's mind that her aunt enjoyed the attention. And no way was Emma going to be partially at fault if things went wrong. "She'd start scheming her flavors by early spring."

"Your aunt was pretty competitive."

Now Emma felt the first smile since she'd arrived at the festival. "Only with the neighbors."

Brody barked out a laugh. The sound was so surprising that Emma couldn't help but join in.

They were approaching the stall now, where nine pies were waiting on different plates, each marked only with a number. Still, Emma could spot Jodie Humphrey's perfectly crimped crust anywhere, and Dawn Tracey's expert latticework. With a heavy heart, she realized that one entry was missing. Viv's. She'd planned a cherry pie this year, with a special secret ingredient that even Emma hadn't been privy to—and now she'd never know what it was.

"I should have made Viv's pie," she said softly.

Brody gave her a sad smile. "It hits in waves, I get it. But don't be hard on yourself. You've had a lot going on this week, from the sounds of it."

More than he could even know, she thought, flicking a glance back toward the fountain, wondering if Wyatt had even started to miss her yet or considered where she'd gone.

"Maybe after this, we can grab a drink and listen to some of the music? I hear they have a great live band this year."

Emma hesitated, thinking that after sampling the pies for the next half hour or so, she might want to go find Sarah or even Leah. Or go home.

But as Brody took a slice of pie, cut it perfectly in half, and handed her a plastic fork, she no longer saw any reason to leave.

"That would be nice," she said.

And it certainly beat sitting around that big old house by herself for one more day while life continued to pass her by.

CHAPTER SEVENTEEN

SADIE

Sadie had almost choked on her coffee when Emma inquired this morning about whether she planned to go to the Founder's Day Festival. As if! Town events were a special version of hell for Sadie. There were smiles from strangers that had left her feeling like everyone knew her story, and she didn't even know their names. It had made her want to grab a book and hide in one of the nooks that she'd discovered early in her days of living in this big, creaking house.

Her aunt had tried to tell her that everyone in town wanted to show them all that Fog's Landing had to offer. Emma preened under that kind of attention, and she was all too happy to befriend everyone in town, accepting their hugs and their offers of candy, like sweets could make everything right.

But Sadie was older, and she knew better. And it hadn't taken her long to figure out that her mother had grown up here, especially when she got the whispers from the women at the grocery store, when they thought she was out of earshot: "Lydia's child. The youngest is a spitting image. Can't help but wonder how Vivian feels about that."

And from then on, nothing that Aunt Vivian could say about the intentions of the community was completely acceptable to Sadie. She still felt like an outsider. Just like her mother had been in this town.

So no, there would be no stopping by the Founder's Day Festival today to sample the town's offerings, no more rides to endure at Emma's begging, no drinks to enjoy now that she was legally old enough to do so.

Still, the festival weekends were the only times each summer that the rest of the town felt free and open to her—when she could go down to the coffee shop or the ice cream parlor without having to engage in conversation. When the town was quiet and she could be left to enjoy it in peace.

Desperate times and all that. She stuffed her laptop into her bag and walked down to the Harborview Café. Her hopes of seeing an unknown face behind the counter, however, were dashed when Sandra's eyes widened the moment Sadie stepped through the door.

For a moment, she contemplated leaving her oversize black sunglasses on, even inside. There was plenty of sunlight, which was a handy excuse. But judging from the way Sandra was looking her up and down, like she'd never seen anyone wear black on black before today, she figured that she'd probably be doing herself a favor by removing a bit of her armor.

"Why, Sadie Burke!" Sandra looked a cross between giddy and scared, as if drama was about to ensue.

Sadie smiled mildly. Scandal wasn't what she was after today; coffee was. She decided to cut right to the chase. "A large latte, please. Skim milk, if you have it."

She didn't know why she bothered with nonfat milk when her caloric consumption these days was higher than it had been in years, thanks to Emma's baking. She hadn't seen the inside of a gym since she left New York, and given her lack of employment, she'd have to cancel her membership before she returned.

Return. Just thinking about New York made her stomach tense up. She eyed the display case now, but the offerings were slim and not as appealing as anything Emma was filling the counters with back at the house.

Correction: back at Vivian's house.

"I heard you were living in the Big Apple!" Sandra said excitedly.

Sadie managed a smile. "I've been in New York for a while now." She could tell by the look in Sandra's eyes that the woman knew exactly how long it had been since Sadie left town, probably right down to the exact date, if Sadie were a betting woman, which she was not. Too much in life was already left up to chance.

"Well, I'm sure it's nice to be back in Fog's Landing. All of you girls together again under one roof." Sandra raised her eyebrows.

"It's unfortunate given the circumstances, as you can imagine," Sadie said pointedly, knowing that would put an end to this conversation.

She took her drink and finally settled at a table with her back to the counter and pulled out her notebook and laptop, eager to get working again on the novel that hadn't been touched in so long that she realized with a bit of a shock that she had forgotten several of the main characters' names—in particular, her heroine's last name and her heroine's dog's name, and even what color hair her heroine was supposed to have.

Sighing with the realization that she'd have to go back and actually read everything over from the beginning, or at least skim it before she dove back in, thus risking discovering that it was complete garbage, Sadie leaned back in her chair near the window and sipped her latte from the ceramic mug. She grinned when she saw Jimmy coming up the gravel path and knocked on the windowpane, getting his attention.

He looked up, brightening when he saw her wave, and then seemed to quicken his pace. A moment later, he was inside, approaching her table.

"I assumed everyone was at the festival."

She gave him a look that told him he should really know better. "Are you headed that way?"

Knowing her opinions on that, he looked torn for a moment and then said, "I'd rather stay and have a coffee with you."

She grinned, happy for the company, and started to clear her things away.

"Are you working on something?" Jimmy gestured to the laptop, but Sadie shook her head and closed it.

Dusting off an ancient manuscript now felt as pointless as trying to apply for anything more than an hourly-rate job in New York. More and more, just the thought of finishing this darn novel felt like a pipe dream. And getting it published? What did she expect? That it would get snatched up by the first editor who read it, or go to a bidding war for a six-figure sum that would allow her to lease a reasonably sized apartment in Manhattan or Brooklyn? And was all this supposed to happen in about two weeks, maybe three or four at best? Because that was about the time frame she had in mind for when the work on the house would be finished and when her reason for staying in Door County ended.

"Just plans for the house," she said, even though she was sure that if she told Jimmy about her book, he'd encourage her, maybe even ask to read over some pages. The only person she'd ever let that deep inside her most private thoughts was Jimmy. He knew how she felt, living at Viv's, missing her parents, wondering why her mother's name was never spoken. Together, they'd searched the attic, even the drawers, looking for clues. He knew how she felt after that awful day with Carter when Leah had stormed away and first Carter and then Sadie had chased her. How she'd felt in the days afterward, when the entire town seemed to judge her more than they ever had already.

"How is it coming along?" he asked, looking genuinely interested.

She dipped her chin at him. "If you're wondering if my sisters approved your paint selections, then you will be pleased to know they did." A satisfied smile curved the corners of his mouth, and she couldn't help but laugh. "How pleased they will be when I pick up a roller is yet to be determined, however."

"There might be a career for you in that!"

"In New York?" She shook her head and reached for her mug.

"Still planning on going back, then." It was more of a statement than a question, and Jimmy's tone was more than a little heavy.

"It's not like I could stay here!" She scoffed. Really, Jimmy. Didn't he know better?

He gave her a look that said he did not, and she let it go.

"We're ordering some new furniture, bedding, that type of thing. The house is large enough for Emma to carve out some living quarters in the back, though she's been strangely quiet about the whole process even though she was the one who suggested it."

"She's probably just struggling with the change," Jimmy said kindly. "She was so close to Viv."

Sadie felt her mouth thin. Yes, she was. Viv had become a true replacement mother for Emma in a way that Sadie had never allowed her to be. It hadn't felt right, even though Viv was special. The way Sadie saw it, she had a mother, but over the years it had felt like Emma forgot her, whereas Sadie tried to hold on.

And Leah . . . she just tried to move forward.

Now, she was torn between loyalty and guilt. "I keep thinking about what we found the other day," she said slowly. She'd thought she'd scoured that house from the attic to the cellar, never producing a single piece of evidence that her mother had ever even lived there. Not a rag doll, not a faded sundress. Not an old drawing or even a Christmas stocking.

But this photo was proof. And for some reason, Viv had kept it, tucked away, in a place that only she would ever look.

"Hold that thought while I get some caffeine," he said and moved to the counter to place his order.

The table was cleared of any evidence of her true intentions by the time he returned. Sadie didn't know why she didn't feel like she could tell him what she was working on, if for no reason than she hadn't felt comfortable opening up to anyone in years. It just led to vulnerability, and vulnerability led to hurt. And she was tired of being hurt. About as tired as she was of being judged.

"So," Jimmy said, dropping into the seat across from her. He drank his coffee black, as opposed to hers with sugar and cream, just like he always had, ever since ninth grade, when they'd tried their first sips and started coming here most days after school to do homework or just delay going home. Delay having to be apart. "Have you told your sisters about the photo?"

Sadie hesitated. "I haven't had the chance." But that wasn't the real reason. Things were tense enough in the house, and mentioning their parents always stirred up more of the past, more feelings and memories that were better forgotten.

"But it's interesting, isn't it? How it was tucked away, in a cookbook of all places."

"Viv must have forgotten about it over the years." Sadie was pensive when she sipped her coffee. "Or maybe she knew that Emma never bothered with those older books."

"Or maybe she hoped that Emma would find it." Jimmy shrugged. "Maybe she wanted to talk about it but didn't know how to bring it up."

Sadie considered it. She could certainly relate to that. And Viv was stubborn—or at least that's what people said when they pointed out how she reminded them of her aunt.

"And your mom has never told you anything, not even now that we're older?"

Jimmy shook his head. "You know my mom isn't one to gossip. And Viv was special to her. Whatever happened . . . I have to assume she took Viv's side."

Viv's side. All signs pointed to a falling-out, of course, but hearing it that way made her feel especially loyal to her mother.

She swallowed hard now against her building emotions. She didn't think of her parents much anymore. She supposed that was the natural order of things with grief. It was the only thing on your mind for a while, and then one day it wasn't. She didn't know which was worse.

"I'll show them eventually." When the time was right. When she'd had time to think about it. When she could actually get Leah to look her in the eye.

Sadie felt a pull from behind her and glanced over her shoulder to see Sandra watching her with interest while pretending to refill the sugar canister at the coffee station.

Turning back to Jimmy, she lowered her voice and leaned across the table. "I think Sandra is more interested in our conversation than she is in making a decent blueberry muffin."

"Then why don't we really give her something to talk about?" Jimmy's grin was mischievous.

He'd always been so straitlaced, balancing out her less conservative energy. But every once in a while, he managed to surprise her. She'd nearly forgotten that about him. And even though she'd worked so hard to forget this town, the people here, and that part of her past that hurt too much to revisit, she'd never wanted to forget Jimmy. Or the way he made her feel.

"What do you have in mind?" she asked, even though she knew that whatever he suggested, he could count her in.

Fifteen minutes later they were in the water, skinny-dipping in broad daylight, something that would have sent Viv straight to her grave if she hadn't already been there.

It wasn't the first time—as kids, they'd often done it on warm summer afternoons after school when they were too impatient to change into their swimsuits first. Later, it had stopped, once they were teenagers and more self-conscious about those things—or at least Jimmy was. But like she'd come to realize about Jimmy, just when she thought she had him all figured out, he always had a way of surprising her. Even now.

Sadie had dutifully closed her eyes when he'd shed his clothes, but she wasn't so sure that he hadn't glanced over his shoulder when he'd politely turned his back while treading water. Not that she cared. This was Jimmy. Jimmy, who had seen her break into tears more than once. Who had held her close, told her everything would be okay, and she'd believed him. Jimmy wasn't just a friend; he was the only one who ever got her and stood by her, no matter what people said or thought about her.

Jimmy didn't need to fit in any more than she did. They were content to be their own people. And maybe that was what had bonded them.

"Damn, Jimmy, have you been working out?" Sadie swam closer to him and gave his arms a little squeeze, nearly sending herself plunging under the water for a second there.

"This is a quiet town. I have to find something to keep me busy in my free time."

"So you're not dating anyone in your free time?" she asked. Jimmy had never dated much back in their teen years, or, come to think of it, not at all. But they were in their thirties now. Surely he wasn't still the same shy boy who would just look away when she asked if he was going to the school dance with anyone.

He shook his head, sending water pellets flying from his hair. It stuck up now in spikes, making him look boyish and handsome all at once.

"I'm busy setting up my practice," he explained.

Sadie gave him a rueful glance. "Makes sense. And then there's the whole living-with-your-mom thing to consider."

"Hey!" He splashed her, playfully, and she laughed. "It's just temporary."

"Three-years temporary?" She widened her eyes at him, but he surprised her by not laughing back for once.

"I've been building a house, actually."

Sadie hadn't thought that there was anything that Jimmy could have said that could shock her, but she was wrong. She stared at him, looking for a hint of amusement in his eyes, something to indicate that he was having fun with her, but his expression was flat, maybe even a little defensive.

"You're serious." It was a statement, not a question, and for some reason, when he nodded his head to confirm it all the same, she felt a strange weight in her chest, like someone had come along and popped the air out of her balloon, taking everything that was light and fun out of this day.

Reminding her that things had changed. That even Jimmy had changed. That there were things about him she didn't know.

That he wasn't just shacked up in his mother's house, temporarily.
He was building an actual house in Fog's Landing.
He was putting down roots.
And she was essentially homeless.

"You can come to see it," he offered, brightening up at the prospect.
"It's not much. And it's taking forever. But I want it to be just right."

Sadie didn't know why she suddenly felt like she was all alone in the
world again. The only one who didn't fit in around town. Didn't fit in
anywhere. She'd thought Jimmy understood that—that he got it. Got
her. When no one else did.

"Sure. I mean, I won't be in town much longer, but before I go." She
shivered, even though it was a warm day and the water wasn't exactly
frigid. She started swimming toward the shore, only then remembering
that she didn't have a towel.

Once again, she hadn't thought things through. Instead, she'd acted
in the moment. Lived for it, really. And how was that working out for her?

"Don't go sneaking a peek!" she warned, even though she knew that
there was no point. Jimmy was her oldest friend, practically a brother, given
that they'd run in and out of each other's houses for years. She'd loved sitting
down to a warm dinner in Mrs. Price's kitchen, who wasn't exactly as good
a cook as her aunt Viv but who somehow reminded her of how it used to
be, back when she had a mother, too, one that knew just what to say and
do and when to ruffle her hair and when to pull her close. Viv had tried,
but it wasn't the same, at least not to her. Sometimes, she envied Jimmy
for still having a mother, but then she remembered that he'd lost a father.

That he understood her.

The water sluiced from her body when she pulled herself up. She
snatched her cotton T-shirt from the rock where it had been warming
in the sun; it stuck to her body, but it would dry fast enough.

Once fully dressed, she turned back to the bay, wringing the water
from her long hair. A strange sensation rolled through her stomach
when she saw Jimmy staring at her, his easy smile gone, replaced with
something more intense and unreadable.

"You sure I can't talk you into joining me at the festival?" he asked, treading water with little effort. Clearly, those hours at the gym had paid off.

She snorted in response even though she didn't exactly have any other plans. Her laptop sat in her bag, a few yards from her bare feet, beside her sandals. She'd dabbled in that book for years, forgotten it, and come back to it. What made her think she could suddenly finish it now?

"I want to get back to the house. I want to take a look at that photo again," she said. She wondered idly if there were more. If Viv had kept things of her mother's, things she hadn't shared.

Maybe she was being just as wrong, not sharing the photo with her sisters yet, but she needed to know what it meant first. Why it was the only trace of their mother in that house. In this town.

He nodded as he began to swim back toward the shore. Dutifully, she snapped her head around to face the road, her curiosity piquing a little when she heard the last splash of water and felt him rummaging for his clothes beside her.

"Well," he said, giving her a grin that belied his disappointment when she turned to face him. "I guess I'm off to brave the festival on my own."

"You really plan to go?" It wasn't like he ever skipped it back when they were kids, but as she'd come to realize, they weren't kids anymore.

Her gaze dropped to his bare chest one last time before he shrugged on his shirt.

"What can I say? I embrace where I live. I like it here."

She nodded. This time she knew it was her smile that revealed her inner disappointment. Much as she and Jimmy might be soulmates or kindred spirits or whatever other term she might assign it, there were some things in life they could never share and would always keep them apart.

And today was a good reminder of that.

CHAPTER EIGHTEEN

EMMA

Emma was enjoying a quiet morning in the kitchen—solitude that she hadn't truly appreciated until now. While she was growing up, the house had been filled with noise and chatter, the sound of the piano being rehearsed over the clicking of Viv's knitting needles or Leah's phone calls with Carter. When her sisters were gone and it was just Viv, there had always been the awareness of someone else in the house, even when it was quiet.

With Leah and Sadie both out for the day, Emma felt like she could finally clear her head and think without the worry of one of them walking into the room, plunking down on a barstool at the big center island, and going on with talks of plans, or worse, not talking at all.

The sun streamed through the big window over the sink where her raspberries were rinsed and waiting to be added to the batter that she'd just finished stirring. Sully was asleep in his bed in the corner, and only the soft chirping of birds could be heard over his gentle snores.

Emma checked on the first batch of muffins through the window of the oven. Experience had taught her that an overly done topping could ruin the entire taste, and, counting to . . . ten, yes, ten, she grabbed her oven mitt and pulled out the pan, setting it to cool on the stove top. She smiled as she bent over to inhale the sweet richness of butter and sugar. It calmed her every time. Centered her. Reminded her that while everything else in her life might be falling down in glorious fashion, some things would always remain the same, and these muffins were proof of that.

After taking the colander from the sink, she carefully stirred the remaining berries into the batter, having waited until the last minute so they would stay firm. Once the next tin was filled, she set it on the middle rack, thinking that it would be nice to have two ovens, not that she especially minded dragging out the experience by baking in batches or swapping out pans on racks so everything was properly heated. Good things came with time; they weren't rushed—another lesson that Viv had taught her about baking.

If only she could accept that the same wisdom applied to life. Sometimes, it felt like she did nothing but wait for good things to come into her life.

A knock at the front door set off Sully's bark, and he sprang from the bed with all the energy of a creature who had never been roused from his slumber in the first place. Emma wiped her hands on her apron and rounded the entranceway into the hall, almost forgetting that the handyman was set to be stopping by until she saw him standing on the other side of the glass-paned door.

"Some watchdog you have there." Brody grinned as Emma let him in.

Sully, the ferocious watchdog that he was, had stopped barking and was now dancing on his hind legs, asking for attention, which Brody happily gave.

"This is Sully," Emma said proudly. She always had to refrain from adding, "Cutest dog in the world." Really, it was obvious.

"I've seen you walking him around town."

While not surprising, because Emma did like to take Sully on long walks—admittedly near Wyatt's place of business, which wasn't exactly close to the house—Emma still thought it funny that she'd never noticed Brody in all this time.

"Well, he's pretty hard not to notice," Emma said, scooping Sully into her arms. He gave her a lick on the cheek before happily settling into the crook of her elbow.

"So he's the reason you couldn't stay too late at the festival," Brody said, looking a little chagrined.

"One of the reasons." She hesitated. "It was a tough week."

That was the understatement of the century. Tough, sad, and completely surprising, and not in a good way.

How was it possible that only a little over a week ago, Viv had still been alive, and Emma had still been going down to the inn each day for her shift, only to return in the evening to have a quiet dinner with her aunt, sometimes interrupted by the excitement of stopping in at Wyatt's pub?

Just thinking about Wyatt made her think of the festival and vice versa, so she tried to think of neither.

"Well, I hope you had a nice time, while you were there." Brody's hopeful expression made the comment more of a question.

She grinned at him, thinking of the laughter they'd shared over Dawn's reaction to winning the contest. She'd hooted so loud and hugged her husband so hard that she'd practically lifted the equally surprised man off the ground. It had been a pure moment of joy and one that even Viv would have had to smile at had she not won the prize for herself.

"I did," she said firmly. Then, realizing that they'd locked eyes for a beat and she wasn't exactly sure what to say next, she cleared her throat and said, "So, I should probably give you a tour. My sister Leah studied design in college, so most of the ideas are hers."

"You're not selling this house, are you?" Brody looked so stricken that Emma could only imagine how Viv would have reacted.

"No," she said, almost as relieved as the man's face before her. "We're . . . turning it into an inn, actually."

"Wow!" Brody seemed pleased by this, but Emma's smile felt thin.

"Yes, well, it's a big house, and it's expensive to maintain. We're on a limited budget for the renovations, though," she warned him.

Brody wiped his boots on the rug and set his toolbox on the bench where Emma and her sisters used to sit and tie their shoes before bolting outside for a day of play. She led him through the upstairs rooms first, where gallons of paint were already stacked in the back bedroom, next to some dustcloths, and then downstairs, explaining the plans for the space as well as she could articulate them, given that she didn't wholeheartedly agree with Leah's ideas, finally ending up in the kitchen just as the timer was starting to go off.

"Oh no!" Setting Sully on the floor, she grabbed an oven mitt and checked the progress of the muffins, sighing in relief that she was wise enough to always set the timer early, because you could always add time but you could never get it back.

Wasn't that the truth? The familiar ache reappeared in her chest, but she distracted herself by pulling out the tin and flicking off the heat switch.

"You made these?" Brody's eyes gleamed boyishly, and Emma half expected him to lick his lips.

"I like to bake. It's just a hobby." And that was all it would ever be now, wasn't it? Her future had been decided for her, for the third time in her life.

"You really should have entered the pie contest!" He looked at her with the same dismay that she'd felt on Saturday.

Emma shrugged and gave him the same excuse she'd told herself. At least it was an honest one. "Like I said. Rough week."

But there was always next year, she told herself. A small consolation for staying in town, especially now that her dreams of Wyatt ever professing his undying love for her had popped like one of the balloons she used to carry home from the festival.

Emma gave a sad smile and took two plates from the cabinet. "My aunt and I baked a lot together, especially when I first moved here. It gave me something to do. It helped with the grief of losing my parents."

"Does it still help?" Brody asked, giving her a pensive look.

Emma thought about it for a moment and gave a little smile. "It does. Especially since Viv passed down all these recipes to me."

"She passed down more than recipes," Brody remarked. When Emma just stared at him, he gestured to the walls. "She passed down this house. Look at this place! This isn't just a house. This thing is an heirloom."

Emma swallowed hard. It was. And unlike the recipes, which were Viv's alone, this house didn't just belong to her aunt; it belonged to her family. To her history.

Even, a long time ago, to her mother.

"You miss her." It wasn't a question but a statement, and when Emma turned around, she saw a shared emotion in Brody's gaze.

"I do," she said matter-of-factly, suspecting that he felt the same way about his grandmother. With a brave smile, she lifted a muffin from the tin that had already cooled and plated it. "You'll probably need some sustenance to tackle this house."

"You weren't saving these for something special?" Brody looked warily at her, but it didn't stop him from happily accepting the plate.

Emma laughed. "No. My sisters both just pick at their food, and I can't exactly offer anything to Sully here, though that never stops him from begging." As if to prove her point, Sully let out an impatient bark and then resumed sitting directly at Brody's feet, his dark eyes never straying from the muffin.

Brody laughed. "He's hard to resist."

"Tell me about it." Emma grinned. "He's the best guy a girl can have."

Brody gave her a curious look, and Emma felt her cheeks heat. Did he know about her crush on Wyatt? Did Wyatt even know? To have heard Viv tell it, half the town knew because of the way she lost her "good sense" whenever the man was around.

Flustered, Emma gestured to the muffins. "Please, have as many as you'd like. It will just give me an excuse to make more." Not that she needed an excuse, but she hated to see any food go to waste.

Brody took a large bite, consuming nearly half the muffin in the first attempt. "Wow," he said. "This is really good."

She couldn't deny the smile even though she knew he was probably just being polite. It was free food, the man was hungry, and who could resist a fresh berry muffin?

"I just followed the recipe," she said, though she also knew it was a very good recipe. And she had tweaked it a bit over the years until she had her base just right. Her trick was a little extra butter.

"Seriously, though, these are way better than anything I've eaten over at the Harborview Café."

She couldn't disagree with that. "Sandra should stick to what she's good at, which is making coffee." And sticking her nose into other people's business. "Speaking of which, I'm sorry I don't have any to offer you. I could make a pot?"

Brody held up a hand and swallowed the rest of his muffin. "No worries. I have a job to do anyway, and we still haven't discussed a timeline."

"Oh . . ." Emma raised her eyebrows. She hadn't considered that. "I guess as quickly as possible. The sooner we can open this place for business, the better."

"Trying to get in on the summer tourists?"

Something like that. "My sisters won't be in town much longer," she explained, realizing with a jolt how true that was. Leah had her girls to get home to, and Ted was surely missing her by now. Sadie remained vague about the details of her life, but there was no doubt that she was itching to get back to New York. Just the way she dressed all in black—in the middle of summer, in Door County—was a testament to her innermost thoughts, her way of showing that she didn't want to be here any more than she fit in.

"And then it will be all on you," Brody said, voicing her inner thoughts.

Just like all those years ago, they were both leaving her in the fallout of the mess they had created.

Only maybe that wasn't fair. Maybe this time it was Viv's mess.

Brody tipped his head and walked to the back door, looking through the glass. "Do you need any work done on that carriage house back there?"

"Oh, it's just used for storage, really. No, just the house. The biggest hurdle will be converting the mudroom and the back two rooms into a livable space."

He gave her his full attention and a little hint of a knowing smile. "Something tells me that you're not too excited about that."

Emma sighed, deciding not to vent her problems to this poor man, especially when he had a long list of work to do and, as they'd both come to discover just now, a short timeline.

"It's just a lot of change at once. I'm still getting used to the idea."

"Well, I'll probably start upstairs so I don't disturb you too much."

"I'll be here in the kitchen if you need me. Or another muffin," she added, noticing how his gaze kept flicking to the tin. "Here." She set another one on his plate. "One for the road. And please, help yourself. I mean it."

"I might take you up on that," Brody said, flashing her a grin that pulled one straight from her too.

She was still smiling long after she'd heard the pounding of his boots come to a stop in one of the rooms above her. She looked at her muffin tins and then at Sully and popped a corner of a muffin top into her mouth, enjoying the way the sour raspberries perfectly complemented the sweetness of the cake.

"Maybe it won't be so bad, after all," she told Sully, but he just let his eyes hood before curling up into a ball in his soft bed near the window.

Or maybe it would, Emma thought with a sigh before taking a bigger bite of the muffin.

The routine continued each day that week. Emma baked away her hours, and Brody arrived to a freshly baked good: there were blueberry scones on Tuesday, Emma's signature cinnamon Bundt cake on Wednesday, and chocolate éclairs on Thursday.

While Emma baked each morning, Leah called her children and Sadie stayed locked up in her room until she decided to make an effort with a paint roller. The back two spare rooms were finished, their closets cleared, and the donation pile of items that were too old to be used for guests was growing: threadbare sheets and faded towels, pillows that had lost half their feathers over the years.

By the time Sarah called Thursday evening and asked if Emma would be up for drinks that night, Emma couldn't wait to get out of the house.

"This was just the excuse I needed," she told Sarah when she met her at the base of her porch steps at seven, freshly showered and wearing her most comfortable and flattering jeans and a dressier blouse.

"You act like you're a prisoner!" Sarah laughed as they began their walk into town. "You're free now, Emma." She stopped, giving a deep frown. "Sorry. That was really insensitive."

"It's okay. I thought the same thing myself, except that I can't leave Fog's Landing."

Sarah's eyes widened. "Don't tell me because of Wyatt!"

Wyatt was simply a perk of staying. Emma shook her head. "Not with all the plans going on."

She hesitated, knowing that the time had come to tell Sarah what they were up to—if Carter hadn't already let her in on the details.

Sarah listened with wide eyes, but instead of begging her to stay on at the inn or encouraging her to leave, she stopped walking and said, "But is this what you want? To stay in Fog's Landing forever?"

Emma swallowed hard and then pressed on, toward the bar, which was now visible just ahead. "Isn't that how life works? You don't always get what you want."

She stared at the building up ahead, thinking of Wyatt being inside, picturing him behind the bar in faded jeans and a threadbare cotton T-shirt, wondering what she would say to him when she went inside. Would it be like the festival had never happened, like his girlfriend didn't exist? Would they go back to how they'd always been? He hadn't texted since the festival, and neither had she. Did he even notice? Did he even care?

"But it could be worse," Sarah was saying. "I mean, you get to keep the house. But you also get your own business!"

But was it the business she wanted? And did it even matter? She hadn't gone after what she wanted. There was always an excuse.

"Think about it. No more boss to report to, not that I mind Pamela," Sarah was quick to add. She gave Emma a playful nudge with her elbow. "Hey, if things take off, maybe you can hire me one day soon."

Emma was doubtful, but she also realized just how much she would miss seeing her best friend each day. Their duties at the Baybrook Inn didn't always overlap, but there was a camaraderie that they shared, and she enjoyed the teamwork.

"My sisters seem to forget my age most of the time. They're still treating me like I'm a kid and they have the final say. Like they can just boss me around."

"Birth order." Sarah nodded sagely. "Carter still gets a funny look on his face if I mention a date or wear a top he thinks is too revealing. They're just being protective."

"More like selfish," Emma grumbled. "They swoop back into town after all these years while I've been the one doing my part, taking on all the responsibility, and they act like they know what's best and that I should just be quiet and listen."

"Then speak up!" Sarah said. "Come on, Emma. You're almost thirty. If you don't take control of your life, then you can't blame anyone else."

"It's funny," Emma said, even though there was nothing amusing about the situation. "I thought that with Leah finally coming back, she'd just make everything okay. I know she thinks she's helping, but it's like she just created more problems."

"Then tell her," Sarah pressed.

"If I tell her, then we still have the problem of the house. And if I tell her . . ." Sadie would leave if she had no reason to stay and help with the plans. She and Leah wouldn't have a reason to speak again or even see each other after this. And the family she'd longed for, even given up on having, would be lost again.

This time, forever.

Emma grew silent. "I think . . . I think Leah and Sadie are both trying to make everything okay in their own ways. I think we all are. And until I figure out what I really want, then there's no room for me to shut things down. Not when we all have so much to lose."

Not when she stood to lose more than the house.

Emma looked out over the bay as they rounded the bend. Sarah was right, though. It was time to take control of her life. Starting right now.

"Where to tonight?" Sarah asked, given that there were plenty of options in this tourist area.

"I was thinking we could go to the Dockside Pub," Emma said as they started to approach it. When Sarah's eyes flashed, she said, "Things were weird at the festival. I . . . want to smooth things over."

And see where she stood. Even though she'd never known where they stood.

"It's open mic tonight," she reminded Sarah, even though every Thursday was and Sarah knew it. She'd been the lead in every school play growing up, and was known to sit down at the piano in the inn and regale the visitors with Christmas carols every December. Now, Emma felt a tug in her chest, thinking of how much she'd miss those days. "Maybe you can get up there and serenade us."

Sarah looked hesitant but walked over to the door anyway. She gave Emma a look that said, *Are you sure about this?* and Emma just smiled, even though she wasn't sure of anything anymore. Once her life had been almost painfully routine, and as much as she'd resented it, she embraced it, because it was safe.

But now everything felt unsure and uncertain. And the one thing she could still count on was the way she felt when she saw Wyatt. Like there was nowhere else she wanted to be.

And maybe, that was what she needed right now.

Inside, her eyes swept the room quickly and promptly landed on Wyatt. His jeans were faded, his T-shirt tight, revealing the cords of his muscles as he helped set the stage area with the sound equipment. His dark hair flopped over one eye, and his face broke out into a wide grin that made Emma's stomach completely flip over when he spotted them.

"Looks like there's no awkwardness from the festival," Emma whispered, releasing a breath.

No awkwardness maybe. But no change either.

The women settled onto two barstools, where they always sat, so Emma could chat with Wyatt.

"Speaking of the festival, I didn't know that you and Brody were so chummy." Sarah picked up a menu, even though she probably had it memorized by now.

Emma did the same, if only to keep from looking back at Wyatt. "You know Brody?"

Sarah's brow wrinkled in confusion. "Of course I know Brody. He's lived here for, like, three years."

"Yeah, well, he's never been out in all the times we have."

"Too busy using all his spare time fixing up his grandparents' house," Sarah replied.

Emma stared at her, baffled. "How do you know all this when I don't? What have I been doing all this time?"

Sarah gave her a knowing look and jutted her chin toward the stage. "Pining over a certain someone, that's what."

She made a show of darting her eyes in Wyatt's direction and then pursing her lips at Emma. Not for the first time, Emma wondered just how many conversations Sarah and Viv had had about their disapproval of the man that Emma . . . loved.

God, it felt wrong to even think it, but there it was. If it wasn't love, then what was it?

"That's complicated," she said.

Sarah raised an eyebrow, but her eyes were tender. "Honey, it's only as complicated as you make it."

Emma wasn't up for another lecture about Wyatt, especially when he was in earshot. Besides, there was nothing she could really say in her own defense. She had pined after the man.

"Enough about that. So, you know Brody. And now he's fixing up the house."

Sarah adjusted her handbag straps on the back of her stool. "Handsome, isn't he?"

"Is he? I . . . hadn't noticed," Emma said lightly.

Sarah dipped her chin, giving Emma a hard stare. "Now, I find that impossible to believe. Failing to notice a newcomer to town, sure. But when he's staring you right in the face?"

Emma gave a little smile. "If you think he's so handsome, why aren't you dating him?" Sarah was single most of the time. She went out on dates, from setups to dating-app dates, but lived by the motto that when the time was right, she'd meet Mr. Right.

"I flirted with him one time at a bar, back when he first moved here."

"And where was I that night?" Emma asked.

"Probably home with Viv, watching old movies."

Oh, true.

Sarah sighed. "Anyway, it was clear he wasn't interested in me, so I never mentioned it."

"So he's single, then?"

Sarah's grin turned coy. "Why? Are you interested?"

"Please." Emma scoffed. "You know I—"

"Only have eyes for a certain unavailable man," Sarah finished. She rolled her eyes.

"It's not that," Emma argued. She felt herself frowning, and she didn't want to argue with Sarah. They rarely argued, and when they did, it was usually over Wyatt. But tonight she just wanted to have a good time. God knew she needed it.

"I have the house to worry about. And my sisters," she added.

And everything else, she thought. Because soon her sisters would be gone, back to the lives that they'd chosen. And she'd be left behind. Again.

Stuck with the life she'd been given.

"Speaking of sisters," Sarah said. "Isn't that Sadie over there in the corner?"

Emma turned on her barstool and saw Sadie and Jimmy over in a dark corner, each with a drink in hand. She waited until her sister looked up to wave, but her attention was quickly snagged back to the bar when Wyatt's voice said, "What'll it be, ladies?"

As if he had to ask!

Emma felt her insides go soft when she looked into those beautiful blue eyes, and for a moment she nearly forgot what she usually ordered. Luckily, Wyatt remembered. He always remembered.

A moment later they were both served their drinks (white wine for Sarah and a strawberry margarita for Emma—only in the summertime, and always with a cocktail umbrella). Emma took hers with a nervous smile, wondering if Wyatt was going to mention the festival, but instead one of the guys called from the stage area, and he walked off to deal with it.

Emma followed him with her eyes until they suddenly locked with Sadie's.

"I'm surprised to see you here," Sadie remarked as she approached the bar.

"Hey, Sarah! Come over here and test the mic for us!" Wyatt called, and Emma pinched her mouth together, wishing she'd taken voice lessons instead of piano all those years.

She didn't even realize how long she had been staring until Sadie laughed softly and said, "Earth to Emma. What are you looking at?" She looked over at the staging area and then nodded her head knowingly. "More like who are you looking at?"

"No one," Emma said defensively.

But it was impossible to get anything past Sadie. Sure enough, she raised a single eyebrow and took a sip of her drink. Whiskey, from the smell of it. *Not very ladylike,* Viv would have said. But then, Viv was known to enjoy cracking open a cold beer every July Fourth, drinking straight from the can and telling Emma that in the privacy of one's own home, anything went.

But not pining over Wyatt Bale.

"Oh, I see. The tall, good-looking one with the biceps that could even make Superman jealous."

"Please!" Emma scoffed, but her gaze snapped to Wyatt's arms; she felt flattered on his behalf. He did have wonderful arms, and when she closed her eyes, she could still sense their pressure against her body when he hugged her.

"He was the one at the service, wasn't he? You were talking to him on the porch. You said his name was Wyatt, right?"

"He's a friend," Emma said, feeling her cheeks heat as she darted a glance at him, hoping for once that he wouldn't come back to the bar for a while.

"Friends don't look like that, Em." Sadie laughed.

Emma frowned. No, they didn't. And she had certainly never looked at him as just a friend.

"You like him, don't you?"

"It doesn't matter," Emma said, sipping her drink miserably. Sarah was practicing the opening lyrics of one of her favorite songs. A few people clapped.

"Does he know?" Sadie pressed, her eyes gleaming in a way that immediately got Emma's back up.

"No," she said firmly. At least she didn't think he did.

"Why not?" Sadie insisted.

Emma just shook her head. The last thing she wanted to do was get into this conversation, not when Wyatt could walk over at any time.

"You want me to pass a note or something?" Now Sadie grinned, and for a moment, Emma was hit with a flash of her sister's younger self, that mischievous, fun-loving spirit. She'd always had an edge, but she'd been warm too. Even happy once.

"Pass who a note?" Sarah asked, hopping back on her barstool.

"The hot guy over there that Emma's so obviously crushing on," Sadie said. Then, catching herself, she said, "Sarah. It's been a long time."

Sarah grinned. Any tension regarding Carter wasn't sensed, and Emma knew that she wouldn't bring it up.

"It has been. So, are you going to join us for a drink?"

Sadie pointed her chin toward the table where Jimmy sat nursing his beer. "I'm here with Jimmy. But I'm around for a while, so another night? I'm under the impression that my sister might be a regular here."

"Well, it's open mic night," Emma said defensively.

Sarah and Sadie exchanged a glance that Emma didn't exactly like.

"Whatever you need to tell yourself." Sadie patted her shoulder and then walked back to her table. A moment later, Emma could hear her sister's laugh clear across the room. Maybe she was laughing at Emma, or maybe she was laughing at something Jimmy had said.

Either way, the sound of her sister's laughter, a sound she hadn't heard in so many years, made Emma's heart swell with a mixture of joy and nostalgia.

And for tonight at least, she was happy that she'd insisted they come in here. And even Viv wasn't shaking her head in the heavens in total disapproval.

CHAPTER NINETEEN

LEAII

Leah woke the next morning to the smell of coffee and cinnamon, and for a moment, she thought she was home again.

Not home in this big, rambling Victorian with its creaky floorboards and secret hideaways but home in her suburban saltbox house, with its four standard rooms downstairs and four upstairs. With Ted brewing coffee in their sunny kitchen. She opened her eyes to reality and blinked as she stared out the window, her mind falling back to the past, but this time the more recent past. To the festival. To her talk with Carter.

And just like when she thought of her ex-husband, her heart gave a little pull for all the love she'd known and lost.

Or maybe somehow hadn't been able to keep.

Deciding that she'd had about enough of that, she tossed the quilt off and swung her legs over the side of the bed. The house was cool now that Viv had installed central air sometime in her absence, and she grabbed her sweatshirt from her suitcase and opened the door, not surprised to see Sadie's bedroom was firmly closed off, no sign of life coming from it.

She wasn't going to think about what Carter had said about her sister. Not today. Maybe not ever.

Instead, she'd go downstairs and get some coffee. Talk to Emma. Call her girls.

Get to work on this old house. If she got an early enough start, she might be able to do a full coat of paint on Viv's bedroom today. It would be a lovely soft gray blue, surprisingly one of the shades that Sadie had suggested. With white linens and the view of the bay on full display, it would be the best room in the house.

In the kitchen, Emma was pulling a pan of cinnamon rolls from the oven, Sully sitting patiently a few feet away, watching her every move.

"I think he's hoping for a treat," Leah commented. She opened the cabinet in search of a mug but felt restless already. The sounds and smells were too familiar, awakening a part of her life that she'd tried to forget. One that hurt to remember.

"Shh," Emma warned. She expertly flipped a pancake. "Don't say the magic word."

Sure enough, Sully had come to life and was now standing on his hind legs, his tongue hanging out in anticipation of a scrap, his eyes full of hope.

Without hesitating, Emma tore off a plain corner of the pancake and fed it to him.

"He's spoiled," she admitted, chagrined.

"I can see that." Leah laughed. "My girls have been after me for a dog for years. If they saw him, I'd never hear the end of it."

"Oh, I do hope they meet him!" Emma's gaze searched hers. "I mean, you will bring them up, right? Now that you and Sadie . . ."

Leah knew where her sister was going with this. Now that she'd done it, come back, even faced Sadie—and Carter—there was nothing to stop her from returning.

But somehow she couldn't bring herself to look that far ahead. Not when she was still trying to just get through today.

Emma pulled a mixing bowl from the baker's rack and began measuring out flour.

"Are you always baking something?" Leah asked, not that she was complaining.

Emma gave a little shrug. "It passes the time. And . . . it makes me happy."

Happy. There was that word again.

"Maybe I should try it," Leah said thoughtfully, even though she cringed at the thought of all the cleanup that inevitably followed.

Emma worked methodically for a moment, as if she had something to say. "But you have your daughters. A husband. A beautiful house. What more could you need?"

Leah thought for a moment about what Carter had said the other day, about the way that her sisters viewed her life—how Sadie saw it.

It was an image that she'd maintained, long before today, back when she was running her kids around every day, coming home to an empty house, cooking dinners that no one seemed to enjoy, not even herself, her husband always the first to leave the table with an excuse.

She told herself that she had a full life. That she didn't need anything more.

What she'd never accepted was that she didn't have a full heart.

And how could she, when so much was missing?

Now, looking at her youngest sister, all grown up, yet still so very much the same, she knew that she didn't want to keep this distance between them.

"Need and want aren't always the same," she said. "But you're right. I'm not sure I need anything more than I have." She smiled, thinking of her two girls, sisters, who she could only hope would grow up to stay closer to each other than she had with Emma. Or Sadie.

"But want?" Emma was looking at her.

"Oh, who doesn't want something more?" she said with a shrug. But the truth was that she hadn't known what she wanted or what was missing.

Not until she'd come back here.

"Seems to me that you're enjoying working on the plans for the house," Emma pointed out. "It's like my baking. It passes the time. And . . . it makes you happy. Doesn't it?"

Leah nodded thoughtfully. "You know, I think it does. But then, that's just my part in this venture. You'll be handling the real business. I'm just helping to set it up."

Emma's brow pinched, and she gave a little nod, focusing on her task of sifting the flour into the large bowl.

"You were out late last night," Leah remarked, wondering just what her sister had gotten up to and if it was the reason for her baking frenzy this morning.

Emma's face seemed to cloud over, and she pushed a loose strand of hair from her forehead with the back of her hand. "Oh, I went for a drink with Sarah. Sadie was there with Jimmy. If I'd known it was going to be a family reunion, I would have invited you."

No, thanks, Leah thought. But seeing Emma's kind smile, she managed to say, "I called the girls."

They'd been gone for two long weeks. The longest amount of time she'd ever been apart from them, but somehow, it felt longer, like the distance was greater being here in Fog's Landing in this old house, with her sisters. The part of her life before they'd ever been born.

The part that she'd never shared.

She added a splash of cream to her coffee and took a sip. "I think I'll go to the hardware store and pick up some more paint rollers," she said. "And stop by some of those home-goods stores, see if there's anything worth buying for the inn."

It was just an excuse to get out, really. To not have to talk about her personal life. To not have to reveal that she didn't have a clue what she was doing, but that at least for today, she had a plan.

"You don't want a cinnamon roll?" Emma looked a little hurt.

Leah grinned. "I think Sully wants them more." And Brody, she thought, thinking of how much the handyman had enjoyed Emma's sweets all week.

That cheered her sister right up, and she gave a shrug, turning back to the stove. "Your loss. But I might bring a plate over to Mrs. Price and Jimmy."

Leah leaned into the island before she went upstairs to shower. "I didn't have a chance to ask. Did you have a nice time at the festival?" It had been a busy week, and they'd all been preoccupied with the plans for the house.

Even with her back to Leah, she seemed to stiffen. She flicked off the burner and then slowly nodded her head. "I did. It was . . . more fun than I thought it would be. All things considered," she added quickly.

Leah nodded. She'd briefly seen her sister before Sarah had met up with her and Carter, but after that, she hadn't been able to find her in the crowd.

"What about you?" Emma asked. "I saw you talking to Carter . . ." She opened her eyes wide as if she wasn't sure if she should say any more.

"It's fine. Carter and I . . . we've called a truce."

"Oh?" Emma looked hopeful, and Leah knew it had everything to do with Sadie and not Carter.

Deciding to set her hopes straight, Leah said, "He did us a big favor, coming through with the loan, so the least I can do is focus on the present and not the past."

"And it all worked out anyway," Emma said, her voice questioning. "I mean, you have Ted and the girls now. You have the life you always wanted."

Leah nodded thoughtfully and pulled back from the counter.

The life she always wanted.

Carter had kept one promise. He and Leah had bumped into each other, nearly every day since the festival. At the bookshop, where Carter was stocking up on the paperback thrillers he'd enjoyed for as long as Leah could remember and she was buying the latest beach read by her favorite author. At the coffee shop, when they were getting their daily caffeine fix, and even at the flower shop that afternoon, when Leah was visiting Leslie, and Carter was picking up a birthday bouquet for his mother.

This was everything that Leah had once feared—the exact reason she had stayed away. But the more she saw him around town, the more she looked forward to it. Since the festival, their conversations had been light and friendly, focusing on the present instead of their shared past. The interactions were pleasant. Maybe even enjoyable.

"You still bring your mother flowers on her birthday," Leah mused as she and Carter wandered through the flower shop while Leslie took down an order over the phone.

"I couldn't stop now. What would she think of me?" Carter pulled a face of horror, one that made Leah laugh. "But I do try to mix it up each year. The problem is, I'm running out of ideas."

"Ever try a plant instead?"

Carter nodded. "Even a tree. I've bought her three trees and planted them myself."

Leah laughed. "Now, that I wish I had seen."

"You should stop by the house sometime, then. I'm sure my mother would be happy to see you."

Leah grew quiet as she turned her back to him and focused on a mixed arrangement. "Maybe," she said because she wasn't sure she could reject the offer any more than she could accept it.

"Well, I have time—Mom's birthday isn't until next week. I was in Sister Bay today, so I thought I'd stop in for some inspiration. But maybe you'll come up with something brilliant between now and then."

"Me?" Leah laughed out loud. "What about Leslie? She's the expert."

She turned to her friend, who had just hung up the phone and was now jotting down details of the order. Leslie glanced up and shook her head.

"Oh, no. I've been down this road before. Everything I suggest, he says he's already done."

"Ever heard of a classic?" Leah asked him. "Some things never get boring or go out of style."

Carter seemed to hold her eyes for a beat. "Oh, I know."

His voice was gruff, and he cleared his throat before checking his watch. With a clap of his hands, he said, "Looks like I'm going to be late for a meeting. Leslie, I'll be back."

"Oh, I know." She gave a good-natured laugh.

"Leah. I'll see you around?"

This time it wasn't so much of a promise but a question, and he was looking at her for direction. The trouble was that she didn't know how to answer him, not when she wasn't sure what to tell herself.

Instead, she gave a tight smile, exhaling only when he'd finally left and had disappeared from the view out the window.

Finally turning to Leslie, she saw her friend giving her a knowing look from across the room.

"What?"

"You know what." Leslie tapped her pen against the counter. "You and Carter. Getting along. Like old times."

"It's easier that way," Leah replied as she approached the counter.

"Is that all it is?"

No. But that was all it could be. For a lot of reasons. And Leslie should know that.

Instead of indulging this conversation further, she went back to the purpose of her visit and said, "So that list. I want to be able to thank everyone who sent flowers for my aunt."

"Of course." Leslie snapped back into professional mode and rummaged under the counter for a moment, finally producing a long inventory sheet. "A lot of people loved Vivian," she said gently.

At the mere mention of her aunt's name, Leah felt the backs of her eyes prickle, and she gave a firm nod, reminding herself that this was true even though she knew Sadie was still claiming people had loved Viv only for her money. It wasn't true. They loved her for her generous spirit, among other fine attributes.

"Before you go." Leslie seemed to hesitate for a moment, her expression suddenly looking pained. "There's something I should tell you."

More bad news? Leah couldn't imagine what it could be.

"I think you should know, if you don't already . . ." Leslie pulled in a breath and blew it out. "Carter and I went out a few times. When he first moved back to town. Nothing ever happened. It was clear that we didn't click, romantically, and we agreed to just be friends like we always have."

"Oh." Leah swallowed hard, but her mouth suddenly felt as dry as cotton. She realized that she was nodding and blinking rapidly at the same time. "Okay."

But something inside her was screaming that no, that wasn't okay. Leslie was her friend. She knew what Carter had done. And she'd been there, the third wheel oftentimes, all through their relationship, joining them at the movies, eventually at the local pubs.

"It felt forced, and I had the impression that he had feelings for someone else." Leslie's gaze searched hers. "I just . . . wanted you to know."

"Well, thanks for telling me," Leah said. "But . . . it doesn't matter. Carter and I are just . . ." She was going to say *friends*, but that felt wrong. They'd never been just friends before, and why should they be now, when she was just passing through town, when they hadn't seen each other in over a decade, when he'd broken her heart so badly?

But to say they were less than that would be equally impossible.

There was a bond there. One that she couldn't deny. And one she didn't want to.

Carter and Leslie. It still bothered her to think of him with someone else, even when she knew it shouldn't. She'd moved on, gotten married. Had an entire life with another man. Of course he would have done the same.

Except now she was single. And he was too.

And that made things . . . complicated.

"Anyway, it's fine. Really." She gave Leslie a pat on the hand and tucked the list into her handbag. "Well, I should probably get back. Drinks one night next week?"

Leslie looked relieved when she smiled. "Yes, please. I want to get as much time with you as I can before you leave again."

Leave again. Leah didn't want to think about it right now. Not any more than she'd once thought about staying.

By Saturday, the work on the house was obvious. Brody was ticking off the repairs on the list nearly as quickly as Leah was adding to them. The house was old, and she noticed something new every day that would need to be addressed before they could open the place to guests. The colors that Sadie had chosen for the walls were remarkably suitable for the space, and the few rooms that were already touched up with soothing blues and natural greens made Leah dream of how the finished space would be with crisp new bed linens and curtains, fresh flowers on the end tables, and cozy throws draped over slipcovered armchairs.

She hadn't felt this excited about something other than her children since she and Ted had first purchased their home, and she decided to stroll through some of the shops in town for little touches that would set the inn apart from the rest of the competition.

Weekends in Door County were always busy, especially in the summertime. The sidewalks were already crowded when Leah walked into town, refusing her the space she craved. Still, she decided to see the upside of it: she could blend in, like she had at the festival, instead of being singled out—or rather called out—for her absence. For how good it was that she had returned. For how much it would have meant to her aunt.

Her heart was heavy when she wandered through the shops, many of which had changed hands since she'd lived here, keeping up with current trends, offering everything from cute wall plaques to irreverent coasters.

The restaurants had remained, however, many of which were housed off the lobbies of the inns that lined the street, the fortunate ones with their backs to the water, offering a premium view.

Leah was yet to brave dining out alone since the separation. She saved eating out for the days her girls were with her, but knew that the day she'd go solo was inevitable. Already Chloe preferred the company of her friends, and it wasn't like she could drag her kids to one of the movies she had hoped to see in the theater either. She couldn't always rely on her girlfriends, not when they were married and had families to tend to seven days a week like she once did.

But now her stomach rumbled, and she didn't want to go back to the house yet. She stopped on the sidewalk, looking out toward the water and planning her next move, when a deep voice came from behind.

"Hello again."

She realized that while she'd been staring into the distance, she hadn't even noticed the man walking toward her. Now, her heart skipped a beat when she locked eyes with Carter, the grin he gave her making her stomach twist in a way that made her regret telling him the truth about her circumstances.

He knew she was divorced. Single, precisely. And where did that leave them?

The same place as before, she told herself firmly. Nothing about the past had changed, and therefore nothing about the future could either.

"I'm surprised to see you," she remarked.

"Pleasantly so?" He stopped before her.

"Don't push it," she warned, but she couldn't fight her smile. "I was just about to grab some lunch."

As soon as she said it, she wasn't sure if that had come out as an invitation or an excuse to part ways. And she wasn't sure which she preferred just now.

He gave a little shrug. "I could join you. Unless you're meeting someone. Or . . . if you prefer to be alone."

Leah was certain that she did not want to be alone, not that she'd admit as much. "I'm not meeting anyone. Is LuAnn's still serving up that grilled fish sandwich?"

His mouth lifted into a slow grin. "Only the best in town. Come on; if we hurry, we can get a spot near the water."

They sped off, laughing at the silliness of it. They were too old to be racing just for one of the prime picnic tables along the waterfront, but somehow, being back with Carter, Leah felt like a kid. Like her old self. Not the woman she'd become whose dreams had been set aside for a new plan.

It would all change when she went back. When her kids were in her arms again, under her roof, complaining about breakfast options and arguing over which television show to watch.

But here, in her old stomping grounds, she was just Leah. The Leah that Carter once knew. It was a side of her that Ted had never seen because she'd never shared.

Now, she couldn't help wishing she had. Not with Ted, of course. But with her girls.

"There's one table," she said, out of breath, pointing to the weather-warped table closest to the water.

"Grab it!" Carter all but shouted, with an intensity that made her feel like she was running for something a heck of a lot more important than an old picnic table.

Still, she felt triumphant when she sat down, claiming it as theirs. *Theirs.* Just the word was sobering. She watched Carter approach the take-out window of the old building, which was hardly more than a shack, containing only a few tables inside, near the bar, for the locals in the winter months. She caught her breath, but her heart still wouldn't slow down.

What was she doing? Spending time with Carter like this?

Worse, enjoying it?

Carter looked equally satisfied when he carried over the two paper-wrapped sandwiches and a stack of napkins.

"Oh, that smells good," Leah said, already anticipating the first bite.

"You have to admit it was worth coming back to town just for LuAnn's cooking." He grinned and took a big bite.

"How often do you come here?" she asked, closing her eyes at the familiar taste.

"Oh, a few times a month at least. Fog's Landing is a small town, but there's never a shortage of decent food in Door County."

"True." She thought about him going on dates on those food outings. Or talking to women in the bars.

Pushing the image from her mind, she reached for a napkin, knowing she was making a mess of herself and she didn't even care.

"You don't mind being back, then?" She wasn't sure if she was opening a wound. But she had to know, for some reason. Was Carter happy?

Because she wasn't sure that she was. Not completely, at least. And not even before she and Ted had called it quits.

"It's not always so bad," he said with a shrug. "I know more about everyone in this town than the newspaper's gossip columnist."

She laughed, then gave him a little frown. "Please tell me there's not really a gossip columnist."

"You mean you haven't picked up the *Gazette* since you've been back?" His grin turned wicked. "Just kidding. But it wouldn't surprise you, would it?"

She shook her head. "No. This town is small, at least for the locals. That's one thing I actually sort of miss."

"The only thing?" He glanced at her sidelong, holding her stare.

Finally, she looked away, taking in the cliffs on the other side where the park pushed out into the water, disrupting the view. "No, not the only thing."

He seemed to hesitate for a moment and then said, "You didn't need to stay away so long, you know."

She knew that now, but back when she was younger, when the hurt was still fresh, she hadn't. Now, she was filled with regret for all the lost time, for the memories she could have made right here, with her girls. And Viv. She was sorry about Viv.

"I got caught up in my life," she said truthfully. "Once you have kids, it's all consuming."

"And your career plans?"

"I worked at a kitchen-design place until Chloe came along." It had been a starter job, and that wouldn't be enough experience to help her find a position in the industry now. "Like I said. Kids . . . my life took a different turn."

"Life doesn't always turn out like we expect it to," he said, giving her a sad smile.

She nodded at that, thinking of the plans she'd made for herself, the path she'd carved. She'd wavered, then decided to stay the course. But it was too late.

And there had been many days when she'd wondered what might have been if she'd never strayed. If she'd just stayed put. Held on. To this town. To the man sitting beside her.

Until one day she'd stopped thinking about this town and this man at all. Focused on the life she did have. Made the best of it. Even loved it at times.

But that hadn't been enough.

"Working on the house has reminded me of what I enjoyed once. The project of seeing potential in a space and making it beautiful."

"It shows," Carter remarked. "You light up when you talk about it."

"I haven't had a chance to flex that muscle in a while," she mused. "I created the sweetest bedrooms for the girls when they were little, but now they're putting their own mark on things." Just like she was doing with Vivian's house, she thought, wondering if Viv would approve of the changes. "Speaking of the changes to the house, we've decided to have an estate sale for some things that we won't keep but that are too nice to just throw away."

"Heck, every dime counts, right?" Carter said, reminding her for a moment of what had brought about this truce, what was tying them together. The loan. The end goal.

"That's true," she admitted. Then, feeling a strange sense of distance between them that she didn't like, she added, "All day tomorrow, if you want to stop by."

He grinned at her. "Is that an invitation?"

She twisted her mouth, fighting off a smile. "I wouldn't turn away a paying customer."

He laughed. "I might, then. Good idea."

"It wasn't actually my idea . . ." Sadie had come up with it that morning, and impulsive as it was, it was too good not to agree. The rooms would need more clearing out as the work continued, and it didn't feel right not to treat Viv's things as the treasures that they were.

"Ah." Carter nodded. "Let me guess. Sadie."

Leah set the sandwich on its wrapper. "Hey, I'm not going to shoot down a good idea just because it came from her."

"I can see you two still aren't on good terms, then."

"Why is it so important to you that we are?" she asked.

"I just know how upset she was when you left. We both were."

His gaze was steady on hers, and for a moment, Leah fought the urge to ask what he meant by that, or to argue with him, tell him she highly doubted that, even though that wasn't true, at least not now. Even now, after all these years, she could read his expressions so well, and what she saw now was sadness, regret, and honesty.

"It wasn't all her fault, Leah."

Leah pulled in a breath. She had been bracing for this conversation, and now it was here.

"I know," she admitted. "But . . . she's my sister."

"And I was your boyfriend. Until you dumped me," he added.

"I didn't dump you," she clarified. "We were . . . taking a break."

"Because you wanted one." He cocked an eyebrow. He knew he had her there.

A moment passed when no one moved. He knew, she supposed, that this was another decision point. They could argue about the past, or they could move on, let it slide into the place where it belonged, no longer defining who they were. Maybe not even who they were to each other.

But forgive Sadie?

Carter had acted on a rebound. But Sadie—what was her reason? What had Leah ever done to her?

"Sadie. She's so . . . defensive. So . . . angry." She thought about how Sadie had acted this week, alternating between silence and defiance, stubbornly refusing to acknowledge her part in anything, seeming annoyed that Leah should still care.

But she did care. She cared because it had cost her—and not just the chance of a future with Carter. It had cost her that house and all the memories she'd made in it. It had cost her more time with Viv, and moments she'd never been able to have with Emma. It had cost her a safe place to return to for holidays or just because.

But more than anything, it had cost her that bond that she and Sadie once shared. That sisterly love that, as the eldest two, they alone had shared.

Once their parents had died, Sadie was the person she'd known the longest and the best. The one who knew her as a child, all those memories that only she could share.

And now they were lost. Along with so much else.

"She's hurt," Carter said.

"Well, that makes two of us."

"So isn't that your answer? Stop the pain, Leah. You have an opportunity right now."

She nodded. One that might never happen again, was what he was saying. What she already knew.

"I'll think about it," she said as she stood and wiped the crumbs from her legs. But the truth was that she wasn't so sure she could ever forgive Sadie.

Just like she wasn't so sure that she'd ever be able to completely forgive Carter.

She could move on, and she had. But that was different. And that was something she'd had far too much experience with in life.

CHAPTER TWENTY

SADIE

By ten the next morning, Sadie was already regretting even muttering the words "estate sale." She'd thought she was offering up something useful, since compared to her sisters, her contribution to this venture seemed to be minimal. What had she been thinking, inviting the public into the house again, this time to literally search through their drawers? But she'd been thinking of the house. And the money. And all this stuff that would be pretty damn hard to haul away on their own.

She and her sisters had spent the entire night arguing over the price of the items, with Emma putting the most value on everything and, according to Emma, Sadie placing the least.

She'd been up since six to start again, and it didn't take a detective to notice that some of the tags she'd placed on the old dressers, coatracks, and candlesticks had been updated while she slept.

Whatever. If it all meant that much to Emma, so be it. It was Emma's house, after all. Emma and Viv's.

Still, she felt a strange wound open up when she noticed that someone had set tags on the old books in the back den. Astonished, she began snatching off the tags as quick as her fingers would allow her. These books were her escape, her joy, and even her sorrow at times. The few times she ever allowed herself to cry were usually over something that happened in a book. A sad ending—or sometimes a deservedly happy one—could send her sobbing into a pillow, her throat raw even hours later as she digested the experience she had just had.

These books had been her world, more than this house ever was. They were all hers. And now one of her sisters had gone and tagged them to give away to complete strangers!

In fairness, she knew that anyone who came through the house today would be not a complete stranger but a friend of Viv's. No doubt looking to see what more they could take from the old, rich spinster.

Well, they wouldn't be taking the books! Not Viv's books. Not Sadie's.

She peered closely at the handwriting, recognizing it as Leah's, and, even though she knew she should probably just count to ten and let it go, she couldn't.

She stormed into the kitchen, the tags tight in her grasp, waving them at both her sisters, who were standing at the island, sipping coffee, their expressions now both frozen and confused.

"So you thought you could just give away the one thing in this house that meant something to me?"

Emma's eyes were so wide that for a moment, Sadie feared she might cry. And then she'd really feel like a jerk. But she was tired of dancing around everyone's emotions, hiding out in her room, and disappearing from the house for long stretches. Her sisters might have put all the plans for the house in motion without her input, but they couldn't just completely do with it as they pleased without thinking of her at all.

"Calm down," Leah said firmly. "If you want the books so badly, we won't sell them. They've just been collecting dust for fifteen years."

It was a jab at how long she'd been gone. How long she'd abandoned Viv. Emma.

"I'm not the only one who hasn't stepped foot in this house in fifteen years," she said archly.

"Guys . . ." Emma sounded like she might cry. "Don't scare Sully."

Sadie looked at her sharply. "Oh, please, Emma. I'm not even shouting." But she was shouting, she realized, and Leah—well, Leah looked like she was ready to get down on the ground and tackle her.

For a moment, Sadie almost laughed at the thought.

"Why can't you just shake hands and move on?" Emma said now.

Sadie opened her mouth and then closed it, realizing it was what Viv had always told them when they were little and they'd argue over silly things, things that she couldn't even remember anymore, other than how Leah hadn't liked the way Sadie was hanging too many Christmas ornaments in a cluster one year.

Something in her heart pulled when she remembered that—how she'd been so annoyed that Leah was trying to make it her tree, her holiday, her decorations. When all Leah was really trying to do was make everything beautiful.

And better.

"Okay then." She lifted her chin and jutted her hand out, her eyes blazing as her heart hammered in her chest, waiting to see if Leah would take it.

Leah looked about as shocked by the gesture as Emma, and after what felt like enough time that Sadie should really just give up, and for good—like, pack her bags and leave this house to them to sort out, the books included—Leah, slowly, held out her hand.

Emma let out a little gasp, but other than that, the room was eerily quiet. Even Sully had stopped crunching his food to watch what was happening.

Sadie felt her sister take her hand. The long, thin fingers. The soft palm. The very hand that she'd held so tightly that first day they'd arrived at this house. Holding on for dear life.

It felt so familiar. So full of love. Like wherever she was, with that hand in hers, she was home.

Clearing her throat now, Sadie pumped her arm up and down and then snatched back her hand.

Emma was grinning ear to ear. "There!" she said as if that made everything right again.

But maybe it did, Sadie thought, glancing over at Leah, who seemed to be fighting off a shy smile, lowering her head, muttering something about getting to work if they were going to make today worth their while.

At least the tension was starting to thaw, but still, Leah's smile felt frozen as they walked the rooms and tagged the remaining items, and they hadn't mentioned the past. Not the bad parts of it, anyway.

Maybe they'd been trained to do that from a young age, when their parents died, when Viv refused to even discuss their mother, and all that darkness just faded away. Maybe that was better.

But looking at her sister now as they put away the pens and the slips of paper and took in the space as it was for the last time, she didn't think so. The past was the one thing they all shared and couldn't face together. And it was what had driven them apart and kept them that way.

Sadie's eyes darted to the cookbooks. None were tagged. The photo was safe and sound where Viv had left it. She was doubly relieved to look at her watch and note the time—nearly eleven. "I'll be back in a couple of hours. Jimmy's going to show me the house he's building. I'll put the sign out front on my way."

No one argued. They all knew it would be best if Sadie weren't around to greet the lookie-loos.

"Jimmy, huh?" Emma gave a little smile that bordered on suggestive.

"Yes, Jimmy. Why do you say it like that?"

"Oh, nothing. I mean, it's just funny that you're both back in town, after all this time. All grown up."

"I'm not back in town," Sadie clarified. Her cheeks felt hot, and she was now more grateful than ever to have an excuse to leave this house.

Really! What was Emma getting at? She didn't know what was more preposterous: that there could ever be anything more than friendship between her and Jimmy, or that she was back in town for even one day longer than necessary.

———— ❧❦ ————

Linda Price was outside tending to her flower bed when Sadie cut across the yard. In her sixties, she had gray hair cut into a neat bob, and her brown eyes were bright under her straw hat.

"Is that a sign for an estate sale?" The woman shielded her eyes with her hand when she stared over at the large homemade poster.

"We're clearing some stuff out," Sadie said. "Please. Go over and take what's special to you. Free of charge. Viv would have wanted that."

Linda stood up, wincing as she unbent her knees, and then smiled. "I hear you're turning the house into an inn."

Even though Jimmy had told her that his mother wouldn't have a problem with it, Sadie asked nervously, "So you don't mind?"

"Mind?" Linda's laugh was as clear and melodic as the wind chimes that hung from Aunt Vivian's front porch. "I think it's a brilliant idea. Vivian would be thrilled. She always did prefer that house to be filled. The only time I ever saw her smile slip was when she was alone in there."

Sadie pushed back the guilt that kept coming back in waves. It was so much easier to keep under wraps from hundreds of miles away, in a city that never grew quiet, when she was always rushing off to the next best thing, even if she wasn't planning two steps ahead.

She was relieved when the screen door whined as it opened and Jimmy stepped outside, giving her a slow grin.

"Don't work too hard, Mom."

"Oh, you." Linda brushed him away with her hand. "Always fussing over me."

But it was clear from the pink in her cheeks that she was pleased.

Sadie waited until they were in the car to say to Jimmy, "Do you think she's lonely? Without Viv, I mean? They were like sisters."

And she knew firsthand how difficult it was to lose one. Only this was different. Linda and Vivian hadn't had a falling-out. There was no chance of a reunion.

Sadie wondered how she'd feel if something happened to Leah before they had a chance to mend things, but then she shook that off. She was feeling sentimental—conflicted, really. And stressed about the future. Leah had played just as big a part in things as she had. And Leah had moved on with her life quite nicely.

"She doesn't say so, but it can't be easy for her. They *were* like sisters, especially after . . ."

"After my mother moved away." Sadie grew quiet as they drove out of town, onto country back roads and miles of fields and forest that weren't yet developed and maybe never would be. "Anyway," she said, forcing a bright tone that she almost felt. "Tell me all about the house."

Jimmy's smile grew bashful. "It's just a house, Sadie. Just like all the others. Somewhere to live."

He made it sound so easy, like it was a given, when she knew that it wasn't.

"Out here, where no one lives?"

"On the other side of the peninsula," he explained, and she knew that was only a matter of miles. Door County was long and narrow, meaning they'd be there in no time.

Sadie didn't know why she suddenly felt nervous.

"So you want some space. I get it."

He glanced at her sidelong. "You always do."

They fell into silence, the fields and trees eventually giving way to small buildings and houses and a view of Lake Michigan that spanned miles. Here, the lots were bigger, and the land was less developed. Away from the busy Main Streets of all the towns and the restaurants and shops that only ever seemed to trade hands, not close.

It was quiet over here, and the water stretched out before them like a navy blanket, interrupted only by the large sailboats in the distance. Sadie looked out the car window, trying to picture Jimmy living out here.

"How'd you find the lot?"

He gave her a funny look. "A real estate agent, of course."

"Of course." Still, the idea felt so foreign to her. She didn't have a rental apartment to return to in New York, and here Jimmy was, actually building a house!

"What about the plans? The building?" She couldn't imagine what went into such a thing.

But Jimmy just shook his head and gave a low laugh as he eased off the accelerator and swung right, where the main road turned private. Possibly, this was even some sort of driveway.

"Anyone ever tell you that you overthink things?"

She looked ruefully out the window. "Only you."

But only Jimmy said a lot of things, because only Jimmy really knew her in a way that even her sisters didn't.

"So you're staying in town but not really," she commented.

"I don't mind my space," Jimmy agreed. "And after living with my mother for three years . . ."

Sadie laughed. "Admit it. You loved her cooking."

His grin was broad, while his eyes remained on the road. "I love her cooking. Always did. Always will. There are some things that never change."

He glanced at her sidelong, and her heart gave a little pull.

"I suppose there are," she said quietly. She looked away, out the window again. She'd always been able to count on Jimmy. Then. Now. She could lose her parents, her house, then her sisters and her childhood home. Jobs, apartments, boyfriends. They all came and went.

But Jimmy was her sure thing. Even when he wasn't with her.

Even sometimes, she realized with shame, when she didn't even think of him.

Jimmy rolled the car to a stop and pointed through the trees. "There it is."

Sadie blinked, following the lead of his finger. She wasn't sure what she'd expected, but somehow, this wasn't it.

Before her stood a nearly fully erected house—and not a small house. No, this was a large, dare she say family-size, home with a three-car garage and a front porch, or at least the makings of one.

Piles of lumber sat under tarps, and as they climbed out of the car and approached, she saw that the inside was still just framed. But the outside . . .

"Wow, you were serious."

"You seem surprised by that," Jimmy said. He dipped his head back, looking proud at the huge building before him.

"Well, it's just that . . . it's a house!" And it was: not just a foundation, like she'd expected, or maybe just a clearing with a place for a house, but an actual proper house with four walls and a roof and, from the size of it, probably even a formal dining room. "It's just so . . . so grown up."

"Well, we are grown up, Sadie," he said, giving her a slow grin as he came to stand closer to her. For a moment they stood there, side by side, staring at the great big structure complete with a winding driveway that backed up into a dense forest.

Jimmy was building a house. He was putting down roots. In Fog's Landing of all places.

"So, you never have any plans to leave, then? This is it? You're going to spend the rest of your life here, in this town?"

"You make that sound like a bad thing," he said, a frown pulling at his forehead.

She felt something prickle, her defenses rising. "For some of us, it is."

"Oh, come on, Sadie. You don't think anyone is really still hung up on what happened all those years ago, do you? We were kids back then. And kids do stupid things sometimes."

She knew he was being kind, if not a little dismissive. She knew that he wasn't calling her stupid, only what she'd done. And maybe it had been. But it had been real to her. Too real. Real enough to change the course of her life, again.

"Besides, you and I both know that you were just looking for an excuse to get out of this town and that house, and you didn't know how."

"Are you saying that I, like, sabotaged myself?" She stared at him in shock, even angrier when she saw the little shrug he gave her. "Are you serious, Jimmy? My God! My life has been awful since that happened!

Leah only started speaking to me again because she had to. Because we're both here—because Viv . . . died." Her throat burned, and she had the horrible fear that she might start to cry, even though Jimmy had been the one person she didn't mind seeing her cry. Until now.

"And Viv is gone. Gone, and I never got to say goodbye. Even Emma seemed surprised that I came back for the funeral. It was like they all assumed that I stopped caring, when it was the other way around."

"You know Viv loved you," Jimmy said. "A lot of people got hurt in that mess. A lot of people's lives took . . . another direction."

"Are you talking about Carter? How he's been stuck here, working for his dad, when he might have been married to Leah, living somewhere else, raising their kids?" She shook her head bitterly. "As the saying goes, it takes two to tango, but somehow I took all the heat."

"Carter came back. No one thinks about it anymore when they see him," Jimmy said firmly. "It's your . . . your absence that drew so much attention to things."

She stared at him in horror. "Are you saying that I brought this on myself?"

He didn't say anything for a moment, giving her her answer. She took a step back and then another. "Wow, Jimmy. Just . . . wow. I would have thought you of all people would have understood."

"It's Jim, by the way," he said, his jaw set in a way she'd never seen it before.

She blinked, unsure of what he meant.

He took a step toward her, his big, beautiful future behind himself rising tall in the form of a house. "Jimmy's what people called me as a kid. You're the only one who still calls me that."

"Oh." Well, she hadn't known. Or done it to offend him. To her, he was Jimmy. Her best friend. Her trusted person. And now, she didn't know who he was. "Well, okay. I'll say that from now on."

If they even ever spoke to each other again after this conversation.

"You're the only person who calls me Jimmy because you're the only one who is still stuck in the past, Sadie. But everyone has grown up and moved on. Heck, you've moved away. So have I."

"And you came back."

"And so did you," he countered. He was close to her now, so close that she could see the flecks of brown in his otherwise green eyes. "And you don't have to go. You can stay too. Put down roots. Make this place your home."

She shook her head. "Impossible."

"Why? Is New York so great? Because it doesn't sound like you have much waiting for you there."

"And what do I have for me here, Jimmy? I mean, Jim?" It didn't sound right on her lips. He wasn't Jim to her. He'd always be Jimmy, and maybe that was just the problem.

"You have me," he said simply.

"You know it's not that simple," she told him.

He shrugged, but there was a strange shadow that had fallen over his eyes. "Life is as difficult as you make it."

She bristled, hating that word. *Difficult.* Had he chosen it on purpose? Surely he knew what people said, what they'd always said, even when she was young, long before that incident with Carter. She was the most difficult of the three Burke sisters. Weren't the middle children supposed to be more agreeable?

"Look at me," he said, seeming to relax. "When I was working for that big law firm, I was putting in seventy, eighty hours a week. And that was an easy week. I was running on a hamster wheel; I was never caught up. No time for a social life or friends. I didn't even get to enjoy all the great restaurants the city was known for. It got to a point where I didn't even know what I was chasing anymore. And I certainly wasn't going to ever reach it. Not like that."

"What was it you wanted?"

He pulled in a breath and then cracked a smile, opening his arms wide. "This, I suppose. A nice life. A happy life. A good day's work, a home to come back to. Maybe a family waiting for me. A wife that's my partner and my best friend."

"Hey," she said, feeling a spark of jealousy at this picturesque image. "I thought I was your best friend."

His gaze locked on hers for a moment, and then he looked away and cleared his throat.

"Sometimes everything we're chasing was right here in front of us all along."

Sadie didn't know what he meant by that, but she knew that they weren't coming from the same place. Her experiences in this town had been, well, difficult. His, not so much.

"It's different for you, coming back here. It's not that—" She stopped herself. Shared a smile with him, one that came easily. She'd been about to say *simple*.

But could it be that simple? She'd been running away more than chasing a life, but one thing was certain, and that was that she didn't even know what she was running to anymore.

Could her life be that simple? Or was it only ever going to be . . . difficult?

"I should be getting back. My sisters need my help at the house."

It was a good excuse, but still an excuse. Her sisters were probably equal parts relieved for her absence and resentful of it at the same time. But right now, being there at least gave her a purpose. To clean it up. Make it shine. Turn it into something new.

It was the only thing in her future that felt certain.

And the only other thing that she was even sure of right now was that she had to get away. From this house. From Jimmy. From every reminder of the past and every dashed hope for the future.

She had to get out of this town. And this time, for good.

CHAPTER
TWENTY-ONE
EMMA

The time had come for Emma to return to work. Just in time to give her notice. A generous one, but one all the same.

She didn't know what made her feel sicker to her stomach—the thought of letting Pamela down, the thought of putting an end to a reliable income, or the thought of committing to a life alone in that big old house, where she'd no doubt end up like Aunt Viv, never married, loved by the community, spoiling her nieces instead of her own children.

She waited until the end of her shift, which was only the morning, because Pamela had insisted on easing her back in, because she was kind like that. Had taught her all there was to know about the hospitality industry, especially the part about always keeping the guests happy. But that part had come naturally, hadn't it? Emma was used to keeping everyone else around her happy.

Which made this conversation especially difficult.

Pamela was in the lobby, fluffing the welcome table's fresh flowers, which Leslie delivered twice weekly. It was a sunny day, and all the guests had left shortly after breakfast, most on the bicycles that the inn provided for them, others on foot. Emma knew that they wouldn't return until four or five, and even then it would just be to pop in and freshen up before leaving for dinner in Fish Creek or Williams Bay. She'd seen the notes and the reservations that had been requested and garnered. The mornings and evenings were the busiest times, the afternoons often slow, allowing for Sarah and Pamela and Emma to tend to the day-to-day business of the inn. The little things that went on behind the scenes that kept the place operating.

Little things like tidying the throw pillows on the furniture in the lobby. Making sure that there was enough chopped wood for a fire that evening. Seeing that they didn't run out of the soap and shampoo that the guests kept on stealing—a statement, Pamela insisted, that proved they liked what the inn was offering.

That was certainly one way of looking at it. Emma could only hope that Pamela would see the bright side of the news she was about to deliver.

"Oh, Emma!" Pamela looked up with a smile. "I didn't see you standing there. Guess I'm still getting used to having you back."

Oh, no. Emma's insides seemed to turn to jelly, and she had the sudden urge to abort this mission altogether. She could put it off for another day, surely.

But eventually, that day would come.

With a watery smile, she said, "I'm afraid you won't like what I have to say."

"Don't tell me a bathtub overflowed!"

That had happened exactly once, in 1999, ruining the carpet and the ceiling of the room below, not to mention upsetting the guests who were literally rained on in their sleep. It was one of many incidents that Pamela still brought up to this day.

"No, nothing that bad," Emma assured her. She gestured to the couch in the bay window. "Can we sit?"

"Oh no." Pamela's shoulders sagged, and Emma knew at that moment that Pamela understood. She was leaving her. She just didn't know why.

"I knew this time would come. We haven't been able to offer you the most glamorous position, I'm afraid. And the guests can be hard to deal with."

Emma gave a chuckle. Oh, she knew.

"Actually, I'm not leaving the industry, though. I was taught by the best! But with Viv gone, my sisters and I had to decide what to do about the house. And we've decided to make it a small inn. I hope you're not mad."

"Mad?" Pamela cried. "Why, that is a brilliant idea. My little protégée. I couldn't be prouder."

She pulled Emma in for a long, hard hug, and Emma accepted it, realizing with a prickle in her eyes just how much she needed it—the hug and the words. Two things that Viv could no longer offer.

The truth was coming out, one piece at a time, like secret ingredients that, once revealed, made the recipe complete.

And now it was Emma's turn for honesty.

Sarah was right. She should just tell Wyatt how she felt about him. Once and for all. Admit her feelings, and see if he shared them. If just being friends wasn't enough for her, then it was time to get on with it—say her piece and hear his out, firmly, clearly, no more confusion. Maybe he'd take her into his arms and kiss her, telling her that this was what he had been waiting to hear, that he'd been wondering how she felt, that he didn't want to ruin what they had by making a move . . .

Or maybe he'd say he wanted to remain friends, and then she would know. Once and for all, she could be sure.

She had nothing to lose.

Accept her pride. And her dreams. And hope.

Right. She was doing this. Today. Because if she didn't do it today, then tomorrow would be just like yesterday and all the days before, and next year might end up like the previous year—or worse.

Her chest seized on a terrible thought. Maybe Wyatt would end up marrying Allie, never knowing Emma's true feelings.

Maybe she and Wyatt would live happily ever after in this town. He running his pub, and she the inn. She'd bake all his favorite sweets, and he'd enjoy them heartily. They'd have three children, and she'd teach them her favorite recipes in this very kitchen.

It would be enough. It would be more than enough.

She'd been in the kitchen for hours, the evidence of her struggle on full display in the form of a strawberry pie, blueberry tarts, cinnamon-streusel cake, and of course, double-fudge brownies.

By the time she'd turned off the oven, hung up her apron, and hurried out the door, she was already having a different conversation with herself. One that echoed a little too much of what Viv had been saying for years. "A man like Wyatt doesn't need to work up the courage" was one of those thoughts. The other, more pressing, being "When a man wants a woman, he does something about it."

She shook those thoughts free. Enough dancing around whatever there was between them. She was a modern woman, and besides, where had Viv's opinions gotten her?

Okay, that was mean. Unforgivable, really, but still, a little true. Viv had never been married or had any beaux in all the time that Emma had lived here. She'd never talked about boyfriends from the past. For all Emma knew, she had never even been in love! So really, her opinion shouldn't matter.

It was time to have it out. Open, honest communication. To know where she stood.

What he felt.

She hurried the entire way to the coffeehouse, her heart turning over as it always did when she first saw him after a few days. He was sitting at a patio table, scrolling through his phone. He held up a hand in greeting when he saw her, a big smile stretching his face in that way that made her wonder for the thousandth time what it would be like to kiss those lips. To have him pull her close against himself, slide his hand down lower as his mouth explored her ear, her neck.

She shook away that fantasy. Swallowed hard. She wasn't here for a usual visit. She was here for a very serious conversation.

"How are things going?" he asked, and it was then that she realized just how much he didn't know. About her sisters, or the plans for the house, or all the work that they'd been doing to get it ready.

That as much as she thought that life here in Fog's Landing never changed, it had changed for her. And today, it was going to change even more. One way or another.

"Busy," she said to sum it all up. There would be time to talk about all that other stuff later, but she could hardly sit here and pretend to have a casual conversation when her heart was pounding so hard that for a moment, she thought she might be sick.

"I feel like we haven't hung out in weeks," Wyatt said, giving her one of those easy grins that made Viv cluck her tongue in disapproval.

Emma did her best to ignore that now. She wasn't looking for advice. She was looking for insight. For the cold hard truth of where they stood once and for all.

"Well, it's been a busy time." She smiled. It didn't come easily.

"I was disappointed that we didn't get to spend more time at the festival." Wyatt leaned into the table, resting his forearms on the wood, locking her gaze with his.

Was it just her, or did his blue eyes seem to positively sparkle?

She swooned a little. She couldn't help it. Or maybe she just wavered. Because wouldn't it be easy to stay just like this forever?

But that was just the problem, she thought as her heart sank a little. She wanted this—her and Wyatt—forever. And she didn't know what the heck Wyatt wanted.

"Oh, you seemed to be in good company," she said nervously. She wished she'd had the sense to grab an iced coffee before sitting down. She would have something to do, to distract herself from that handsome face and those intense eyes that never seemed to leave contact with her.

She watched him carefully now, wondering if he'd pick up on the elephant in the room. The person who was never discussed and barely even mentioned. The girl he had brought to the festival.

The festival that he'd invited her to attend with him. She hadn't imagined it. He had.

Had it been planned? Did he think she wouldn't care?

"About that . . . ," he started, and Emma widened her eyes, not sure if she felt relief or anger.

So it hadn't been planned. He hadn't wanted her to meet his girlfriend. But he had one. And he had her on the side, as Viv liked to say. An old-fashioned saying, Emma always thought, but now it felt so painfully accurate.

She was angry. For the first time since she'd met Wyatt, all those years ago, she was furious with him. Did he know how she felt? The tears she'd cried? The dreams she'd dreamed?

The dreams she'd given up?

Well, it was time to find out.

"I was sort of surprised. I mean, in all these years, I've never met her. I was starting to wonder if she even existed." She laughed, but there was no amusement.

Wyatt's expression changed then. Gone were the charming grin and the sparkling eyes. His jaw seemed to tighten as he leaned back in his chair.

"It's complicated," he said.

"You could say that," she said flatly.

She didn't know where this was coming from, this strange new emotion that emboldened her, made her seek the truth rather than try to deny it. She was facing the worst kind of heartache—or maybe she wasn't.

Maybe not knowing was the worst kind of pain. Having hope where none existed.

"Sometimes . . ." She pulled in a breath, searching for Viv's voice. Thinking that this would really frost her aunt's cookies—feeding into this man's ego.

But she heard nothing. No echoes of disapproval. No roll of thunder or crack of lightning to send her running for shelter—ending this conversation before it could begin.

She was on her own. But somehow, it didn't feel that way. She had her two sisters waiting for her at home. And Sarah, her faithful friend. And Viv, in her heart.

She could do this.

"Sometimes I thought that something was going to happen . . ." Just spit it out, Emma. "Between us."

Wyatt looked pained as he leaned in and gave her what could only be described as a pitying smile. "You're a great girl, Emma. The best."

The air felt like it was being sucked from her lungs with the length of his pause.

But. There would be a *but*, of course.

She was a great girl, just not the girl for him. The best. Just not the best for him.

"It's just . . ."

She wanted to hold up a hand, tell him to save the excuse, because she didn't need to hear it. She already knew. Deep down, maybe she always had. She just hadn't wanted to believe it. She'd wanted to hold out hope. To believe that there could be more for her in this town beyond the confining walls of that old house.

"Allie is pregnant, Emma. We're getting married."

She felt her eyes pop. She had braced herself for any one of a dozen lame and generic excuses as to why Wyatt didn't want to be involved with her, but this was one she hadn't seen coming.

Pregnant. Meaning they were having sex.

Viv's voice had never been clearer: *Of course they are, Emma! She's his girlfriend. Mind you, in my day, a lady would have waited for marriage, but—*

Emma closed her eyes to Viv's voice. To the reality of what Wyatt had just said. To the implications.

Wyatt—her Wyatt—was going to be a father. He was going to have a whole new life. One that she wouldn't be a part of anymore. And all these . . . get-togethers, hangouts, whatever they ever were, would be coming to a grinding halt.

"Married?" It was all she could say, all she could focus on. Had he already proposed? Had he bought the ring? Was he going to expect her opinion on it?

"We've been together for four years." He tipped his head and gave her a long and patient look, like he was hoping she'd understand.

But she didn't. "But you and me—"

"You're my closest friend here in Fog's Landing," Wyatt said. "This doesn't have to change anything."

Oh, yes, it did. It changed everything.

Emma managed to save the tears until she was nearly home, and only then, when the big white house with the gables that harbored the perfect reading nooks and the wraparound porch where the best tea parties and lemonade had been served up appeared in the nearby distance, did she feel the strange mixture of relief and sadness.

The house still stood, looking exactly as it had every year since she'd first come to this town. It was her one constant, the one thing that never changed. Now, though, a good half of the furniture was gone, claimed mostly by friends of Viv's, people who would at least cherish the items, even if they left obvious holes in the rooms, the empty marks a reminder that everything did change, eventually. Even that old house.

Letting the weight of her heartache consume her, Emma hurried her pace, nearly running to the house, eager for the shelter only it could give, for the one place in this world that had always kept her safe, ever since she'd first arrived here, all those years ago, feeling then like she did now. Lost. Scared. Utterly heartbroken.

Back then only one thing about the future had felt certain. That this house would be her home, that it was big and sturdy and cluttered and comfortable, and she had loved it for it.

She realized now, through the pain in her chest, that she still did.

Sully let out a bark the moment she pushed through the front door, reminding her that this house wasn't just hers but his as well. That it wasn't the lumpy velvet couch or the mismatched frames of old photographs on the piano that made it home. It was who filled it. Once, that had been her sisters and Viv. Now, it was her sweet little dog.

She managed to stop the flow of tears as she went to the back of the house, where Sully sat waiting for her near his gate and not exactly patiently. His bed had been upturned, and his toys were scattered. When she bent to open the gate, he stood up on his haunches, greeting her with all the joy as if she'd been gone for weeks or months. It was the kind of love that couldn't be replaced and was never taken for granted.

A smile pushed away her sadness when he licked her salty tears, nearly frantic with excitement at her return. She laughed as she tried to pull away and failed, relinquishing herself to be covered in paw prints and tongue licks as he danced around her.

"Someone's happy to see you."

Emma looked up to see Sadie smiling wryly down at her, but her sister's expression changed quickly.

"What's wrong?"

The tears might have stopped, but Emma could only assume the evidence of them was still there, despite Sully's attempts to lick them away.

She stood, holding Sully, and shook her head. What was there to even say? Too much. That was the problem.

"Where's Leah?" she asked, even though that was sort of dumb. Leah would be wherever Sadie wasn't, even if they were trying to get along better. The tension was still there, dragging the past into the present. Propelling it into the future, even. "Never mind, forget I asked."

"You didn't answer my question." Sadie followed her into the kitchen.

For once, Emma didn't feel like baking. She didn't even know what time it was, and she was surprised to see that she'd been gone only an hour.

Another reminder of how much life could change in such a small amount of time.

Now that the house was still again, she could hear the smooth and steady sound of the paint roller from upstairs. Of course. Leah was right where she'd left her. Brody must have left for an errand, maybe for the day.

"I should go help. With the painting," Emma started to say, but Sadie was having none of that.

"Not right now you're not. For one, because I need a break, which is the reason I was down here to begin with."

That forced a smile out of Emma, because there was truth in that, a selfish but endearing side to Sadie that she'd almost forgotten about—one that reminded her of who her sister was and would always be. And she loved her for it.

Especially now, when Sadie knew exactly what she was doing. For Emma.

"I think it's wine o'clock. Why don't we take some of these treats you've been baking for Brody—" She raised an eyebrow when Emma started to object and then said, "We'll go sit on the porch. Watch the water. Enjoy the breeze."

"All of us?" Emma was doubtful. Their attempts at family bonding these past two weeks had been shaky at best.

But Sadie just pulled open the fridge and plucked a bottle of white wine from the inner shelf. "All of us."

Leah didn't need much encouragement. One holler up the stairs was enough. She came down a moment later in jeans and a T-shirt that didn't bear a single paint stain.

It didn't take long for Emma to summarize the past few years with Wyatt. How she'd met him, how they'd connected. How they'd parted.

"What a jerk," Sadie hissed, reaching for the wine bottle and topping off her glass.

"Maybe not." Emma shrugged. "He never made a move on me. Never tried to kiss me or anything. He was just . . ."

"Leading you on?" Sadie raised one eyebrow so perfectly that Emma couldn't help but laugh. Even Leah joined in.

"I was going to say he was just a friend," Emma finished. She tightened her cardigan around herself and pulled Sully close, stroking his soft fur until she felt calmer.

"Can men and women really be friends, though?" Leah shrugged. "It's just something I've been thinking about lately. It's . . . complicated, isn't it?"

Emma looked at Sadie, knowing that she of all of them should know the answer to that. But for once, Sadie didn't defend her relationship with Jimmy. Or define it.

Emma wondered if something had transpired between them but decided not to push. Besides, she had her own problems today.

"Viv never liked Wyatt," Emma said with a sniff.

She caught a smile passing between her older sisters, enough to almost boost her mood.

"Well, I think that's unanimous," Leah said. "Who can like the guy who broke her sister's heart?"

"Not me," Sadie said, clucking her tongue the way their aunt would have done if she were here. "Should we sic Sully on him?"

Emma managed to laugh again. "Only you can make me laugh at a time like this, Sadie."

Leah nodded. "It's true. You always had a way of distracting us when we needed it. And a way with words."

Now Sadie mumbled something and reached for her glass of wine, but it was clear that she was pleased by what Leah had said. And it was true. Sadie was sharp. In life and in words.

Emma thought about all the stories her sister used to write. If she still kept at it. Or, if like so many other parts of their life, she'd given it up long ago.

Now Emma reached for her glass, needing a little liquid courage. "That's not all that happened today. I gave my notice at the inn. Pamela was flexible. She said that I could stay on until we're ready to open."

"Well, that's good! And now it must feel official." Leah looked so happy for her that Emma felt sick to her stomach.

She swallowed hard. The truth was coming out. But one part remained. "It does feel official. But it doesn't feel good." She looked up at her sisters with big eyes, wondering if she could really go through with this. Knowing that she had to—before it was too late. "When I suggested the inn, I was only thinking of saving the house. I wasn't thinking of being the one running it. Being stuck in this house, all on my own, day after day." Forever and ever.

The room went strangely quiet, but it was Leah who spoke first. "But why didn't you say anything?"

"Because I didn't think I had a choice! Viv left us with this problem. And this was a solution. And then you went and got that loan, Leah, and now we're all on the hook. I had savings. Not much, but some. I . . ." She almost couldn't bring herself to say it, to voice her innermost desires, that little part of herself that she'd set aside for years. "I didn't have the chance to up and leave like the two of you did. I was young, so of course I stayed behind. But I didn't want to stay forever."

"You never said as much!" Leah said, looking almost shocked. "You seemed happy here. Content. This has been your home far longer than either of ours, and there's no denying that you were closest to Viv. You have an entire community, a job, and you never complained."

"What could I have said?" Emma shook her head miserably. "That I've felt stifled all these years? Resentful at times? That I'd lie in bed at night thinking about living a different life? And that now that Viv is gone, I'm racked with guilt?"

"Oh, honey." Leah shook her head. "I thought I was the only one who felt guilty."

"Me too," Sadie said quietly. Another glance passed between the sisters.

"If you don't want to stay in this house, we won't make you." Leah's smile was kind, but the words felt empty.

Life wasn't that simple. It never had been. Baking was simple. Straightforward. That's why she liked it so much.

Emma shook her head. "We're hardly in the position to hire anyone, and that wouldn't feel right anyway. And you have a family to get home to, and Sadie has her apartment in New York."

"No," Sadie said, now managing to silence Emma. "I don't have an apartment anymore. My roommate kicked me out. Said her gross boyfriend needs the space. It's just as well. But . . . I don't exactly have anything to return to."

"Oh!" Emma wondered for a moment if this was the solution, but Sadie had never been shy in her feelings about this town or place.

Sadie just shrugged. "It's okay. I figured I'd find another place. And job. I always have. It's nothing new." Sadie's jaw was pronounced, but the usual defiance in her eyes seemed to be clouded over by something else. Something Emma recognized as fear.

"And I don't have a family to get home to," Leah said softly. "I have my girls. But . . . Ted and I broke up. We're getting divorced. He's with the girls now. It's . . . his turn with them. They were never at camp."

"Leah!" Emma felt her own eyes fill with tears, and she inched closer to her sister to wrap an arm around her. "Why didn't you say anything?"

"With everything going on here? We have this old place to worry about. And I didn't want to add any more stress or worry to you, Emma."

Emma gave her sister a sad smile. "Oh, Leah. Don't you see? I'm not a little girl anymore."

"I guess I'm just so used to being the one everyone turns to—when we were kids, now with my own kids . . ." Leah shrugged, and for the first time since she'd come back, Emma saw how tired she looked.

"I'm always going to need you, Leah. I'm always going to want you. Because you're my sister. And I love you. But I can take care of myself. You don't have to do everything. We're all here, together." Emma gave a pointed look at Sadie.

"It's true, Leah. And the same goes for you, Emma. This isn't all on your shoulders. I know I don't have as much to lose as the two of you if this all goes wrong, but I'm here, trying. I'm really trying."

Emma saw Leah look at her for a long moment. She didn't argue.

"You could have told me about Ted," Emma said to Leah. "You could have let us be there for you for a change."

The idea seemed to be a revelation to Leah. "I guess I thought . . . I thought it was easier to come back here pretending that my life in Chicago was better than it is."

Sadie nodded her head. "I felt the same way."

For a moment, there was silence, and then Emma said, "So what are we going to do?"

Leah's face broke into a smile through her tears. "Find a way. We always do."

Only this time, she wasn't doing it alone.

CHAPTER
TWENTY-TWO

LEAH

When Carter called and asked Leah if she wanted to join him at his mother's birthday dinner on Friday night, two thoughts came to mind.

One was that she wasn't eighteen anymore and that this was both a good and a bad thing, for the obvious reasons (wrinkles) and the not-so-obvious ones (where they stood wasn't any clearer than how she wanted things to be defined).

The other, more pressing thought was that she'd loved Mrs. Maxwell once, and she couldn't imagine passing up the opportunity to celebrate her dinner. And she'd feel like a real jerk for making up an excuse, even though there were plenty at hand, ranging from personal (Carter had slept with her sister, albeit fifteen years ago and when they were on a self-appointed break) to realistic (the house still needed a lot of work if they were going to get it opened as an inn before the end of summer).

"What can I bring?" she asked, knowing that Carter already had the flowers covered.

In the end, they decided that he'd pick her up on his way over, and they'd bring the flowers together, along with a cake that Emma insisted on baking, because she was in the mood to bake a cake anyway, and now she said she wouldn't have to worry about consuming it all on her own later that night in front of an old movie.

What Carter didn't tell her was that he'd be picking her up in the classic Chevy Corvette passed down to him from his grandfather because he always loved tinkering with it.

She felt her jaw go slack as he approached, and then she laughed, long before he'd pulled to a stop and climbed out of the driver's seat, just like he had a hundred times before on their dates.

The image hit her hard and fast before she could brace herself for it. And just for a moment, she felt all that same anticipation—and something else too. Something that, if she didn't know better, felt an awful lot like love.

"I feel like I'm a teenager," she said. "You *look* like a teenager."

"And you look beautiful," he said.

She felt her smile slip, and she looked down at her breezy floral sundress that skimmed her knees, at her beige leather sandals that matched her bag.

"I can't believe this thing still runs," she said, coming down the stairs. She kept her eyes on the car and off the handsome man who didn't seem to look away, no matter how much a part of her wanted him to.

"I only take it out sometimes, for special occasions." He winked and opened the passenger door. "My lady."

My lady. She'd forgotten that. He always said that in jest when he opened the door, and she always smiled, because how could she not?

He cranked up the radio and rolled down the windows (the car had never had air-conditioning, and apparently the heat had gone out recently too), and by the time they arrived at the Maxwell home, Leah's hair was officially windblown.

"I should have brought a brush." She rummaged through her bag, but Carter was already popping the locks.

"You're fine. Besides, this is family."

Family. And the implication was that she was a part of it—or had been, once.

That little knot in her stomach reappeared, that nagging thought that every attempt she'd ever made to have a proper family had somehow blown up in her face, or gotten lost along the way, or slipped through her grasp no matter how tight she held on.

She carefully picked up Emma's cake from her lap while Carter pulled the flowers from the trunk, and they walked up the flagstone path toward the navy door adorned with a brass knocker and a simple white floral wreath.

Through the windows, the house seemed to glow, but if she knew the Maxwells, they'd be outside on their back patio, lit by cozy lanterns and overhead strings of light. There'd be wine and laughter and teasing and singing before Carter's mother blew out the candles.

It would be a picture-perfect night.

But what did it mean? And where could it ever go?

Dinner was simple but delicious and prepared by Sarah so her mother didn't have to cook on her birthday. The conversation was light and easy, like it had always been. By the time the cake was brought out, Leah had consumed two glasses of wine, shown the Maxwells at least a dozen pictures of her daughters, and felt herself almost wishing the night would never end.

"Look at this cake!" Mrs. Maxwell exclaimed when Sarah carried it out on a plate. Two round tiers were frosted in white with a wreath of buttercream flowers in pastel colors.

"I can't take the credit," Leah confessed. "My sister made it."

"Emma is so talented. I've always encouraged her to do something with her skills instead of just keeping it a hobby forever." Sarah carefully set the cake in front of her mother, and the entire table stopped to admire it.

Leah grew quiet, thinking of their conversation the night before. Was this what her sister wanted? It was so obvious, but somehow Leah had been too caught up in her own life, her own problems, to realize that her sisters had some of their own—ones that, like her, they had kept to themselves.

"Let's light the candles," Mr. Maxwell said, already starting the task. After they'd sung, he wrapped an arm over his wife's shoulder. "Now make a wish."

Mrs. Maxwell glanced at Sarah, but her gaze lingered on Carter for a moment before she sucked in a breath and blew out every last candle on the cake.

"That means your wish came true," Sarah announced, handing out dessert plates.

"I hope so," Mrs. Maxwell said mysteriously.

After, when they had said their goodbyes and were walking around the side of the house and through the garden gate, Leah decided to voice her suspicion.

"Do you think your mother's birthday wish had something to do with you?"

Carter's hands were in his pockets, his stride long, his shirtsleeves rolled to the elbows. "That would be just like her."

"I understand. Once I had Chloe, every dream and wish I had for myself became about her happiness." She glanced at him, taking in the wavy brown hair, the strong profile. "I wonder what your mother thinks will make you happy?"

"Well, a grandchild is my bet," he said with a laugh. "And since I'm the oldest and Sarah's love life is pretty nonexistent these days, she's probably placing her bets—or hopes—on me." He jutted his chin toward the small pond at the end of his road where they'd used to sneak away for some quiet time when they were teenagers. "Want to take a walk before you head home?"

Home was technically her house in Chicago, but she didn't correct him. And she didn't turn him down either.

"Sure." But her heart was starting to speed up.

Leah didn't know what she was doing today any more than she knew what she was going to do about tomorrow, or next week, or next month. It didn't matter that she was in her midthirties and there was no one telling her what to do anymore—that it was all on her. That she was supposed to have answers that she didn't.

She was alone. With Carter. Not for the first time since coming back to this town.

And worse was that she was enjoying herself. She couldn't blame the wine—she hadn't had enough to lose her better judgment. No, she could only blame herself for not being able to keep that wall up. For letting him chip away at it, bit by bit, with each grin, with each story, with each laugh.

"Tonight was fun. Being around everyone again. I haven't laughed like this in a long time," she admitted now, as they walked down the quiet street.

"I haven't either," Carter said.

She looked at him suspiciously, not sure she believed it. "I was unhappily married for years. What's your excuse?"

He didn't meet her eyes when he shrugged. "Loneliness."

She considered that for a moment. Only now, being in his company again, being in this town again, tapped into a part of herself that she had denied all this time, did she feel whole.

"You can be with someone and still be lonely," she said. It had been that way with Ted, even if she hadn't realized it at the time. She'd been too caught up in parenting responsibilities, too tired at the end of every long day, to give much thought to what was missing.

Now, though, she knew that so much was.

"You sure can," Carter said slowly.

She frowned now, wondering what he was getting at, thinking back on the conversations they'd had, filling each other in on everything they'd been up to all these years, carefully leaving out the parts of the past that overshadowed this new relationship they were building.

Because that's what it felt like. Even though Leah didn't have a clue what she expected to come of it.

Closure. That had been the plan. But like all the other times, it had morphed into something else, taking on a life of its own.

"You said you had some serious relationships," she said.

"Some were more serious than others," he replied. "But in the end, here I stand. I'm in my midthirties, and I'm alone. Spending a summer evening with my first girlfriend."

First girlfriend. Not *only girlfriend.* But then, what could she expect?

She felt his eyes on her, and she glanced up and then away, feeling nervous in his company even though she'd spent hundreds of days with him before. Thousands, even.

"So why didn't any of them work out? Your relationships, I mean?" she asked, stepping away to create a little space.

He mulled that question over. "It's complicated. But I don't need to tell you that."

No, he didn't.

"There was one relationship that lasted awhile. But . . . in the end, it ended."

She couldn't help but laugh when she caught his smile, visible in the moonlight. "You don't mince words."

"It's that simple, though, isn't it?"

"Sometimes," she said. Because sometimes, like now, it felt very complicated. "But marriage is a big step. And it's no guarantee either."

"For happiness?"

"Or for anything," she said. But she frowned now, thinking that happiness hadn't even been on her mind. She hadn't considered that emotion—however simple or complex it was. She was thinking about other things: promises, trust, security.

Now she wondered when she had stopped being happy. And worse, when she'd stopped trying to be happy.

Carter looked up. "Storm's coming in. I suppose we should call it a night."

If Emma were here, she'd say that was Viv, high above, sending a message. End the night. Leave before things get even more complicated than they already felt. Before she put her heart over her good sense.

They walked back to the car, and Carter opened the door for her. This time he didn't say his usual line, and she got the sense that, like her, he was still feeling out the situation. That he didn't want to push it.

That their past still lingered between them, much as she wished it didn't.

"I forgot that I need to grab a file from my father for work. I'll be right back."

She watched as he hurried to the front door and knocked instead of letting himself inside, reminding her that this wasn't where he lived anymore, that he'd grown up and moved on, just like she had.

Leah watched him out the window for a moment, chatting and laughing with his dad.

She sneezed, twice in a row, from all the pollen the rain was stirring up and rummaged through her handbag for a tissue, thinking that if she were back in Chicago with her girls, she'd be carrying around her giant tote filled with everything from bandages to tissues to the free lollipops she picked up at the car wash, even though Chloe now claimed they were for babies.

Instead, she'd borrowed one of Viv's vintage clutches, and the only thing it contained was a tube of lipstick and her cell phone.

She sneezed again, and this time she opened the glove box, her heart squeezing hard when she saw the navy velvet box under the stack of vehicle papers.

She glanced through the window to check that Carter was still chatting with his father.

She reached her hand inside and pulled out the box, knowing what it was before she even lifted the top. It was a ring. A diamond ring. A round solitaire on a simple white gold band.

She snapped the ring box closed and shoved it back under the papers, then slammed the glove compartment shut.

Her heart was still pounding when Carter opened the door and eased into the driver's seat. He gave her a grin, but his brow furrowed.

"Everything okay?"

"Of course," she quipped, even though everything was far from fine.

"You sure?"

There were few things she was sure of, and this certainly wasn't one of them.

She managed a smile. "Just tired. We've been doing so much work on the house. It'll be an early night for me."

A flicker of disappointment crossed his face, but Carter nodded and started the car.

Leah turned up the radio even though she hated the song that was playing, but she was afraid to say anything more. Blood was rushing in her ears, and she felt shaky and unsure of herself.

Carter had a ring box in his car. He was planning on proposing to someone.

Right when she'd started to fall in love with him again.

Sure enough, the rain had started by the time they reached the old house, and the porch light flickered invitingly. Leah managed a tight smile before opening the car door, grateful for the rain and an excuse to dash quickly inside, no need for a drawn-out goodbye or an explanation.

Leslie's words echoed in her mind as she set her shoes on the mat in the vestibule to dry. "I had the impression that he had feelings for someone else."

Then she flitted to what Carter had said about the long-term relationship he'd had.

Of course. It made sense. Carter was in his midthirties. Most people their age had settled down by now. Married.

Like she had.

Only now she was getting divorced. Starting over. But she didn't feel like she was moving forward.

The house was quiet and dark from the gathering clouds outside. Leah watched through the big bay window as a flash of lightning cut across the bay. She waited a few seconds for the roll of thunder to gauge how close the storm was.

Close, she realized when it came quickly.

Following the light into the kitchen, she saw Emma standing alone at the big island, a glass of wine beside her, a recipe book open next to canisters of sugar and flour.

"Baking?" It felt like a rhetorical question, but it was easier than thinking about her own problems.

Emma gave her a small smile. "Not tonight."

"Don't tell me you're still thinking about that guy," Leah said, even though she suspected this to be the case.

Emma's look was withering. "Wyatt. No. Well, yes. In a way. I guess I was just thinking that now that I know where I stand, and now that you know how I feel, I have no reason to stay here. And that feels . . ."

"Scary?" Leah ventured.

Emma scrunched up her nose. "Sad."

Leah nodded and took out a wineglass, pouring herself pinot from the bottle. Sully jumped out of her way when she scooted out the counter stool beside her sister and settled in for a chat.

"There's a lot of sadness in moving on. You can't really move on without letting something go."

"Is that how you feel? About Ted?"

About Ted. Once, about this house.

"I wasn't happy with Ted. I know that now. But somehow holding on to what you know is easier." She shook her head, brushing away a tear before it could fall. "It just seemed easier than being honest with myself."

"I understand," said a voice from behind her.

Leah turned on the stool to see Sadie standing in the doorway to the room, looking chagrined at being there.

"Sorry. I didn't mean to overhear."

"It's your house, too," Leah replied.

"Is it, though?" Sadie asked, coming into the room.

"What's that supposed to mean?" Emma asked.

Sadie shrugged and then took another wineglass down from the shelf. "Just that this was Viv's house. And we only came to live here because of what happened. Even though Mom grew up here, there was no trace of her anywhere. I used to look."

"I did too," Leah said quietly.

Sadie seemed to hesitate, but Emma jumped in, rising to Viv's defense. "But Viv loved us. You know that."

Leah and Sadie locked eyes briefly. Yes, they did know that. But Leah also knew that it hadn't been as easy for them as it had for Emma.

"So what haven't you been honest with yourself about?" Leah asked Sadie, even though part of her didn't want to know. Or care. The hard truth was that she did care. And that was why everything still hurt so much when it came to her sister.

"A lot of things. Mostly that I'm not happy in New York. I have to make a change. I just don't know how." She blinked a few times, and for a moment Leah thought she actually might cry, but then she guzzled down her wine and poured another glass. "I'm getting too old to not know where my life is headed."

Leah caught Emma's shocked expression and burst out laughing. Emma didn't take long to follow.

Even Sadie managed to crack a grin.

"You know what Viv would say about this?" Emma said after she stood up and pulled another bottle of wine from the fridge. "That just means we have more to look forward to."

"I'll toast to that," Leah said because she wanted to believe it so badly. Even if she didn't just yet.

She raised her glass to her sisters, and then all clinked with enthusiasm. It was a wish, perhaps, or a hope. Or an unspoken promise.

And maybe, just maybe, Emma was onto something. And Viv was looking down on them. And for the second time in their lives, she'd find a way to make everything be okay.

CHAPTER
TWENTY-THREE
SADIE

Sadie hadn't seen Jimmy since the day he'd driven her out to his house—
not that she was especially looking for him when she came and went
from the house or glanced out the windows that looked out onto his
property.

She wasn't even looking for him when she collected her bag and
went into town, having no real purpose other than a need she couldn't
explain.

It was dumb, really. She could go over, knock on the door, around
dinnertime or afterward. She didn't need an excuse, except that for some
reason, she felt like she did.

Something had shifted between them, more than distance or the
passing of time.

So it wasn't with any hope that she set off into town under the
self-told excuse that she needed to work on her novel since it was the
only thing in life she had going for her, knowing it was lunchtime and
Jimmy might very likely be taking a break at one of the many cafés that
edged the shoreline.

Half an hour of wandering, a quick bite to stave off her grumbling stomach, and a strange sense of disappointment later, she was almost ready to give up when she saw Linda Price waving to her from the next corner.

"Sadie!" Linda beamed as Sadie approached, her eyes flicking, wondering if Jimmy was around. But of course, Jimmy would be at work.

"I keep hoping you'll come by for dinner one night. I'd have stopped by more, but I didn't want to intrude."

Sadie gave the woman a mild smile. "You wouldn't be intruding. I'm sure my sisters would welcome the company."

"So you're all getting along?" Linda looked worried, but before Sadie could answer, she added, "I know how hard it was for her, keeping that house up all on her own. How happy she was when you girls came to join her and add a little life to its walls. Sad circumstances sometimes bring about the most unexpected surprises."

Sadie considered those words. If their parents hadn't died, she probably never would have even met Viv. And why was that, exactly? Why hadn't their mother ever mentioned the house or even this town?

With a sinking feeling, she realized that all this time she'd held Viv responsible, assumed her aunt was at fault for something, when all along, her mother had been hiding the truth too. But why?

She glanced around, this time for one of her sisters, who could easily be out shopping or just enjoying the day, and said, "My aunt never talked about my mother. And my mother never told us about her. We didn't know anything about this town or the house before we came to live here."

Linda looked sad when she nodded. "Family rifts. Seems to run in that house."

Sadie pressed down on her lips. There was no use getting all defensive when the truth was pretty black and white. And everyone knew every dirty detail of what had happened between her and Carter fifteen years ago.

But they didn't know how she felt. Or why she'd done it.

"You have time for a coffee?" Linda surprised her by asking. They'd never been alone before. In the past, Jimmy had always been a buffer, and in the past, Linda had always been the adult looming in the background, gracing them with smiles and offers of milk and cookies.

But now Sadie was an adult. And it was time to start acting like one.

She nodded, and they went into the bookstore café, a little nook where they wouldn't be interrupted, and certainly not on a sunny summer day when everyone else was outside.

They placed their orders and sat at a small iron table. Linda seemed to collect herself while she stirred in cream and sugar, and then more cream and sugar.

"One of my vices," she said with a wink.

Sadie gave a wan smile. "We all have them."

Some just worse than others.

Linda eventually set down her spoon and sighed. "Now that Viv's gone, I suppose that I'm not betraying her by telling you about your mother. It was a sore spot with Viv, you know."

"Oh, I know." But Sadie's heart was starting to pound, and she was wondering if this was such a good idea, if she really wanted to know about something that had happened and couldn't be changed. Her mother was gone, and now her aunt was too.

But then she thought of the picture. Of that house that bore no other evidence that her mother had ever lived there, and she knew that she had to know the truth once and for all.

And this might be her only chance.

"Your aunt was a lot older than your mother, and oh, your mother was the apple of her eye."

"She was?" Sadie was surprised by this, even though it did make sense, regarding the photo.

"Oh, she adored that child!" Linda's smile was wistful as she looked off into the distance, through the window, as if she could look back to a time and place before Sadie had ever come along. "She would dress her up in bows and parade her all over town. Everywhere Viv went, your mother came. And that's how Viv liked it."

"So what happened?" Sadie frowned, wondering how things could have changed.

Linda raised an eyebrow. "What do you think? A man is what happened, dear. Isn't that what always drives people apart? Love. Ironically."

"But Viv was so much older than my mother . . ."

"She was, but by the time your mother was eighteen, she had the attention of a lot of boys in town. Your aunt had started seeing this guy. His family was renting a house in Sister Bay for the summer. He was two years younger than her, which was a bit unusual at the time, but your aunt was so young and radiant." Linda paused. "But then, you know Viv. She was . . . captivating. She could charm anyone with a laugh and a smile."

Her eyes misted over for a second, and she stopped to sip her coffee.

"But your mother was . . . well, she was beautiful. Not to say that Viv wasn't, but your mother was something special."

"Let me guess." Sadie groaned. "Viv's boyfriend dumped her for my mother?"

"He proposed to her, darling. Two weeks after cutting things off with Viv. Your aunt never saw it coming. As the people in town would say, her tears hadn't even dried. And worse was that she heard he'd bought a ring. She just didn't know who it was for." Linda raised her eyebrows. "I still feel sad knowing that she held out hope that it was for her."

"My mom never told her she was seeing him?" Sadie blinked, trying to picture the woman she barely knew, of whom her only memories consisted of trips to the mall for back-to-school clothes, or making lunches every morning and tucking them into brown paper bags, sometimes with little notes, ones that made Sadie always feel a little embarrassed when she was in the cafeteria, but notes she'd kept anyway because she couldn't live with herself if she threw them away.

Now she wondered where those notes were. And how she could have ever let them fade away, forgotten or lost.

"Your mother never wanted to hurt your aunt. She looked up to her. I think she hoped that in time, Viv would come to understand. Love can be unfair. Cruel, even. But powerful. And your mother . . . she was madly in love with your father. And he was with her."

"My father?" Sadie blinked. She pulled up an image of her tall, lanky father with the broad grin and gray eyes that crinkled at the corners when he laughed. He had always been laughing. Always . . . happy. Even after he'd gone and broken Vivian's heart.

Linda nodded. "Those two were meant to be. But Viv, well, I think she saw it as her last chance. And after that, I think she was afraid to trust again. She'd lost her boyfriend. And her sister."

Sadie grew quiet. All she could do was nod.

When she finally felt she could speak, she said, "So my parents eloped." She knew that much; her mother had told her anytime they'd asked to see wedding pictures.

"Just about broke your grandparents' hearts, but I think they understood. Viv never spoke about it, and we all knew better than to mention it. Even when you girls came along."

"I can't imagine what Viv thought when she found out about us."

Now Linda leaned across the table and took her hand. "Never saw the woman cry so hard in her life, not even after your father broke her heart."

"Because she missed my mother?" Sadie stared into Linda's kind eyes.

"Because she had a second chance."

A second chance.

"Thank you, Linda." Sadie stood and followed the woman out onto the sidewalk. All around them were people going about their days seemingly without a care, licking ice cream, chatting about the temperature of the water, and discussing their plans for the day. She gave Linda one more smile, this time of gratitude. "And . . . tell Jimmy I said hi."

Sadie walked away, away from town, and farther around the bay and past the forest preserve. She was used to walking, and she realized now how much she had missed it, how she was eager to be engulfed by a crowd in the next town over, even though it paled in comparison to the streets of New York, where she could get lost in her thoughts, lonely but never really alone.

Here, it was the opposite. She could walk alone, but that feeling of anonymity was gone, replaced with the sense that here people knew her, and not just her name but her story.

The good and the bad parts. And that was the struggle.

Most of the shops on Main Street in Fish Creek catered to tourists. There were gift shops selling everything from hand-painted teacups and matching saucers to stationery to personalized signs. Several boutiques offered merchandise focusing on lake life: blue-and-white-striped pillows, upscale picnic baskets, oversize beach towels, and home goods with a nautical theme.

There were clothing shops ranging from practical to designer, and art galleries featuring prints of local artists—it had always amused the girls when they were younger to spot their own home in some of the renderings.

Now, on a whim, Sadie went inside the next art shop, giving a nod to the shop owner, whom she mercifully didn't recognize. She flicked through the matted prints, many the same copies that she had seen in the windows, some a variety of the same group, all of them of Fog's Landing or the neighboring towns of Egg Harbor or Sister Bay. She moved on to the next rack, to a selection that wasn't shown on the store walls, and sure enough, halfway through the pile was a watercolor of Fog's Landing, and there, across the bay and to the left, poking out of the dense foliage, was their house.

It was one of the better renderings that she'd seen. Painted in shades of blue and green in a way that was just subdued enough to make her feel calm and just realistic enough for her to be able to name each and every building and home she saw. There was the ice cream shop and the old church. The little cottage over near the public beach that had the best waterfront location.

Her own house, of course. Or Viv's. Emma's really, now.

"Can I help you, ma'am?"

Sadie turned to look at the young woman who was staring at her from behind oversize frames that were probably considered "cool," though Sadie was too old to know. Old enough to be called *ma'am*, even though it was killing her not to correct the girl.

Aunt Viv had been a *ma'am*. Whereas Sadie was . . .

Too old to be a *miss*, she supposed. She'd been one the last time she'd been here, in this town. Young and stubborn, impulsive and overly confident, at least on the outside. The side she let show.

No one knew what was really dwelling beneath her thick skin. She kept those thoughts to the pages of the journals she had once scribbled in.

And to her conversations with Jimmy, of course.

Make that Jim, she corrected herself. Just like she was now *ma'am*.

A wash of sadness swept over her, as heavy and dark as the waves in the painting, and even though she should be pinching every penny right now, she announced firmly, "I'll take it."

Because for some reason, she couldn't part with it. Even though once, not so long ago, she couldn't have thought of ever returning.

Now, she wasn't sure it would be so easy to leave again.

Sully was the first to greet her when she returned to the house, butt wiggling and tail wagging, but it was Emma whose expression lit up when she saw the painting.

"It's just a print," Sadie said. Though with the size and the matting, it hadn't exactly come cheap. "I saw our house in it—I mean, Viv's house . . ."

"It's your house as much as mine. It's not Viv's anymore." Emma's eyes looked round when she shook her head. "It still feels weird to say that."

It did, even though Sadie wasn't sure why. She'd left this house fifteen years ago and never really considered returning. And maybe she never would have either. She didn't feel she had any claim to it, not when she'd made the choice to let it go.

Not when she'd never called it her own.

Clearing her throat, she turned her attention back to the painting. "There was just something about it that spoke to me."

"May I?" Emma took it from her hands and held it at arm's length. Leah came in from the kitchen and stood behind them to admire it.

Now Sadie saw new things, even though they were old things, really. Like memories that she'd cast aside and had started to resurface. There was a boat in the water, its sails catching the breeze, and beach umbrellas in a variety of colors. There was a little dog chasing a red ball. And another, scampering after it. The entire town was there, hugging the bay, alive and happy. A typical summer day. The way many had been.

"This makes me think of all those lazy summer afternoons," Emma said, smiling. "I remember waking up in the morning and sprinting out of this house as fast as I could. It felt like every day lasted a month and every week lasted a year."

"Now all the days just get pushed together," Sadie said, frowning. The years too.

"There were a lot of good times," Leah said as she came into the room, a tone of regret in her voice that matched the heaviness in Sadie's own chest.

"This would look perfect over the mantel right here in the front room," Emma said, marching quickly across the sun-filled room. She stopped, turning to Sadie. "But I guess that you'll be bringing it home with you. To New York."

For a moment, Sadie was at a loss for words. She hadn't even considered what she'd do with the print; it was certainly too large to bring on a plane. New York hadn't even been on her mind.

Now, she realized that it hadn't been in her thoughts in days. She'd been too busy helping with the house, buried in a task that didn't just distract her but also seemed to fill her in a way that none of those other jobs in New York had ever been able to do.

"No," she said, shaking her head and forcing a smile. "You're right. It looks perfect right there. It belongs there."

Emma stepped back, and for a moment they all admired it, and for the first time since she'd arrived here, or even longer than that, Sadie felt like she'd done one thing right.

She'd contributed something to this house. Brought something back into it.

Put a smile back on her sisters' faces.

Put one on her own too.

"So, when do you think you will go back to New York?" Emma looked pleasant enough, but Sadie couldn't help but feel immediately tense.

She glanced at Leah. "I don't know. I guess when the house is finished. Or . . . when I'm not needed here anymore. There wouldn't be any reason to stay."

Technically, there wouldn't be. But she was starting to wonder what reason she had to leave.

CHAPTER
TWENTY-FOUR

LEAH

The work on the house was coming along slowly but surely. The once colorful walls were now covered in soft, soothing colors that lent themselves to the natural landscape. The faded quilts in the spare rooms had been washed and folded and tucked away in chests in the attic, replaced with crisp white duvet covers and pillows, and soft throw blankets for a bit of color. The new furniture would arrive in the coming weeks, as the finishing touch, and plans for reimagining the downstairs space to accommodate Emma's living quarters were on hold. It would save money, making it easier to pay back the loan, but the topic of who would actually run the business was yet to be discussed again.

They'd gotten good at that over the years—keeping quiet when things troubled them. But Leah didn't want to live that way anymore.

Sadie was strangely quiet about when she would leave, Emma didn't discuss the house at all, and Leah was counting down the days until her girls were back home.

Home. More and more the thought of returning to that house in the suburbs that had once been their family home, a house that she and

Ted had picked out together, a house where memories were made and promises were broken now felt like a strange concept.

They were all downstairs in the sunroom on Monday, avoiding the sounds of Brody's hammering upstairs—where he was addressing some of the loose floorboards in the hallway that the sisters had learned over time to step around without even thinking—and sipping iced tea, when Leah decided that it couldn't wait anymore.

If Emma didn't want to run the inn, they couldn't exactly make her. But then, they needed a new plan, and quick.

"We need to figure out what to do about the house," Leah said.

"It feels like we're back to the day of Vivian's funeral," Sadie said, looking displeased. "How did we get here?"

Leah didn't know if she meant *here* meaning full circle or *here* as in all three of them, sitting on the sun-faded floral chairs that were grouped around a circular ottoman. There had been a time when they liked to have tea parties in this room or curl up with a good book on rainy days when this room seemed to still manage to bring in the light.

She turned toward the large windows now, looking out over the backyard, which would need some heavy weeding soon, and onto the carriage house, a large space for two cars plus storage with another floor up above.

It was nearly a house in itself. Someone could live there. Manage the inn.

She turned away, shaking off a silly thought.

"It feels weird to let a stranger run it," Leah said.

"No, it feels just wrong. This is our family home—" Emma said.

"But it never felt that way to me," Sadie interrupted. She sighed when Leah and Emma stared at her. "It always felt like Aunt Vivian's house even though our own mother had grown up here. Mom never talked about this town or this house. Viv could have made this a family home, but she made it hers instead."

A flash of the anger Leah always remembered seeing in Sadie's eyes returned for a moment, but she quickly looked away, out the window again.

Leah glanced at Emma, who pulled a face. Sadie wasn't exactly wrong, maybe just wrong about Viv's intentions.

"She wanted us to feel like this was our home too." Emma's expression turned wistful. "Remember how she made quilts for each of us? They're still on our beds."

They were. But they wouldn't be much longer. Transforming those three bedrooms into guest rooms was the last stage of preparing the house for guests. That would be what they did on their final day before they walked out of this house and returned to their lives. To the homes they had made for themselves.

Even if they were now broken. Empty.

"She included us in everything. She gave us free rein of the place. We never had to worry about where we set a glass or if we touched something. We never had to ask permission." Emma blinked rapidly and scooped Sully onto her lap.

"It's true," Leah agreed. "But Sadie's right. It was Viv's house, not our mother's house. Even though it was really both of theirs."

Sadie looked at her in surprise for a minute and then stood up and left the room.

"Is she upset? Where do you think she's going?" Emma whispered.

Leah could only shrug. She couldn't always read her middle sister's moods, not any more now than way back then. Sadie kept her truest thoughts tucked away. She didn't like to show vulnerability. She'd rather run away than face her emotions. Even if it made things harder for her.

Leah frowned for a minute. The same could be said for herself.

A moment later, Sadie returned. She held out a piece of paper. A photograph, Leah saw.

"I found this. In a cookbook of all places. An old one. It's a photo of Vivian and Mom. I was waiting for the right time to share it."

For a moment Leah was angry that Sadie had held on to the photograph, but just as quickly, she understood. Something this big couldn't be brought out under tension or arguments. It had to be something the girls considered together. As a family.

"I never saw this!" Emma reached forward, carefully taking the picture, and Leah leaned in closer to her chair to study it. It was an old photo, faded, the color not as saturated and the picture not as clear as ones taken by more modern technology. An older girl, Viv, was standing in the kitchen, and a little girl, who looked so much like Emma it was almost shocking, was standing in front of her. Both girls were grinning, wide and happy; Viv was hugging their mother from behind, her head tipped adoringly toward her.

"I can't believe how much you look like Mom," Leah said to Emma.

Emma swallowed hard, still staring at the photograph. "I can't believe how happy they looked. What could have happened for Viv to never mention Mom again?"

"Some things hurt too much to talk about," Leah said, meeting Sadie's eyes. "But there must have been something. Because Mom never even told us she had a sister. She never told us anything about this town or her past."

"That's because she wasn't proud of it," Sadie said. With a sigh, she sat down on her chair again. "I talked to Linda. She told me everything."

Now the room went silent. Sadie knew what had happened between their mother and Viv, and she hadn't told them. Anger built in Leah's chest, hot and quick, but she tamped it down and told herself to give Sadie a chance to explain.

Something she hadn't done in the past. Something that she probably owed her.

"I just found out, and I've been waiting for the right time," Sadie explained, clearly reading their reactions. She took a deep breath and then repeated what Linda had said. When she was finished, neither Leah nor Emma moved for a few minutes.

History had repeated itself, right here in this very house. Only this time it hadn't been Viv and their mother . . . and their father. This time a sisterly bond had been broken between Leah and Sadie.

"No wonder Viv wished so much that we'd smooth things over," Leah finally remarked, shaking her head. Viv had tried so hard to convince Leah to stay, and later, to come back. Until eventually, she'd stopped asking altogether.

Leah had always assumed that Viv had finally respected her decision. Now, she saw that Viv understood it. But she didn't agree with it. Because she had known the consequences.

"She saw us as her second chance," Sadie said.

"She'd never have a chance to make things right with Mom, but she always held out hope that the two of you would find a way back to each other," Emma said slowly. "She talked about it. Not often."

"And instead we both left, leaving her here, alone."

"Well, she had me," Emma said, her cheeks turning pink. "But your absence was known. She felt it every day. Now I realize why it hurt her so badly. It touched on her losing her own sister. Long before Mom was really gone."

"But she had you," Sadie pointed out. "Like you said. And you were her favorite."

"Only because I didn't push her away!" Emma accused.

Sadie looked down at the photo. For once she didn't snap or even argue. "I blamed Viv for things I shouldn't have. I didn't understand then. I . . . wish I'd handled things differently. A lot of things," she said, looking Leah in the eye.

Leah saw the hurt pass through her gaze and looked away, back at the photo, at the two smiling sisters who didn't look like anything in the world could have ever driven them apart.

"I wish I'd handled things differently, too," Leah admitted aloud, and maybe for the first time, to herself. "I was upset. And then . . . I just moved on. My new life kept me busy."

"I don't have that excuse. I just ran away from my problems," Sadie said bitterly.

"And you stayed, Emma," Leah said quietly. "I thought it was because you wanted to be here. Now I see that we gave you no other choice."

Emma nodded. "I knew she needed me. I . . . knew that I couldn't leave her."

Leah thought of her youngest sister, who looked so very much like their mother, certainly the most of the three of them, of her bright spirit and brave smile. Of everything she'd set aside. Of everything she'd said the other night.

"I never wanted you to feel trapped here," Leah said.

"I know that," Emma said. "And I didn't always, just . . . sometimes. Sometimes I wanted the opportunity to decide for myself what I wanted, instead of feeling like I didn't have a choice."

"Well, you have a choice now," Leah said.

Emma's eyes went round. "What do you mean?"

Leah knew that she couldn't go back and fix things any more than Viv could go back and fix things with their mother. But that didn't mean she couldn't make things right going forward.

"I mean that I'd like to take over the inn." Her heart was beating with such force that she wasn't sure if it was telling her she was wrong or she was right. It wasn't impulse, though. No, as soon as she said it she knew that it had been in her mind all along, like a dream that she didn't quite dare to reach for, like the last hope of getting things right. Now, she felt more alive than she had in years. And, she realized with a smile, happier too.

"What?" Emma was staring at her with big eyes, and even Sadie looked stunned. Then Emma started shaking her head. "No, Leah. You shouldn't feel compelled to take this on. That wouldn't be fair to you."

"I'd like to run it," Leah said with more conviction. "I need a job anyway, and I think this would be perfect for me. I never got to focus on my career all these years, and I never got to spend the time here that I should have."

Emma sat up straighter. "But . . . but your girls. Won't that make things complicated with Ted?"

"Ted travels all the time anyway," Leah said. She didn't get into the details of their custody arrangement, which came down to certain weekends and large blocks of vacation time, like this past month. "And Door County is only four hours from where I live now."

Four hours. And in all these years, she'd put so much distance between herself and this town that there might as well have been an ocean between them.

"But . . . your house." Emma still looked worried. And not for the first time, Leah was going to make sure to ease that feeling for her little sister.

"I'm selling the house," Leah said. The relief she felt proved that she was making the right choice. No more bad memories. No more feeling of something missing. Her girls knew nothing of their heritage, nothing of her past. She didn't want them to be sitting around one day, learning the truth like she was now. "And selling it will only take the pressure off the situation here too. Besides, I need a fresh start. But more than that, I need a second chance. And this could be it. But only if you'd be willing to share the responsibility or pass it off to me."

"But—"

"No buts," Leah said. "No more excuses. I told you that I was selling my house. Let me invest in your dreams this time."

"But where will you live? The living quarters—"

"Didn't Brody say that he could turn that carriage house into a pretty decent house?" Leah pointed out. "Besides, it might only be temporary."

Emma looked disappointed for a fleeting moment until her mouth curved into a slow grin. "You mean, you and Carter?"

Leah brushed aside her sister's excitement. "Staying or leaving this town isn't about Carter anymore. This is my house too. All of ours."

She looked over at Sadie, but she was still staring at the photograph. "I'm sorry, Leah," she blurted, tears filling her eyes. "I'm so sorry." Leah pulled in a breath. "I know you are," she said sincerely.

Sadie shook her head. "But I need to explain. I need to make things right."

Leah didn't need to hear the reasons behind Sadie's actions fifteen years ago, not anymore. She was tired. Time had passed. And people had been lost.

She wasn't going to lose Sadie. Not again.

But she could tell by the tears that fell down Sadie's cheeks that Sadie needed to say it. And so Leah was going to listen.

"I never loved him. Not like you. It wasn't about that. Having him. Or hurting you. I never even expected you to find out. I guess . . . I didn't think of you at all."

Leah raised her eyebrows. Sadie had always been self-protective, even, at times, selfish. But admitting that was different.

"You had Carter. And"—Sadie turned to Emma—"you had Viv. And I . . . felt lost sometimes. I didn't know where I fit into this house or this town, or even into this family. And you and Carter, you had these plans for this future that you were so certain of, and then you just went and threw them away, and I guess . . . I just wanted to have that kind of certainty too. That kind of guarantee. That beautiful life that you had described."

Emma looked at Leah with the same worried crease on her forehead, and Leah could only shake her head. "I did go and throw it all away. And I regretted it."

"Do you still regret it?" Sadie asked quietly.

Leah closed her eyes for a moment and then opened them with a smile. "No. Because I have my daughters. My life took a different, unexpected path. And it was still beautiful."

"And it can be beautiful again," Emma said. "I want to believe that. For so many years, my future was all planned out for me, airtight, the days turning into years, and it . . . scared me just as much as the unknown." She reached out and took Sadie's hand, and then Leah's.

Leah looked at Sadie, sitting across from her, her eyes red, her cheeks blotchy.

"Can you ever forgive me?" Sadie asked.

"I already have," Leah said, reaching out to take her hand.

"Look at us," Sadie said with a smile. "Just like when we used to play ring-around-the-rosy."

Leah laughed at the memory. Mostly they'd played it for Emma's sake. If she closed her eyes, she could still hear the little girl's giggle echoing in her memory.

She wondered now if Viv and their mother had ever played that game. If Viv could hear her little sister's laughter in the recesses of her mind. If she had longed to go back and have that moment, however fleeting. To savor it one last time.

"There's one thing you didn't say, though, Sadie," Emma said quietly. "Sure, I was closest to Viv. And Leah and Carter were in love. But you . . . you had Jimmy!"

Sadie sniffed and brushed away a tear. "I did. I had Jimmy."

She squeezed Leah's hand, and Leah squeezed back.

Fifteen years later, they were a family again.

And they had Viv to thank for it.

CHAPTER
TWENTY-FIVE
SADIE

So there it was. Leah would stay in the house. Pass it down to her girls one day. It was fitting, of course. Sadie should be relieved that Emma hadn't looked to her to take over the responsibility, only for some reason she wasn't.

It wasn't that she wanted to run the inn. That would mean staying in this town—in the one place where she'd felt so alone and misunderstood.

But she was tired of shutting people out. Tired of being alone.

She'd hated the history that lived in Fog's Landing. But now she saw it as a story that might not be finished. One that she'd shoved under her bed without finishing, much like that old manuscript.

She'd been cleaning out her drawers all morning. Teenage clothes and random items like cheap jewelry, dog-eared young adult novels, and old movie-ticket stubs that Viv hadn't bothered to clean out in all these years.

Or maybe, chose to keep in place.

Sadie shut her bedside-table drawer. Her old belongings filled two trash bags. The room would soon be cleared of all her things. All her memories. It would be as if she had never been here at all.

With a sigh, she pulled open her laptop and skimmed the first few pages of her novel, trying to regain a connection to it and finding herself completely numb. She'd given her main character a dumb name—something that tried too hard to be special and different. Something that she'd have to change. But all that was fixable. It was the big, daunting stuff that always left her stuck. With her book. With life.

A knock on the door pulled Sadie from her thoughts.

"Yes?"

She expected to see Emma, but instead, it was Leah who opened the door and then closed it behind herself.

Sadie felt a flicker of dread. They'd made it this far without killing each other. She'd probably be gone within the next couple of days. A one-way ticket to Manhattan. She'd stay in a cheap motel. Maybe she'd see if her old roommate would have some mercy and let her camp out on the couch until she found something else. At least a job. But she was attractive enough, and she certainly had a long résumé. There were a million restaurants in New York. She'd find something.

She always did.

But the truce they'd made yesterday had stuck, and now Leah looked at her with the truest smile that Sadie had seen since they'd first returned to this old rambling house.

"Sorry, are you working on something?"

Sadie's first thought was to lie. To shield herself from the same reaction she'd received from Neil. From her roommate. From herself most days. She could say she was job searching, which is what she really should have been doing.

But she was tired of keeping everything to herself. Tired of never having anyone to share the hard stuff with. Or the good times.

"It's this novel I've been working on." For so many years she had lost count. "But . . . it's not working. I can't seem to finish it."

"Can I see?" Leah looked so interested as she crossed the room that Sadie saw no choice but to hand over the laptop and then clench her fists while Leah settled onto the end of the bed and read to herself for a few minutes.

Leah laughed a few times, smiled some more, and then looked up at Sadie with wonder in her eyes. "You're really good!"

"You think so?" Sadie blurted. But then, sobering, she said, "You probably have to say that. You're my sister."

Leah gave her a knowing look. One that actually pulled a smile from Sadie.

"This is good. I mean, it's exciting. And fun. Why don't you think you can finish it?"

Good question. And one that Sadie couldn't answer, or hadn't, until now.

"I guess it's because it's just how I am. I don't stick with anything. I don't commit to things. It's . . . easier that way."

Leah looked at her thoughtfully for a moment and then handed back the laptop. "I don't think you're being honest with yourself."

Sadie closed the laptop. There was truth in those words. Spoken by the person who had once known her best. And maybe still did.

"You're a great writer, Sadie. You always were. Even when you would scribble those little stories in school." Leah smiled fondly. "But this book . . . while good, is another escape. Maybe that's why you can't finish it. Or stick with those other things. Jobs. People. Places. Because it's not really you. You're not being yourself."

Sadie pulled in a breath and blew it out quickly. "You're right," she said. She laughed because it was so obvious. "But why is it so hard?"

"I guess because when you're true to yourself and you really put yourself out there for what you really want and what will make you the happiest, there's always that fear that it won't work out."

"You have that too?" Sadie stared at her sister.

"Of course. It's not easy going after what you want most in life. But . . . what's the alternative?"

Sadie nodded slowly. "Can I ask you something? What made you decide to forgive me? Was it Viv being gone?"

Leah sighed. "Honestly, I think it was thinking about my own girls. It would kill me if they went for fifteen years without talking to each other. Or longer. I don't want us to end up like Mom and Aunt Vivian. I want my girls to know this house. But I also want them to know their aunt."

Sadie gave a little smile. "I'd like that too." She looked up to see Emma standing in the doorway, as if she was afraid to interrupt.

"It's fine," she said, smiling widely. "There's room on the bed for all of us."

Emma grinned and quickly joined them, tucking her legs up under herself so she could face them both.

"It's strange to think that this might be one of the last times we all sit in here together like this," Emma mused. "It's even stranger to think of guests sleeping in these rooms that were ours for so long."

Sadie nodded. The house had been all of theirs all along. It was theirs to share. To love. To live in. To do with as they pleased.

And what they could all agree on was that they wanted to preserve it. The sordid history and all.

It wasn't until Sadie had time to think about this that she knew that this was what she'd wanted all along, even when she'd fought against it, told herself that this wasn't her town or her home or her roots. She'd pushed away the things she loved most. The people too.

But now she wanted to fight for something else.

"I'd like to help out," she said, feeling a little breathless. "Maybe run the front desk."

The room fell silent as her sisters stared at her. For one terrifying moment, Sadie thought they might say no, they had it covered. She'd turned her back on this place; what did she expect?

Finally, it was Leah who spoke. "You mean you want to stay in Fog's Landing?"

"It's my home," Sadie said at long last. It didn't feel as strange as she had thought it would. It felt . . . good. "It's taken me a long time to see that, and now that I've found it, I don't want to lose it again."

Her heart was hammering, waiting to see what Leah would say, if she'd open the door or close it again.

But Leah just smiled and said, "This is your home for as long as you want it to be."

Sadie felt the weight she'd carried on her shoulders for so long finally roll away. Leah had given her permission to not move on but stay.

And she'd given herself the permission to finally embrace what she needed most in life. What she wanted. What she loved.

It wasn't difficult to find Jimmy, and not because he lived next door. His office was in town, not far from the bank, and there was a handy bench outside shaded by the boughs of a large maple.

Sadie planted herself on it that afternoon, and while she waited, she thought about the plans for her book. Her new book. The story of her heart.

She was so engrossed in her notes that she stopped checking her watch, and she startled when she felt someone drop onto the bench beside her, reminding her that there was another world, all around her.

"Jimmy!" She blinked, then, correcting herself, said, "Jim. I . . . I was waiting for you."

"You were hard at work. I was almost afraid to interrupt you." He pointed to the notebook in her hand.

"It's an idea I had. For a story." About three girls. Sisters. Whose lives all turned out okay in the end. Maybe even for the better. "It's from the viewpoint of a house that has witnessed a lot over the years." She grinned, excited about the idea. "I guess you could say I've been inspired."

He was nodding, grinning at her, his eyes roving around her face in a way that made her set aside the notebook and her thoughts and put all her focus on him.

"Can we take a walk?" she asked, motioning to the path leading down toward the waterfront.

Jimmy hesitated for a minute and then stood. "Sure. We're going the same way anyway."

Going the same way. Sadie tucked her notebook and pen into her bag and stood, hoping that he was right. That they were done drifting apart, going their separate ways.

"How's the house coming along?" he asked as they stepped aside from larger rocks and reached the sandy shore. The question was pleasant, conversational, but stiff. And there was a tension in his tone that she didn't like any more than the way he struggled to meet her eyes.

"Fine. Should be done soon enough. Leah and Emma and I have been doing the painting, and Brody's been fixing things up. The big project will be the carriage house. But the bigger news is that Leah's going to move into it with her girls. Turns out that she never mentioned she was divorced."

Now he looked at her in surprise. "She never told you?"

Sadie gave him a knowing look. "We didn't tell each other a lot of things. But all that's changed now. A lot has changed."

He nodded slowly, giving her a sad smile. "I'm happy to hear that, Sadie. You needed that closure."

She did. Even though she hadn't even known it until now.

"So I guess there's nothing left for you to do here?" Jimmy picked up a stone and tossed it into the water.

"Not specifically, no." But there was nothing more for her to do in New York either. At least here, she had a purpose.

"So I take it that you'll be heading out soon?" His voice sounded strained, even forced, and he didn't look her in the eye, even though she was still staring at him.

"I'm not going back to New York. There's nothing for me there." There never was, she thought. She was chasing something she'd never find.

"And here?" He stopped walking and turned to face her, his eyes questioning, wary. "You swore you'd never come back here."

"What can I say? I grew up." She grinned at him.

"So what are you going to do?"

She shrugged. "I'll help Leah with the inn. Get to know my nieces. Catch my breath a bit." Just saying it now was a weight off her shoulders. For the first time since she was a child, she felt hopeful.

So hopeful that she wasn't so sure she was ready to let it go just yet.

But then she thought of what Leah had said. And she thought of the alternative.

She stared at Jimmy—make that Jim. At the man he had become, with his broad shoulders and square jaw, the lines around his eyes and mouth that gave him character, created by each laugh and smile, moments that she'd shared.

"In New York, I was always running. Chasing something, and I never knew what. I kept reaching for the next thing, whatever came along. Some might call it hustling, but looking back, I was drowning. Desperate, even. And it's only since I've been back here that I realize how unhappy I was, how I could never find what I was looking for. At least not there."

"I'm exhausted just thinking about it." Jimmy grinned, easing whatever tension remained between them. But as he stepped forward, his brow pinched. "You'd be happy here, though? In this sleepy little town? It's not very exciting."

"Exciting is overrated," Sadie said. "I've had enough for one lifetime. What I want now is . . ."

She stopped, swallowing hard, realizing that she'd never dared to articulate what it was she truly wanted. Because she'd never really known. Until now.

"This," she said, feeling the breath leave her body. A smile stretched on her face, and she blinked back tears that she didn't try to fight. Tears of relief. And happiness.

"I want this. I want to wake up every day to the sun and the breeze off the lake, and I want to walk down the street and wave to people I've known most of my life. I want people to know my name. I want to come home to my family, to a house that I know and I love. One that's filled with memories, even the bad ones. I want a purpose that isn't just about how to pay for the monthly rent but to know that my life is filled with people and history. And you."

She looked up at him, feeling her heart banging in her chest, so hard that for a moment she wondered if he could hear it too. This was it: it was all out there, everything on the line. It might work out; it might not. Either way, she'd be okay.

She had her sisters waiting for her back at the house. A bed with a quilt on it that had been made by her aunt, who had taken her in and loved her, who had found a way to move on and fill her heart, even after it had been broken.

And she could too. If she had to.

"Jimmy—" She stopped herself, shaking her head. "Sorry, I mean Jim."

But he just shook his head as a slow smile tugged at the corner of his mouth. "It's Jimmy to you. It always was. Always will be."

Jimmy. She didn't know if she said it or thought it, but she just knew that it would all be okay. That he understood, just like he always did. He got her in a way that others didn't, stood by her even longer, and knew her even when years lapsed, filled only with silence and memories that she'd forgotten.

And when he reached out and took her hands, she didn't push him off; she held on tighter. Because she was finally running toward her future. Which had been right here, in her past, all along.

"Are you going to make me wait to kiss you?" he asked with a lopsided grin.

She laughed and tipped her chin up to him. "We've waited long enough."

CHAPTER TWENTY-SIX

EMMA

Both her sisters would be staying in Fog's Landing. It didn't seem possible. It didn't feel real. And all Emma could think about was how happy this would make Viv.

And what a shame it was that she didn't even know it.

Emma hooked Sully's lead to his collar. It was a cooler day, perfect for a long walk, and Emma needed to get out of that house, at least for a while. Only this time she wasn't hiding from her sisters or feeling stir crazy. This time she wanted to walk around this town and enjoy it with fresh eyes. Think about how her mother had walked in these very steps.

The mother she looked so much like.

Was that why she had always had such a special bond with her aunt? She'd never know for sure, but she wouldn't change it either. Viv had been her family. Was her family. As much as her mother had been.

And still was, she thought, looking up to the cloudless blue sky.

Sully let out a yip and quickened his pace, something that she knew she needed to get under control because technically she was supposed to be walking him, not the other way around.

She halted when she saw a tall man with dark hair walking in her direction.

"Wyatt." She hadn't seen him since their awful conversation at the café, but now she realized she hadn't properly talked to him since before Viv died. Once there had been a time when he knew every detail of her life because she was willing to share it.

Now she stopped herself, wondering when he stopped asking.

And when she stopped caring.

"Emma!" He looked so happy to see her that she could only frown where once she would have all but swooned.

Her smile felt tense as he approached, oblivious to her feelings.

She could almost hear Vivian snort.

Now, Emma stared at him as he came near. He still had the same wide grin, those same sparkling eyes, that hair that she'd once dreamed of raking her hands through.

But for some reason, she no longer felt anything. He was a good-looking guy. Probably he knew it too. He'd been a friend to her at times when she needed one the most.

But he'd been oblivious to her feelings. And how much he'd hurt her.

"How's my boy?" Wyatt stooped down to scratch Sully behind the ears, and Sully gladly accepted the affection.

Now Emma stifled an eye roll. She felt like how Aunt Viv must have every time Emma got a hop in her step after receiving a text from the man who was now grinning up at her as if everything between them was just fine.

As if they could just carry on as if she hadn't laid her heart on the line. Given it away.

Wasted it on someone who only ever saw her as a friend and could never be anything more than that.

But was that even a friend? Emma wasn't so sure.

"I haven't seen you around!" he exclaimed, rising to stand in front of her. She'd forgotten how tall he was. In time, she'd forget more. But for now, she had also completely forgotten how her heart used to speed up at the mere sound of his voice. The mention of his name.

No, she hadn't reached out, and he hadn't either, but maybe that was for the best.

More like definitely for the best, she told herself. She tightened her hold on Sully's lead.

"I've been busy. My sisters and I have been fixing up the house. We're opening an inn, hopefully by September."

They'd finally agreed on that, and not just because they had made so much progress on the house. Their futures were becoming clearer now that they'd opened up to each other.

And been honest with themselves.

"An inn!" Wyatt looked so surprised that for a moment, Emma felt sad at the distance that had grown between them. But then she thought of Sarah, her true friend. And her sisters.

Her best friends. The ones who had her back, supported her dreams, and in the end, never let her down.

"I'm headed over to the pub to get a band set up," Wyatt said. He tipped his head. "Maybe we can hang out after."

Hang out. How she'd come to loathe that term long before she understood its meaning. It was vague, noncommittal, like Wyatt himself.

"Maybe," she said, equally vague.

Wyatt frowned. "Nothing has to change between us, Emma."

"But it does," she said, firmly but not unkindly. "You're getting married. You're going to be a father. Your entire life is changing."

But so was hers. In more ways than she could even think about right now, and certainly more than she cared to share. In time, Wyatt would find out her plan and what she'd decided to do with her life. In time, they might even be friends. But not now. Right now, Emma had other things that needed her attention. And other people who needed her time.

"I should go. Sully needs a good long walk, and I promised my sisters I'd be back by dinner." They were all cooking today. And she didn't mind sharing the kitchen.

"I'll see you around, Emma," Wyatt said, a little sadly.

Emma looked at him for a moment, thinking of how undefined that comment was, how she'd lived like that for too many years, hanging on his words, reading into the subtle meaning behind them, and now couldn't imagine living like that for one more day.

She was going places. Where, she didn't know. But she knew one thing for certain, and that was that Wyatt wasn't part of her plans.

He never had been.

Brody was packing up his toolbox in the kitchen when she entered the house through the back door. Sully scampered straight to his water bowl, plunging his entire face below the surface and then lapping it up happily.

"Work here is almost done!" Brody gave her a grin, but there was something hesitant in his eyes, as if he was sort of sorry to say it.

Emma understood. She'd gotten used to having him around.

Really, she liked seeing him. Talking to him. And not just because he was another dynamic in the house. She liked the way he looked at her when she talked. How she felt when she was around him. Not all swoony and jittery but relaxed, at peace. Happy.

Like herself.

"You don't look as excited as I'd expected," he remarked.

"Yes and no. Plans have changed."

"Oh?"

"My sister's going to be the one taking over the inn, actually. Leah. She's going to move here with her two daughters and live in the carriage house, like you suggested." She almost couldn't even believe what she was about to say next: "And Sadie will help out too. With the front desk."

"And what will you do?"

Emma had been asking herself the same question all night and morning, each day ever since her talk with her sisters. She had the entire world in her hands, and with Leah offering to buy her out with the proceeds of her Chicago house, she had the money to pursue anything she wanted.

"Honestly, I don't know yet. I'm still figuring that out." Still grappling with the fact that just when she was free to move away, her sisters had come back.

"At a crossroads?"

She thought about that for a minute. "More like . . . starting a new chapter."

She couldn't fight the excitement that was building up inside her, nearly as big as the apprehension of the unknown. All her life, someone had been there, guiding her, even if she didn't like having decisions made for her.

Now, she was on her own. Except that she wasn't. Her sisters might not be telling her what to do anymore, and Viv might not be leaning on her, but they were all still there in the background. In her head.

In her heart.

And even though she hadn't heard Viv's voice in a while, she felt like she could hear it now, left behind by the whispers of the wind that blew in off the water. Telling her everything she already knew, deep down.

"So if you're not going to be running the inn, I guess that means I work for your sister now, not you." He looked at her for a moment, suddenly seeming a little shy.

Emma's smile was slow. "That's true. I'm not sure who I'll bake for."

His grin broadened. "Oh, I could think of a few places. Harborview Café could do with your baked goods, for one."

Emma considered this. "That's where we met."

"See?" His eyes twinkled. But then, they always seemed to light up when they talked. "It's a lucky place. Good things happen there."

They did. And good things happened here, too, right in this house.

"Maybe you and I could actually sit down and have a coffee there next time," Brody said.

Emma looked at him. "You mean . . . like to hang out?"

His grin turned bashful. "I was thinking more like a date."

A date. Emma felt a flush rise up in her cheeks. She glanced down at Sully, who was now watching her with intense brown eyes, water dripping from half the fur on his face. She waited for a sound, a little voice in her ear that warned her to use her better judgment.

But all she heard was the pounding of her own heart. Beating in a way it hadn't in quite some time.

"That would be nice." And this time, she was pretty sure she was the one with a twinkle in her eyes.

"Yeah?" Brody's grin broadened, revealing dimples she wasn't sure she'd ever noticed before.

But then, there was a lot that she hadn't noticed. And it didn't stop with Brody.

Emma was still smiling long after Brody had left for the day with a promise to meet for coffee this Saturday at ten.

"Knock, knock." Leah poked her head around the kitchen door and grinned. "I didn't want to interrupt." She stepped farther into the room, looking pleased. "Seems like you and Brody have hit it off."

"He's a nice guy," Emma said. "And I think Viv would have approved."

Sadie came into the room and plucked an apple from the fruit bowl on the counter. "The hot contractor? Yeah, Viv would have approved. She'd have to be blind not to approve."

Emma shook her head ruefully. "It's not that he's attractive." Though he was. "He's . . . genuine. He's a guy that I think you can trust."

"I'd sure hope so! We've entrusted this house to him," Sadie said, but from the way she fought off a smile and gave Emma a little wink, it was clear that she wasn't thinking about the house at all.

"Well, the bulk of the work in the house is finished. I guess Brody will be tackling the carriage house starting next week." Leah gazed out the window over the sink.

"So you haven't rethought your decision, then?" Emma braced herself, wondering if her voice came out as tight as her chest suddenly felt.

She didn't want Leah to go back to Chicago. But not for the reasons she'd once had.

Leah turned around and smiled. "Not in the least."

"Well, I have," Emma said, letting out a breath. "I don't think I'm ready to leave."

"Nope," said Sadie. "You're going."

Leah caught Sadie's eye and grinned. "I couldn't agree more."

"But—" Emma stared from one sister to the next. Were they seriously on the same side? She didn't know whether to laugh or cry. "You're telling me what to do again?"

"Yep," Sadie said, but a smile curved her mouth. "And we're giving you the boot."

"You're kicking me out of my own house?"

Leah tipped her head. "It will always be your home, Emma. But there's a whole world out there waiting for you to discover it."

"We all set aside the things we love most for too long," Sadie said, stepping closer. "I gave up my writing. Leah gave up her passion for design. And you put your baking on the back burner to shoulder responsibility."

"I know." But Emma also knew they'd set aside the people they loved most for too long as well.

She swallowed hard and glanced over at Sully. His big brown eyes were so earnest and honest that they always brought out the same traits in her. He made her a better person.

But so had Viv. And even Wyatt. And Sarah. And her sisters.

She looked at them both now and took a deep breath, hoping that she wasn't going to regret what she was about to say but knowing that now was the time to listen to her heart. It hadn't always guided her best, and she knew better than anyone just how much it had been at war with her head, but this time, she knew it was leading her in the right direction. It was telling her what she needed to do.

And where she was meant to be.

"For a long time, that's all I wanted to do," she said. "I couldn't wait to get out, to see the world. To go to culinary school or live in France. Or New York."

Sadie gave a sad smile. "It's not all it's cracked up to be."

"I thought . . . I thought someday I'd be free. To do just that. And then Viv died."

Leah groaned. "And then we came in and dumped this inn on you."

"But it was your idea," Sadie reminded her.

"I know. I was thinking of the house. I wasn't thinking it all the way through." Emma shook her head. "I didn't want this. I thought . . . for a long time I thought that it could be enough for me to live here. With Wyatt."

Now it was Sadie who groaned, but Emma held up a hand.

"I know. I was chasing a dream with that. But not now. Now I'm not chasing anything but the future I always wanted. The future that was right here, all along. Wyatt or no Wyatt."

"What are you saying?" Leah asked, frowning.

"This is my home. And I can't imagine living anywhere else. Visiting, traveling, yes. But these walls hold our memories. The happiest and saddest ones of my life."

"But your baking—"

Emma shook her head. "Don't you see? I finally have my customers. I have my built-in audience, guests who will be staying in this very house. And I was thinking that once we get this place finished, I might walk down to the café and see if I might offer up my services to Sandra too."

"That's a fantastic idea!" Leah grinned.

"It wasn't completely mine," Emma admitted.

Sadie and Leah exchanged a knowing look. "A certain handyman?"

Emma couldn't hide her smile, but she shook her head. "That's not the reason I want to stay, if that's what you're thinking. It's just the thought of leaving this place, now that I finally have the choice . . . well, it's like there's no choice at all. This house is all we have of our past. And it's all I have of my life. It's . . . an heirloom," she said, thinking of what else Brody had said.

"An heirloom." Sadie looked at Leah, but it was Emma who scooped up Sully and grinned.

"The Heirloom Inn," Emma announced.

It was everything that Viv deserved. And everything that she would have wanted. For all of them.

CHAPTER
TWENTY-SEVEN

LEAH

The day had come to leave Fog's Landing. But this time, Leah wasn't leaving without a proper goodbye.

Emma had told her where Carter lived. It was just one of a few things about Carter that she didn't know, and she wasn't at all surprised to see that he'd bought the house they'd always walked by together, not big, but small. A little cottage down near the beachfront, the house with the best view of the water.

The house in the painting that Sadie had brought home.

Home. It was a word that had a new meaning, a word that brought a feeling that nothing else could match. A sense of comfort and joy. And security.

And above all, happiness.

Leah stood at the base of the flagstone path, staring at the cottage, thinking of Carter inside. And she was happy for him. That one thing had gone as planned. Sometimes, that was enough.

She'd thought about what she would say the entire walk over, which wasn't far enough for her to form the words. Maybe even an extra mile or ten wouldn't have been long enough. There was a lot left unsaid between the two of them. A lot that she wished she could say. And take back.

So when she started up the path and Carter came outside, she decided to start with the most obvious.

"I saw you through the window," he said, grinning. "Do you want to come inside?"

She'd never been inside the cottage before. When she was a kid, it had been owned by an elderly couple who kept to themselves. As tempting as it was, she shook her head.

"I came by because . . ." She hesitated. "Because I'm heading back to Chicago—"

The frown on his face made her stop, and she didn't even know what to say now. Where to begin. Maybe that she was happy for him. That he'd found someone he loved. Settled into the house that he'd always talked about. That it wasn't quite like he'd dreamed but almost.

Her life was almost like she'd dreamed too. In some ways worse. In many ways, better.

"Today?" he asked, coming off the stoop as she approached.

She nodded. "My girls are coming back tomorrow. It's already been a month!"

"A month." He shook his head and then pushed out a sigh. "Guess I got used to having you around. Guess this is goodbye, then."

"That's not the only reason why I stopped by," she said. "I'm going to be selling my house so I can pay off that loan sooner than expected."

For some reason, Carter didn't look as pleased by this remark as she thought he would be. Instead, he shifted his weight on his feet, scuffing a toe at the ground before looking up at her sheepishly.

"You don't have to do that."

"Well, I can," she replied. "And I want to." She looked at him quizzically. "You yourself said the interest rate was high. I thought . . ." She thought that maybe they'd reached a place where they could be happy for each other.

"You didn't qualify for a loan," Carter said firmly and then closed his eyes, groaning a little.

"What do you mean, we didn't qualify for a loan? But you said—"
Leah stopped there as understanding took hold.

"Oh my God," she whispered. "You put up the money, didn't you?"

Carter grimaced. "I didn't plan to ever tell you. I knew you'd pay it back, and even if you didn't . . ."

"But why? So you could clear your conscience?" Maybe it wasn't fair of her, but she had to know.

"Because I care about you, Leah!" Carter all but shouted. "I always did. Heck, maybe I always will. And I care about that house." He pointed to it, visible around the curve of the bay. "I care about all of you. Yes, even Sadie, but not in the way that you think. Never in that way."

She nodded. It was sensitive territory, but she knew it was true.

"I was almost a part of that family. A part of me will always feel like I was a part of it. That house has history. Our history. The bad, but the good too. Memories that I couldn't let go of."

Memories to hold on to. She nodded. She got it. But a loan from Carter?

"What if I couldn't pay it back?" she asked.

But he just smiled. "I knew you would. You're a person of your word."

"But the risk—"

"Was worth taking," he said.

"Because you believed I'd pay you back no matter what?"

"Because I believe in you. And your talent," he said. "I didn't do this because of the hotel industry or even to preserve that house. I did it because I knew you would be able to do something amazing with that old place. And because it kept you here a little longer."

She stared at him, trying to digest his words, not finding any of her own.

"I never stopped loving you, Leah," he said, staring her in the eyes.

She blinked a few times. The world around them seemed to grow quiet.

"I wanted to believe that," she said, swallowing hard.

"But it wasn't that simple," Carter said. "You broke up with me."

"So you keep saying." Leah stared at him, wondering if that was really the version of events that he had believed all these years.

Realizing that it was.

"I thought . . . I thought it was just a break. To see what we wanted."

"And what it told me was that I wanted you. You broke my heart, Leah."

Leah fought back the tears that prickled her eyes. All this time, she'd only thought of how she'd felt that night. In the days afterward.

She'd never thought of the days leading up to it.

"A break that you wanted. I would have been happy staying just as we were. Together. Forever," he added quietly.

Leah let that sink in a moment. "I hurt you."

She hadn't stopped to consider that then. She'd been too hurt herself.

"It was a long time ago," Carter said with a wan smile, but Leah shook her head.

"It was a long time ago, but it can still hurt." She knew that. Even as a married woman, even after her children were born, thinking of the circumstances that had led to her leaving Fog's Landing still had as much force as any happy memory she had with Carter. Or Sadie.

"Hurt enough to keep me away all these years. To never even bring my girls back." She shook her head, thinking of the time that she'd lost. "I didn't want them asking questions. About my past. About . . . my sisters. It became easier to just stay away."

"You regret that?" Carter asked.

She nodded. "I do. Aunt Vivian is gone now, and my girls barely knew her. She came to see us, but it wasn't the same."

Her life in Chicago was busy, consisting of school runs and after-school classes and clubs for the girls, harried dinners, and homework. There were none of those lazy, long days like Emma had spoken about. There was always something on the calendar, cutting time into sections instead of stretching it out.

There was always something to do. But was there anything to look forward to?

"That break told me that I wanted you too. That's why I came back."

He looked at her in surprise. "It never had to happen. It shouldn't have happened."

Some of it, no, but if it hadn't, she wouldn't have had her girls.

"A lot of time has passed," she said quietly. All the anger was gone, replaced by something else. Sadness, she supposed, for what might have been.

And hope for what could still be.

But then she remembered the ring.

"We've both moved on."

Carter's brow flinched, but he didn't protest.

"It's okay, Carter," she said, giving him a sad smile. "I saw the ring."

He stared at her, confusion furrowing his brow.

"In your glove box," she explained. "I needed a tissue the night of your mother's birthday, and I saw the ring box, and I looked inside." She shook her head. "It's okay. I have no room to speak. Heck, I was the one who got married. We're in our midthirties. Of course you've had serious relationships. Of course you've thought about proposing. Or plan to."

She'd made a mistake, a long time ago, letting him go like that. She just didn't know how quickly she would lose him. And how quickly she would realize that she didn't want to.

"That ring was for you," he said firmly.

Now she was the one to stare at him in question. "But . . . you haven't seen me in—"

"Fifteen years." He nodded. "Planned to drive you out to the lake-side, have a picnic, get down on one knee . . ." He shook his head. "I guess I couldn't bring myself to take it out."

Realization landed hard and deep like a rock in her stomach. Fifteen years. He'd kept that ring in his glove box for fifteen years.

"I don't drive that car much. Just a few times each summer when I need to clear my head. Eventually, that ring just became a part of the car. A part of the past, you could say."

A part of the past. Of course.

There was no reason for the disappointment that weighed heavily in her chest, but it was there all the same. A reminder of what almost was, or could have been.

"I was going to propose that night before you said we should take a break. Guess we were always on the opposite page," Carter said with a shrug.

"Maybe," Leah said, feeling her heart seize up in her chest. For the second time in her life, she was at a crossroads, only instead of taking the safe route, she could think of nothing less appealing.

"What do you mean?" Carter's gaze was wary, but there was hope in his question.

Hope that matched the swell of her chest.

"I mean I'm back now. And now there's no reason to stay away anymore."

"But you just said you were leaving," he said.

She smiled. "My girls are coming home. And I need to get it ready to sell."

"But your girls—"

"Would love it here," she said, looking him in the eye. "And our life back in Chicago is busy but . . . empty. Here the girls could have everything I had. The lake. The community. Family."

"And you? Would you be happy here?" Carter was watching her carefully, but Leah didn't need any more time to think about it.

She nodded, knowing that she'd made the right decision.

"I think it's the best chance I've got."

"A second chance," he said. "For both of us."

Leah leaned forward, letting him wrap his arms around her waist and pull her close. His kiss was soft and warm, tentative at first, but then oh so familiar.

It felt like a thousand of the kisses they'd once shared and brand new all at once.

But more than anything, it felt like home.

EPILOGUE

Today the old Victorian house on Water Street officially becomes the Heirloom Inn.

The brightly colored walls of my day are covered up, painted soothing shades of blue that draw upon the lake waters that I loved to swim in as a girl with my sister. Back then, she turned to me for everything, from teaching her those first tentative strokes to making sure I'd catch her when she jumped off the old fallen log into the cold bay. The temperature never bothered her—she was fearless, my sister. And I loved her for that spirit. It was contagious, and it lived inside me, long after she'd left Fog's Landing, long after she'd gone.

The house is full of children's laughter again. Chloe and Annie are more alike than they realize, but all that will come in good time. For now, they have to figure out their own paths and follow their own dreams, with some stumbles along the way. The move hasn't been easy for Chloe, just like it wasn't easy on Sadie, my special niece, the one I always kept a watchful eye on, even when she set her face in stone. The people here in town who knew me so well liked to say that she reminded them of me, and they were right. In Sadie, I saw something of myself. Someone whose heart had been broken. Who shut herself off from the world. Who wasn't ever ready to open that door and let someone in . . .

Until three little girls stood clutching their hands on that porch.

Now those girls are all grown and content. Leah and Carter are back together, and maybe a part of them was never really apart. There are people out there who are just meant to be. Like Lydia and the boy I once loved.

I didn't like to talk about my sister. Not because I hated her but because I loved her, and it was too late to tell her that. I regret that. And I regret not telling the girls about her, stories from when she was young. But Linda was there, and she remembers. And now that that photo has been found, the stories have started to come out. I'd forgotten about that photo, tucked away in one of the cooking books that Lydia liked best. It wasn't ever meant to be found. But then, I hadn't baked in all the years since Lydia left. It was Emma who brought me back to it. Who reminded me of what I loved the most.

It was fitting, perhaps, that the youngest of my nieces would look so much like my dear sister. The image I had of her, once just a faded memory, returned in the form of the greatest gift with the purest heart. I held on to her a little too closely for that reason, perhaps. Couldn't bear the thought of losing her a second time. And much as I knew she dreamed of other possibilities, I knew that deep down, Emma loved that house as much as I did. And that she'd take care of it long after I was gone.

There's Emma now, baking a pie in the kitchen, still trying to figure out the secret ingredient I intended to use for my festival entry this year. She'll never know for certain what it was (a squeeze of lime, just a squeeze), but she'll have fun trying and making it her own. And that handsome fellow of hers will enjoy taste-testing it.

She'll still turn to face me when she's walking that sweet pup of hers, or when the wind chimes jingle their soft song on the front porch, or when she crosses paths with that *ladies' man* who I once thought stole far too much of her time, but now I see she was biding her time until she knew where she belonged.

She doesn't need my guidance so much anymore. She's figured things out just fine on her own. But when she searches for me, I'll still be there, even if I don't always whisper the answers. She knows what I would say.

And so I watch from afar, as our family home opens its doors once more, to new visitors, new people, and eventually, new generations.

"Should we put up the sign and make it official?" Leah pokes her head into the kitchen to ask.

Brody lifts his toolbox from the counter and says he's ready. Leah calls the girls. Carter chases them into the front hall, where they are joined by Sadie and Jimmy and my dearest friend, Linda.

"It's a perfect day," Linda says now, because she, too, is thrilled by the life that has been brought back into this house, the people that have come along to fill the holes in her heart from those she has lost.

Emma scoops up her little dog and lets him lick her face, and then—oh! Oh, then he kisses her *lips*. I'm sure she thinks that pinch on my lips she imagines now was from disapproval, but it was always because I was trying to keep from bursting out laughing. Of all the girls, Emma has so much love to give, and I gave her that dog for the same reason that I gave out my money to any of my friends who needed it. Because what is life without love? It isn't always requited, or paid back, and sometimes it ends too soon or too suddenly, but without it, all that you have is an empty house and no memories to live on inside it. And oh, I never wanted that for anyone. Especially not for Emma.

"I just wish Viv could be here to see us," she says wistfully now.

Oh, my special girl.

There are days she won't think of me so often, and that will be for the best. It's what I would want for her. But today, she needs me to be a part of the celebration. She needs to know that the house, while changing, will always be our home.

And so I watch while Emma steps out onto the front porch and her face lifts. She calls out to Leah and Sadie, and everyone comes filing out of the house I lived in every single day of my life and never left. And never will, in some way.

They are pointing to the clear blue sky with smiles of disbelief, wonder, and joy, where, rising high over the bay, is a rainbow.

ACKNOWLEDGMENTS

Thank you as always to my longtime agent, Paige Wheeler, for her ongoing encouragement and support. Her insight in the early stages of this manuscript was invaluable, and I'm so grateful for her commitment to this project. Many thanks of course to my editor Lauren Plude, whose sharp eye and sincere understanding of my characters helped shape this story into its final form. Her enthusiasm for this book is appreciated more than I can possibly express.

And a heartfelt thank-you to my readers, old and new, who make it all possible.

ABOUT THE AUTHOR

Olivia Miles is a *USA Today* bestselling author of heartwarming women's fiction and small-town contemporary romance. RT Book Reviews hailed her as "an expert at creating a sweet romantic plot." She has frequently been ranked as an Amazon Top 100 author, and her books have appeared on several bestseller lists, including Amazon, Barnes & Noble, BookScan, and *USA Today*. Olivia lives on the shore of Lake Michigan with her family and an adorable pair of dogs.